TORSTEN'S GAMBLE

VIRGINIE MARCONATO

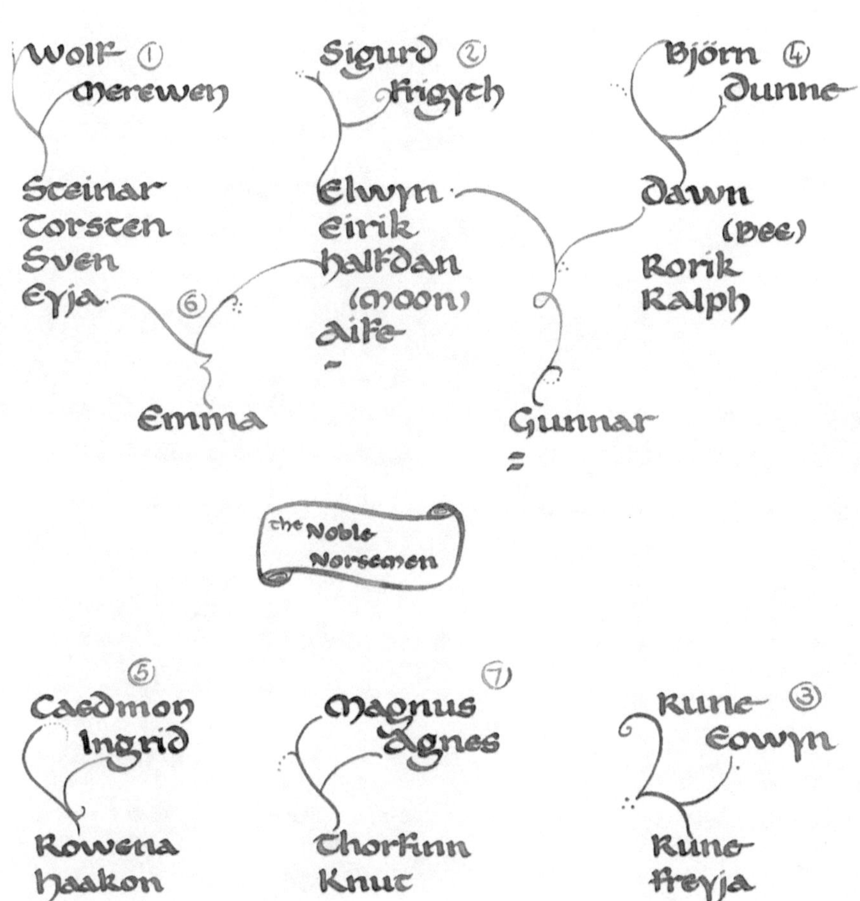

Wolf ①
Merewen

Steinar
Torsten
Sven
Eyja ⑥

Emma

Sigurd ②
Frigyth

Elwyn
Eirik
Halfdan
(Moon)
Aife

Gunnar

Björn ④
Dunne

Dawn
(Bee)
Rorik
Ralph

the Noble Norsemen

Caedmon ⑤
Ingrid

Rowena
Haakon

Magnus ⑦
Agnes

Thorfinn
Knut

Rune ③
Eowyn

Rune
Freyja

PROLOGUE

"I'm in love with Sven."

As she made the very personal admission, Aife fell onto the bench next to Cwenthryth, who was feeding her newborn daughter, Sanna. Being married to Steinar, who was none other than Sven's older brother, her friend was the perfect person to confide in.

"Are you really?" Cwenthryth sounded cautious.

"How can I not be? Have you seen him? Isn't he the most appealing man?" Aife insisted when her friend remained silent. She didn't look anywhere near as convinced—or excited at the prospect of becoming her sister-in-law—as she should be.

"He looks just like my husband, so, of course, I will tell you he's an exceptionally handsome man. But I—"

"But nothing."

Having arrived in the village only a year ago, Cwenthryth could not know that Sven was not the first, or even the second or third man Aife had fallen for over the years. And this was really why she was the ideal person to discuss this with. She would not judge her or remind her that she had once claimed to be in love with Thorfinn—and Haakon.

Yes, the list was rather long... Unfortunately, over the last few years, Aife seemed to have developed a habit of being attracted to men who were already in love with someone else and only saw her as a friend. Sven was no different—for now. But that would soon change. She would woo him because unlike the others, he was not involved with anyone special. On the contrary, he seemed to go from conquest to conquest, which meant that she could easily be the next one. And once she was in his bed, she would make sure to stay there, and burrow her way to his heart. It seemed as good a plan as any.

"You do know that he doesn't seem ready to, er, settle down, for want of a better word," Cwenthryth carried on, placing a kiss on her daughter's head. "You might find it hard to convince him."

"I know that."

But no one was ready to settle until they met the right person, were they? What mattered was that he, at least, didn't have someone important in his life already, someone she could never compete with. Aife was tired of being alone, of being asked when she was going to find someone. At first it hadn't bothered her, since the question rarely betrayed malicious intent, but she would soon enter her thirtieth year. All the friends she had grown up with—the female ones at least—had found someone who made them happy. Why not her as well?

Aife raised her chin.

"I'll find a way to gain his interest, don't you worry. You married Steinar when everyone was convinced he would never marry again. Mark my words, I, too, will end up married to one of Wolf's sons."

1

EAST ANGLIA, SUMMER 1071

Torsten stretched on the pallet, only half awake. Another dawn, followed by another morning, then another afternoon, each more tedious than the last. Days were following one another with frustrating predictability, blurring into a mass of discontent he was finding hard to extricate himself from. Why he'd been feeling so dejected of late, he wasn't sure. Only...that was not quite the truth, was it?.

If he were completely honest, he had a fair idea why he felt so wretched.

His eldest brother, Steinar, had recently remarried. His new wife, a Saxon named Cwenthryth, was much more suited to his needs than his first wife had been, and had just given him the little girl he'd always dreamed of. His younger brother, Sven, was being as carefree as usual and bedding all the willing women he could find, of which there were many. His sister, Eyja, was happier than ever with her two girls and her husband Moon, who also happened to be his best friend. His parents' love was growing stronger every day.

In other words, everyone in his family was content with their lives, right where they wanted to be.

Everyone except him.

He wanted more. Or...*something,* at least. But what that something might be, he wasn't sure. That was one of the problems, he realized in a sudden burst of clarity. He'd lost his sense of purpose, along with the will to want anything. His situation was so dire that he had started to hope fate would do what he seemed incapable of doing, and place what he needed right in front of him.

Of course, he would still have to recognize it for what it was when the moment came.

As he was crossing his hands under his head, his gaze landed on the bulge tenting his blanket. He was hard. That wasn't new either, and little cause for excitement. Any healthy man of thirty summers woke up hard in the morning. Closing his eyes again, Torsten started to stroke himself idly. Could he make the most of the opportunity? Yes. Why not? It was not as if he was in any hurry to get up, or had a woman who could see to his needs later. His mind was dissatisfied and he had no idea how to remedy it, but he could at least offer his body this small satisfaction.

The blanket was thrown to one side with decision.

His hand landed on his shaft, hard and ready for him. Sleeping naked had its advantages, it would seem; he was able to see to his needs in an instant.

It only took a few strokes for heat to start gathering in his loins. He was close, but he already knew this would be a hollow satisfaction, a releasing of tension, nothing more. As usual.

He increased the speed of his strokes, doing his best to conjure up lewd images able to spur him on. This was always the difficult part for him, because he didn't have a wealth of experience to draw from, quite the opposite. Even worse, if he started to think too hard about the experience he did have, he might well never manage to bring this to its natural conclusion.

Just when he was starting to despair, he heard a laugh outside his window. It was such a rich, evocative, dirty laugh that his cock gave a twitch. It was the laugh of someone intent on seducing the man she was talking to, and even if it had not been directed at him, it did what his imagination had not been able to do. It sent his arousal spiking. The woman laughed again, and the throaty sound pierced his spine, pushing him over the edge.

Torsten sat up and groaned as pleasure shot out of him in thick, white spurts that coated his tightly corded stomach. The warmth of his seed scalded his skin, which had become excessively sensitive. He blinked, disconcerted by the strength of a release that had seemed to be wrenched from depths he didn't even know he possessed.

He fell flat on his back, his breathing ragged and his fingers clenching repeatedly.

Well. *That* had been unprecedented, definitely more satisfying than a mere releasing of tension. And it was all thanks to the mysterious woman laughing outside his window. Who had she been? He had no idea but he would make sure to find out. Surely no two women possessed such a laugh.

Full of a motivation he had not felt for months, Torsten stood up and wiped his stomach with the piece of cloth he kept by the basin of water. Then he got dressed and picked up the comb he was currently working on. Of the three brothers, he was the most artistically inclined. Steinar was best suited to tasks requiring physical strength and stamina, and Sven... Well, Sven had yet to find his special talent. Luring women into bed with little more than a smile and a wink didn't count.

Torsten started to decorate the bone shaft with an intricate leaf design mirroring a coil of ivy climbing a young tree. It would be one of his finest pieces, he thought while he carved, observing how regularly the teeth had been sawn, how smooth the polished antler had become. Not that the perfection of the piece mattered, of course, as he had no one special to give it to. He might have the skill and patience to create beautiful objects, but he didn't have anyone to lavish them on.

The burst of optimism created by this morning's unexpected pleasure was quickly starting to dissipate. If he didn't do anything, soon he would find himself submerged in gloom again. He didn't want that, not today.

Abandoning the comb on the table, Torsten made his way to Steinar's hut. When he was in a grim mood, nothing was guaranteed to lift his spirits more than seeing his new little niece, Sanna, who was only two months old and the most beautiful child he had ever seen, with big dark eyes and hair as black as her mother's. With such a mane, it would not be too long before she needed a comb. He smiled at the thought.

Yes. If he hadn't found anyone else to give it to before the winter, he would gift the ivy comb to little Sanna.

"EDITA WILL BE VISITING US SOON."

"Will she?" Aife worked hard to infuse enthusiasm into her voice but wasn't sure she succeeded.

"Yes. Birgit writes me that she recently lost her husband, Eowald, and needs the distraction. It might be that she arrives before the end of the week, as she was set to leave shortly after the missive was given to the peddler who delivered it earlier today."

Aife nodded and helped herself to another slice of dried apple but did not pass any comment. Her mother had come to visit this afternoon, bearing a letter from her youngest sister, who lived in Mercia. Unfortunately, the news it contained was not the best. Her cousin lived a long way away, which was the reason why they didn't see one another too often. Edita was only a couple of years older than she was, fully Saxon, unlike Aife who had a Danish father, and completely different to her.

The two cousins had gotten along well enough as children, but the last time they'd met, some four years ago, Aife had been disappointed. Edita had been very quick to point out that she had wed her husband the summer she had turned seventeen. The man, a rich merchant ten years older than her, had pursued her relentlessly, while Aife and her younger sister, Hedda, were both still unmarried, aged five-and-twenty and three-and-twenty respectively. What she would say now didn't bear thinking about, and this time Aife would be alone to bear the brunt of the attacks. Hedda had left the village two years ago, to go to Denmark. Alone amongst the five siblings, she had decided to go live in their father's country, having been fascinated by his stories from a young age. It had been hard to see her go and they all missed her dearly. No doubt Aife would miss her even more when she had to face Edita alone.

But perhaps being widowed had dulled her cousin's sharpest edges and restored her to the girl she had once been? One could only hope.

Unfortunately, it didn't take Aife long to see that nothing had changed. Three days after they had received the letter warning them of her visit, Edita herself arrived. As soon as she opened her mouth that night, Aife understood that her behavior would be just as bad as before, if not worse. Far from being heartbroken or even simply listless, her cousin announced that she had already chosen her next husband, one of Eowald's closest friends, and then spent the whole meal boasting about her stroke of luck.

"Wulfric has been in love with me all that time, and I only found out now, if you'll believe it. He's been waiting for years in secret, hoping I would one day become available to marry him."

"Some loyal friend he makes, waiting for his friend to die so he can wed his widow," her father, Sigurd, mumbled under his breath—and in Norse. This earned him a sharp, disapproving glance from his wife who, Saxon though she may be, had learned to speak his tongue. But Aife agreed with her father. It seemed particularly underhanded on this Wulfric's part to lust after Eowald's wife and then pounce as soon as he was dead.

An uncharitable thought crossed her mind. Edita's husband had been one of the richest men in the village. Could it be that his friend was more interested in the money this marriage could bring than the bride herself? It was a possibility, because Aife didn't see how anyone could fall in love with someone as conceited and frivolous as Edita had become.

She excused herself as soon as the table had been cleared and went back to her hut, leaving her poor parents to prepare a pallet for Edita.

The following morning, her cousin spotted her drawing water at the well and walked over to her. There was no way to avoid her, and just as Aife had feared, the conversation soon turned to Wulfric and what he thought of his future bride's beauty.

"He says I don't look like a woman entering my fourth decade. According to him, I have the complexion of a maid and the figure of a woman half my age."

Mm. This Wulfric definitely sounded like a flatterer. Not that Edita was ugly or deformed by any means but this was the tenth outrageous compliment Aife had heard that morning. More suspicious than ever, she couldn't help but ask what he looked like. All she knew for certain was that he had to be at least a decade older than his bride-to-be.

"Oh, you know, he has brown hair and eyes. He's taller than me."

No doubt this uninspiring description could apply to all the men in the Saxon village, so Aife was none the wiser. Of course she didn't really care, she had just wanted to stop Edita from boasting about her own looks. Just as she was wondering how to change the subject altogether, their cousin Bee's friend, Sigrid, walked over to them, her young son perched on her hip.

Seizing the opportunity, Aife introduced the two women to one another. Perhaps having a third person present would render this conversation more bearable. It could not make things worse anyway.

"Sigrid, this is Edita, my and Bee's cousin. She is visiting us from Mercia for the first time."

"Yes, and I can already predict that it won't be the last," Edita simpered, throwing a coy glance over to the forge, where the blacksmith's son, Knut, was sharpening a sword while talking to his friend Arne. The men's hair was wet and their chests were bare, indicating that they had just come back from a dip in the river. "The men here are simply too incredible to be believed. Perhaps I should have come here before I found my second husband. I'm a widow you see," she specified for Sigrid's benefit. "And after Eowald, who was darker than most, a Norseman would have been a pleasant change. A very, *very* pleasant change."

Well. What would Wulfric make of this, Aife wondered? Would he praise his future wife for her candidness in front of strangers? Would he commend her on her impeccable tastes when it came to judging male beauty? Somehow she doubted it.

"Yes, the men here are rather impressive, but do not be fooled by their appearance," Sigrid surprised her by saying. "My husband, for all his brawn, is so lazy that, more often than not, I have to use the axe myself if I want to keep the fire going. In the bedroom, it's not always better."

"I'm sorry to hear that." The gleam in Edita's eyes indicated that she was anything but sorry. Aife was getting more and more ill at ease. Really, what had possessed Sigrid to make such a personal remark to a stranger?

"Oh I don't mean for me. No, believe me, in bed at least, Bo is more than vigorous. But I was told only yesterday by a friend who lives in another village that she tried to bed one of the men from here a few years ago and he could not even...rise to the occasion, shall we say. Such a disappointment, as you can imagine."

Edita giggled, delighting in the juicy piece of information. "Indeed. But this is something that could never happen to me, I don't think. I cannot imagine any man, Norse or Saxon, would find it hard to rise to the occasion in my bed. Not that I'm suggesting your friend is not attractive enough to rouse a man's desire, of course," she added with a swift glance in Aife's direction. The meaning of that involuntary glance was clear.

She didn't think *her* attractive enough to rouse a man's desire.

Aife's stomach roiled. It seemed she had been wrong to hope the discussion would take a turn for the better if someone else joined them. Edita had told her many times she thought her too small and slender to please a man, and it seemed her opinion hadn't changed. "Men like to have something to hold on to while they take their pleasure," she'd added with a competent air, looking at her own ample bosom.

"Could you share with us the name of the disappointing lover?" Edita leaned conspiratorially toward Sigrid, who giggled.

"Why would you want to know that?" Aife could not help but ask, her irritation barely concealed. Surely her cousin didn't have any intention of seducing anyone with her next wedding already planned, did she? But perhaps she did, and that was precisely why she had come here, far away from her village. "You don't know anyone here, so the name will mean nothing to you."

"I might not know anyone but you do. It wouldn't do for you

to try your luck with him, would it? Imagine that. You finally get a man into your bed, only to find out he cannot perform. It would be a pity, don't you think?"

Sigrid hid her smile in her son's hair. Clearly it amused her to imagine the scene. Could this get more humiliating?

"Well, I don't need to know, thank you."

The only man she was interested in was Sven, and she doubted that this was whom Sigrid was talking about. His ability to perform was all too well attested—she had heard about it from at least half a dozen women. They could not all be lying.

"Tell me it's not that one at least," Edita whispered nodding at Knut, who had started swinging the sword this way and that to test the blade's balance. Aife had to admit he cut an impressive figure, even if, in her opinion, he wasn't as attractive as Sven.

"No. It's not him," Sigrid whispered back, clearly admiring the way the man's muscles flexed and twisted with each movement. "It's Torsten, Wolf's son. I might as well tell you, since you're bound to hear it sooner or later. I already told Gudrun and we all know she cannot keep a secret."

"Why on earth would you do something like that?" Aife erupted, goaded beyond endurance.

She had never liked the woman, but this seemed particularly petty, even for her. Because she was right. Before the summer was over, the baker's wife would have made sure the whole village knew about Torsten's failing. Why would anyone want to expose him to ridicule thus? Aife liked Torsten, the quietest of Wolf's three sons. He was one of her best friends, and she hated him being the object of such discussions. Either he really was impotent, and it was certainly no cause for mockery, or he was not, and this rumor could only hurt his feelings. In any case, he didn't deserve having his personal life exposed by people who had no idea what they were talking about.

Neither woman answered, as at that precise moment, Knut

threw the sword in the air and caught the blade between his two palms. Edita and Sigrid cheered and started clapping. He gave an extravagant bow in their direction, Arne soon imitating him.

"Well, seeing as you don't need me, I'll go draw more water," Aife mumbled, already making her way to the well.

Let the two women gossip and gawp at half-naked men all they wanted, she would have no part in it. As she walked away, bucket in hand, doubts started to assault her. Was she jealous of her cousin's generous physique? Was she so annoyed because deep down she knew she could not rouse a man's desire? Her lack of womanly attributes might be the real reason she could not attract a man's attention. For years she had wondered what it was about her that made men see her only as a friend. Perhaps she now had her answer. Edita had been cruel, but perhaps she had finally allowed her to understand where the problem lay.

But her figure would not change now. It was too late, she was a grown woman. So, was she destined to live in the village where she'd been born without ever being seen as the woman she had become? As a lover, and then a wife?

Aife had the honesty to acknowledge that she was not the most stunning of women. In her mind, she had always compared unfavorably to her younger sister, Hedda, who'd always been more feminine.

It was not just her lack of curves that made her blend into the background, though. Her blonde hair and blue eyes were attractive enough, she supposed. But she did not have any special talent or trait of personality that stood out and made her unique in any way. She was sensible, rather than imaginative and wild like her friend, Eyja. Unlike Bee, who never lost patience with anyone, Aife quickly got frustrated when people did things she didn't approve of or understand. She was not shy but neither did she find it easy to talk to strangers and make them feel welcome like Rowena did. She liked to help but, unlike Cwenthryth, who had become the village midwife, she had not yet found the best way to do it.

So what was she to do?

How would she ever manage to catch the man of her dreams? There had to be a way of getting Sven's attention and make him see she could be much more than a friend.

But what?

2

———

Would the nails be ready? Magnus had told him he needed a couple of days to finish them, and it had been three days. Perhaps it was worth asking. The blacksmith was a man of his word, and Torsten wanted to fix the fence around the sheep enclosure as soon as possible. The animals had not escaped yet, but it was only a matter of time before one found a way out of the faulty construction and the whole herd scattered in the fields beyond. Maybe all hundred nails would not be ready yet but he could at least start with the ones that were.

He made his way to the smithy as soon as he had broken his fast.

A woman was at the back of the forge, talking to someone he couldn't see. She had her back turned to him and her hair was covered by a hood, but he recognized her voice and her petite frame. It was Aife, his friend Moon's sister. He would have waved to her, but she was too absorbed in her conversation to notice him. It didn't matter, he could say hello later. Besides, judging from the lack of noise coming from the forge, it was a good moment to see Magnus, who would not be hammering away while they talked. He extended his hand to the door, ready to push it open.

Just then, Aife laughed.

The pearly, husky, provocative sound shot straight to Torsten's cock. That laugh... He would have recognized it anywhere. It was the one he'd heard the other morning, when he'd stroked himself to the best release of his life, the laugh he had obsessed about for days.

How had he not recognized it at the time?

Because he'd never imagined that Aife could ever set his loins on fire, that was why. She was his best friend's little sister, someone he'd known from birth, not some sultry temptress. He should know, he'd spent enough time with her without ever once becoming aroused. She was sweet, not seductive, a friend, not a potential conquest. Except that now he knew she hid a wicked side to her. No woman could laugh thus and be only sweet innocence. She might not know it herself, but Aife had the means of setting men's loins on fire.

If he'd been capable of blushing, he would have blushed. How was he to face her? Twice now, he had stroked himself to an explosive release thanks to her. The first time when he'd heard her laugh, then the following morning when he had relived the exquisite moment in all its glory.

Torsten had promised himself he would find the woman who had inflamed his imagination, but now that he had, he wasn't sure what to make of the revelation. Because it was useless. Aife was not someone he could be with in that way. They were friends, nothing more. She would most likely be horrified if she knew what he'd done, and rightly so.

Still, an irresistible force drew him to her. He had to find out more.

Ignoring the forge door, he walked over to her—which was

when he saw who had caused her to laugh in that provocative way.

Sven. His bloody brother.

Everything crumpled inside Torsten. Of course, it had to be him. The man had the ability to send women mad with lust without even trying. But Aife couldn't have fallen into that trap, surely? Having known him from birth, she should be not only impervious to his charm, but also well aware of his wayward reputation and his unwillingness to settle. Wasn't he the last man she should allow near her? Not that Sven would hurt her, of course, but their relationship could lead nowhere.

Well, he reflected bitterly, perhaps she didn't want it to lead anywhere. If she were only interested in a few nights of pleasure, then she had definitely gone to the right man. Personable and carefree, his younger brother had always been the charmer of the family. Steinar, the eldest, was the exact opposite, serious, reliable, married at a young age, and then too busy building a family to worry about other women. As to himself...

Torsten was like neither of them in temperament, nor did he look like a Norse deity. Alone out of Wolf's four children, he had inherited their Saxon mother's looks. His hair had a definite auburn tint to it, his eyes were not blue, but brown. Not quite as dark as Merewen's, but still unusual for a Norseman. He was also the shortest of the three brothers, though not by much, and his physique was more lithe than powerful. If Sven and Steinar were sturdy oaks, he was a silver birch sapling.

How could he compete? The answer was simple: he couldn't. Women did not flock to him in search of nights of passion or think him manly enough to be a protective husband.

Ever since the three of them had grown into men, he'd felt transparent, stuck between two striking men, and never had he felt more inadequate than in this moment, when he was forced to watch the first ever woman who'd roused his desire try to lure his little brother into bed. What a fool he really was. He'd been aroused by her laugh, and it turned out that she had only used it to tempt another man—his own brother. She had not known he was only yards away, being coaxed into release by her sultry voice.

Not only that, but the mysterious woman he had sworn to find was one he had known all his life and the furthest thing from sultry he could imagine.

How humiliating.

"Torsten! Come, you'll want to hear this," Sven called out.

Should he refuse? Explain he'd come to see Magnus and disappear into to the forge? Yes, probably. And yet somehow his feet started moving of their own accord. A moment later he was coming to a halt in front of his smiling brother.

"Listen to this. Aife was telling me what Emma did the other day."

Moon and Eyja's daughter, Emma, was a little bundle of mischief. At any other time, Torsten would have delighted in hearing what she had done. Right now, though, he cared not a fig. Nevertheless, staying silent would only alert Sven and Aife to the fact that something was wrong, so he forced himself to ask the question.

"What did she do now?"

"She walked into Aife's hut while she was making pottage. Our lovely niece decided to help by adding her own special ingredient to the pot."

A pause. Torsten understood that he was expected to ask what that ingredient might be. But how could he behave naturally when his mind was buzzing with confusion and his lower body was throbbing with need? By the gods, but never had taking part in a conversation cost him more.

"What did she choose?" he managed to say. "A beetle?"

Aife giggled. Torsten's chest tightened. Not for him, the

sensual, throaty laugh she had used for his brother. For him, there was only the familiar, friendly giggle, the one everyone else got.

"No, even worse, as a beetle would easily have been retrieved and discarded. Sand!" Sven guffawed. "The imp threw a handful of sand into the pot of boiling water. Fortunately, Aife had yet to add the vegetables or the whole thing would have been ruined."

Torsten smiled, wondering why he felt so hollow. He should have shared in the laughter. Instead, his mouth felt as if he'd been forced to eat a spoonful of the sandy pottage.

"Yes, that is fortunate," he said automatically.

Sven arched a brow "Are you all right, brother?" he asked, laughing no longer.

"Of course."

He was perfectly all right, if one forgot the hole expanding in his chest, the burning need to make Aife laugh in that sensual way, and the inexplicable, paralyzing urge to draw her into his arms and kiss her.

Kiss her? Torsten blinked. What the bloody hell was that about?

He rarely felt desire for a woman, and he never, most definitely *never* fantasized about kissing a friend. Of course he didn't, it simply wasn't done. What next? Would he start lusting after men?

An awkward silence settled between the three of them, then Sven spoke again, excitement in his voice. "If you will excuse me, I see Freydis over there. I wanted a word with her."

Aife's heart fell to the bottom of her stomach when Sven strode away in the direction of the well without waiting for their answer. A word. Was that what he wanted them to believe, that he meant to *talk* to Freydis? She exchanged a quick glance with Torsten, who appeared just as dubious as she was. Indeed for a moment it appeared as if he would call his brother back, but

Sven had already forgotten about them; his attention was wholly on the blonde woman sitting on the bench in the shade of the massive oak.

The woman he wanted to seduce.

This was hopeless. She might well make him laugh with her stories, but he was not interested in making her his, like he was with Freydis. Why? She couldn't understand. It was not as if he only liked buxom or tall women, Over the years she had seen him with lovers of all shapes, sizes, and even ages. Freydis herself was on the slender side, and her bosom was no bigger than hers was. So why was he not looking at her in the same heated way? What was wrong with her?

"If you'll excuse me as well, I have nails to retrieve from Magnus," Torsten mumbled, clearly aware her thoughts had scattered now that Sven was no longer with them.

Guilt sliced through her. She hadn't meant to make him feel inadequate or boring. Just because she felt transparent and unimportant didn't mean she should make him feel the same way. He was a good friend, one of the best men she knew and... well, he looked different that morning.

"Are you all right?" she asked, her attention wholly back on him.

Sven had been right, he looked preoccupied, for want of a better word, and she wondered if something had upset him. Had he heard whispers about his supposed lack of virility? Was that what the matter was? Had Gudrun started to repeat what Sigrid had told her? Her heart went out to him. It would be awful if that were the case. She still had no idea if she should believe the story of him being unable to bed the woman from the other village, but she hated that it could hurt him.

"I'll be all right," he said, sounding rather dejected.

"Can I help in any way?"

He stared at her but didn't answer. Just then in the corner of her eye she saw Sven and Freydis stand up from the bench. In a moment they would be gone, and she had no illusion as to where they were going, or rather what they would be doing once they got there.

She threw herself into Torsten's arms before she could think.

"Kiss me," she breathed, wrapping her arms around his neck.

He didn't move, only blinked, his disbelief obvious. No wonder. Barely a moment ago she'd asked how she could help him overcome his dejection. It would look as if she thought she could simply kiss it away, a ridiculous proposition, admittedly. But it was too late to back down now. In the distance, Freydis laughed.

Aife acted on instinct.

Lifting herself onto her tiptoes, she placed her lips on Torsten's mouth. He froze and for a few heartbeats they remained glued to one another, eyes open wide in disbelief. Then something totally unexpected happened. What had been meant to be a mere touching of lips, a way to show Sven that she, too, could be kissed, turned into something wild and utterly out of her control. All it took to spark the change was for Torsten's hands to close around her waist.

Instantly, Aife melted.

Her eyes closed, her lower body pressed itself against his, her fingers wove themselves into his hair and her tongue darted out of her mouth, coming to tease the corner of his. As if he'd been expecting her to do that, he opened for her, and his taste, spicy and masculine, hit her with the force of a wave crashing ashore. A groan escaped her throat. She hadn't imagined for a moment that he would taste so irresistible, smell so alluring, or feel so perfect against her. Kissing an old friend should feel weird, not familiar, and kissing someone by surprise should be awkward, not arousing. And yet... And yet being in Torsten's arms felt as natural as breathing, and the feel of his lips on hers stirred a dark desire in an unsuspected part of her, one buried deep in her soul.

Why was that?

She'd only meant for the kiss to last long enough for Sven to see them before leaving, but she ended up forgetting everything and making the most of the incredible moment. Because it was incredible. This kiss was unlike any she had ever shared, and the feelings it provoked inside her were completely new. Though Aife was not as experienced as she would have liked, she was not completely innocent either. As a young girl, she had kissed a handful of village boys. Recently, as she'd grown more selective, such opportunities had become rarer. She just hadn't seen the point.

What was certain was that none of the kisses she'd received had felt half as decadent or as...meant to be.

The ground under her feet became unstable, so much so that Torsten had to lean her again the back of the forge to steady her. He did so effortlessly, without breaking the contact of their lips. Aife moaned her appreciation, savoring his confidence as well as his honeyed taste. Who would have thought Torsten would be so manly? So delicious?

Eventually, she forced herself to draw away. When she finally dared to look at Torsten, his deep brown eyes were swirling in a mixture of emotions amongst which she recognized desire, confusion, and anger. Oh, what had she done? She had kissed someone she was not interested in wooing and who felt nothing for her other than friendship.

She had kissed one brother when she wanted another one.

It had been a stupid thing to do, but for a moment she had been blinded by jealousy and resentment, unable to think. Sven had been talking to her, enjoying her story and laughing, looking at her with his amazing blue eyes. It had been perfect.

And yet as soon as Freydis had arrived, he'd forgotten about her and rushed to the wretched woman's side. This was clear proof that she was a friend to him, nothing more, someone he didn't have to worry about pleasing, someone whose feelings he didn't need to spare. Well perhaps he would take an interest in her as a woman if he saw that others did. Weren't men competitive and inclined to jealousy? He had dismissed her to go to Freydis, and she had wanted to make him see that she didn't mind, because she had her own man. For weeks she had tried to make Sven see her differently and it hadn't worked.

It was time to try something new.

"What was that?" Torsten's voice was hoarse, and no wonder. If she, who had initiated what looked like a seduction, didn't quite understand the desire flooding her as soon as their lips had touched or couldn't make sense of the sensations the kiss had provoked in her, he would be utterly baffled.

"I don't know. Forgive me, I just...wanted to kiss you." That wasn't a lie even if, admittedly, she hadn't wanted to kiss him for the reason women usually kissed men.

They were still pressed close to one another, his hands were still about her waist, keeping her upright against the wall of the forge, for which she was grateful, for her legs didn't yet feel able to support her. Really, she had been utterly taken by surprise by the intensity of the moment. But how could she not, considering what happened?

Aife swallowed, not having expected that being pressed against Torsten would feel so right. It was as if, physically, they were a perfect fit. Hulking men were all very well and good to look at from a distance, but Aife was only a short woman, and rather slender. It didn't take a lot to make her feel uncomfortable. In fact, when she stood next to Sven, she often thought that they would appear ridiculous to onlookers. Torsten, by contrast, was masculine without being overpowering, strong enough to make her feel feminine, but not overwhelmed. He also looked... well, impossibly handsome, she now realized.

Had his jaw always been so strong? His lips so full? His eyes so fascinating? From close-up she could see that they were not just brown, as she'd always thought. There was a whole range of emotions swirling underneath the surface, like clouds gathering before a storm. The blue eyes she was used to gazing into, living as she did in a Norse community, seemed flatter somehow, less mysterious.

She glanced over to the bench by the oak. Sven and Freydis were gone, which did not surprise her. The kiss had lasted much longer than she had meant it to last, and it had turned her world on its head.

Aife disentangled herself from Torsten's arms, feeling caught out. It was time to forget the fleeting madness overcoming her and revert to a more normal behavior. They were friends, not lovers, and she was in love with his brother. She had told Cwenthryth as much only the other day, so she could not be admiring another man's eyes or reveling in the heat of his embrace.

"Do you often feel the urge to kiss men like this?" Torsten rasped. By the gods, even his voice was different today, husky, as rough as a cat's tongue, and the effect on her was just as thrilling as a lick from the animal would be.

"No, I don't."

Would he believe her? Would he tell his brother what she had done? Did she want him to? What would be Sven's reaction if he knew that she and his brother had kissed? Would he even care? What would happen now?

Questions she didn't have the answer to jostled in her mind.

Just then the door of the forge opened on Magnus. Oblivious to the tension between them, the blacksmith gestured at Torsten, a smile on his face.

"Ah, you're just in time. Come. I've finished the last nail."

AIFE HAD KISSED HIM.

Torsten still could not believe what had happened earlier that day. Right after the preposterous thought that he would like to kiss a friend had crossed his mind, *she* had kissed *him*. Apparently, she had felt the inexplicable urge too, though why that might be, he could not fathom. His desire had been roused by the realization that she was the woman whose laugh had inflamed his imagination, but what had pushed her to kiss him?

She had looked as bewildered as he'd felt afterward, and more than a little guilty. He could understand the feeling. This was Aife, a woman he had known all her life, his best friend's sister. She was only a year younger than he was, and by an extraordinary coincidence, she had been born on the same day as he had, on the day their Saxon mothers called Michaelmas.

Which, he acknowledged with a frown, was neither here nor there. It didn't create any particular bond between them. It didn't make her special to him anymore than it made him special to her. They should never have kissed. And yet they had done just that. It had not been a quick, sweet kiss either, quite the opposite. It had been hot and wild, decadent, almost scandalous considering they had been out in the open, in full view of everyone. She had ground herself against him in flagrant invitation, woven her fingers in his hair to keep him close and swirled her tongue around his in a sensual dance. He had almost lifted her into his arms and used the wall at her back for support, while he settled himself between her spread legs and rubbed against her heat to ease the ache in his body.

Because his cock had gone hard at her proximity—rock hard, even.

Knowing how difficult he usually found it to get aroused, Torsten had never imagined that such a thing could happen during a mere kiss, with Aife of all people. What would he have thought if she had kissed him only a few days ago, before he'd heard her laugh, he could not imagine. It would have been even more disconcerting, and he probably wouldn't have gotten aroused.

Perhaps it was for the best that she had taken the initiative to kiss him first, because he couldn't bear to think what she would have done if he had kissed her with no warning and no explanation, in the middle of the village. Would she have slapped him or—

"Are you going to hammer the nails in place or what?" Steinar's disgruntled growl cut through his confused thoughts. "I won't be able to hold the plank in place forever. 'Tis heavy, in case you hadn't noticed."

Recalled to the task at hand, Torsten lifted his hammer. A group of men had assembled to finish building the hut for Thorfinn and Rowena. The two of them had married the year before, and Rowena had just given birth to twins. The home they'd had until then would quickly become too small for the growing family, and everyone had agreed to build a new, bigger one by the river.

Torsten had been amongst the first to volunteer for the day, as it provided him with the perfect excuse to avoid Aife. He was unsure how they could face one another after the passionate kiss they'd shared. It was not as if they could become a couple, was it? They were just friends. What had happened was a mistake—it would never happen again. Perhaps they would manage to put it behind them.

"What's up with you, anyway?" his brother asked in his usual gruff manner. "You seem distracted today."

"Perhaps because I am distracted," Torsten growled back. He could be gruff too, if the mood took him. "And perhaps it is none of your business why."

Steinar shrugged, not in the least perturbed by this less-than-gracious answer. "All right, have it your way. I don't really care anyway. As long as you keep hammering, you can think what the bloody hell you want. But I don't intend to remain stuck here all day. I have a wife and children to go back to."

Yes, Torsten thought as he pounded a dozen nails into submission, and wasn't that the whole problem?

He didn't have anyone to go back to.

3

———

Aife came to an abrupt halt, wondering what to do.

Torsten was in the field on the other side of the path, hammering the nails Magnus had given him two days ago to the fence of the sheep enclosure. There simply was no way to reach the village without walking past him and being seen. But was it such a bad thing? After what had happened outside the forge, it was imperative they cleared the air without delay. The last thing she wanted was for things between them to become awkward. They were friends, had practically grown up together, and she would hate for her moment of madness to ruin what they had. Torsten was a dear friend, and she couldn't imagine not having him in her life because of a stupid mistake.

Damn it all, why did *he* have to be in front of her when she'd taken the foolish decision to provoke Sven's jealousy? Anyone else would have been better. Torsten was the last man she should have kissed, considering he was the brother of the man she was trying to attract. Or perhaps Steinar would have been the worst choice. After all, he was married, and to a woman who was a good friend. Yes, kissing him would have been even more awkward, but knowing this did little to ease her mind.

While she built up the courage to go to Torsten, she remained hidden amongst the trees, watching him plant a sturdy post next to a crumbling one, which he then uprooted and threw into a pile behind him. After taking a swig out of his wineskin, he repeated the whole process. It was fascinating to watch because he was swinging his heavy-looking mallet with disconcerting ease, his movements both elegant and strong.

Eventually, stiffening her spine, Aife walked straight to him. The more she waited, the more flushed she seemed to become. It would not do. Better to get it over with.

"Good morning," she said, putting her basket full of herbs down next to the pile of discarded wooden posts. Her foraging had been successful that morning. She had all the St John's wort she needed for making her tinctures and oils, and she had even found some late flowering meadowsweet. The blooms' scent wafted around her, adding a sweetness to the moment.

"Good morning."

Torsten straightened up and wiped his brow with his rolled-up shirt sleeve. The gesture drew attention to both his strong wrist and neck. Out of nowhere, Aife reflected that watching Knut swing the sword the other day had not caused her blood to heat up in the way her blood was heating up now, even though he had been bare-chested. How odd.

"You're repairing the fence, I see." As soon as the words left her mouth she regretted them. Of course he was repairing the fence, that much was obvious, and not worth commenting on. So much for things not being awkward between them...

"I am. It was long overdue."

Mercifully, he didn't seem to think her an idiot for telling him what he already knew.

"You were up early," he commented, nodding at the basket when silence threatened to settle between them.

"Yes. I couldn't sleep so I thought I might as well make the most of the cool morning air to go foraging."

"And you found some meadowsweet?" Mm. It seemed she wasn't the only one inclined to point out the obvious today. This was bad.

"Yes. I didn't dare hope I would find some so late in the season, but there it was, in the shadow of a tree, waiting for me. I will use it tonight to flavor the cream I plan to eat with what's left of the berries I gathered yesterday. I'll go ask Bee if she can give me some of her milk. I ran out yesterday, when I made gruel for Eirik, who stayed to eat with me in the evening. Serves me well for inviting him, when we all know he eats like a horse."

Oh, dear, that was just as awful as she had feared. She was rambling on about cream and gruel. Torsten, who knew her better than most, would know she had a tendency to do that when she was ill at ease. And she was certainly ill at ease right now.

But how could she not? She'd hoped the next time they talked she would see him for the friend he'd always been, and not for the man who had given her the most sinful kiss of her life. So far, it hadn't worked. Because he had never looked more appealing than he did this morning, flushed from his exertions, with his sleeves rolled up over his forearms and his shirt gaping at the collar. Lifting his head up to the skies, he took a few long pulls from his wineskin. Aife watched the muscles of his neck contract every time he swallowed, and her core started to spasm, mirroring the action. By the time he'd stopped drinking, all the moisture had left her mouth and there was a persistent, buzzing noise in her ears. At first she wondered if she wasn't going to faint, but then she noticed that, attracted by the flowers in her basket, a dozen bees had started to fly around them. Oh, of course. That was the source of the buzzing... She really was losing her mind.

She absent-mindedly swatted one of the bees away when it flew too close to her face. A heartbeat later a sharp pain pierced the fleshy part of her thumb.

"What's the matter?" Torsten asked when she cried out in pain.

"I've been stung." Silly her! Couldn't she have guessed this would happen if she hit the insects?

"Let me see." Taking the hand she was cradling in his, Torsten examined the place that was throbbing fiercely. "Look, the stinger is still embedded. It will have to come out immediately."

"Yes."

Aife could see the little fluffy dart sticking out of her skin, but her mind had gone blank and her body felt strangely numb. Torsten's hand was so warm, he was looking at her with such concern... When she made to seize the bee sting between her thumb and forefinger, he stopped her.

"No, wait, not like this. It will only make the pain worse, squeeze more of the venom in. There's a much better way. Trust me, I've been stung more times than I recall." With those words, Torsten drew his eating knife from the sheath at his belt and carefully scraped the stinger from her finger. "All right?"

"All right." The pain was still quite fierce, but it didn't seem to matter.

"Come, let's go to the river. Putting your hand in cold water will help."

Without waiting for her response, he led her to the other side of the field. When they reached the river, Torsten knelt next to her and plunged the hand he was still holding into the fast-flowing water. The cold did ease the worst of the pain, reducing it to a dull throbbing.

"I've never been stung before," she explained after a while, feeling rather silly for her overreacting.

Torsten gave her a small smile. "Well, there's a first time for everything, and I don't know many people who go through life without being stung at some point or other."

Why did his words sound so evocative? Was it possible that the bee venom had gone to her head, turning her into a complete ninny? No, she'd been like that before being stung, while watching Torsten work, while watching him drink.

"I-I suppose it was inevitable," she stammered.

"Is it still painful?"

"No. Not really, thank you." Besides, the distraction had helped restore some semblance of normality between them. Perhaps she should be grateful to the bee.

"Good. Come. Let's go get your basket."

Holding her by the elbow, Torsten helped her back to her feet. Aife allowed him to steady her, looking into his eyes all the while. And then, as if sucked in by the clouds she could see swirling in them, she pushed herself up on her tiptoes, and placed a swift kiss on Torsten's lips. She blinked. What was happening to her? She'd had no intention of kissing him, she'd only meant to thank him. Only, for a moment it had seemed like the natural thing to do.

"Sorry, I don't know why I did that," she murmured, lowering back down. "There was no need, we're alone."

"No need? Alone? What does that mean?" Torsten stilled, his fingers tightening around her elbow. "I think you should explain yourself," he warned when she remained silent.

Aife started to tremble. The moment to explain why she had kissed him the other day had come, and it was every bit as frightening as she had imagined. How would he react?

"I kissed you now because I wanted to thank you, and seeing as we already kissed once it didn't seem so odd to do it a second time." She paused, knowing he wasn't really asking about today's chaste kiss but about the decadent one they had shared by the forge. "And, as for the other day, I kissed you because I thought it would help..."

Her voice trailed. Lost to her shame and unable to be honest, she wasn't making much sense, but somehow Torsten understood the situation better than if she had given him a lengthy explanation.

"I see. You didn't kiss me out of desire for me. You used me, having a purpose in mind."

"I..." What could Aife say? She *had* used him. Should she deny it? Would he even believe her? Wasn't it better to try and be honest? "Being a friend, I didn't think you'd mind."

"Mind?" He blinked at her, incredulity on his face, and she kicked herself for sounding so callous, so blunt, so stupid. She hadn't meant it like this.

"What I mean," she hurried to specify before he stormed away in outrage, "is that I know you don't have feelings for me so I didn't think you would mind helping me."

He crossed his arms over his chest. "I wouldn't mind helping you. In what way?" He had not stormed away, but neither did he seem ready to relent. She would have to be clearer.

Aife bit her bottom lip because this was the difficult part. He might not mind helping her in principle, but the man she was trying to seduce and stir into action was his own brother. He might mind that. Perhaps she had better come up with another, more acceptable explanation.

"I had seen my cousin, Edita, walk by the forge when I kissed you," she improvised. "She's visiting from Mercia."

"Yes, I know." He still didn't see what this had to do with anything.

"Well, the truth is, I cannot stand her!" Aife exploded, as years of resentment and restrained feelings burst out of her. "For years she's been flaunting the appeal she exerts over men, belittling me in the process. She never misses an opportunity to mock me for being too small, too slender, unable to get any man interested in me, and I'm tired of it, do you hear? Tired of hearing her tell me she already has another husband in mind, someone who's been in love with her for years, while I'm nine-and-twenty and still unwed. I saw her walk past, arch a supercilious brow at me, and I snapped. I'm not proud of it, but I snapped. I did the first thing that came to my mind to show her that I, too, could appeal to men. I thought that if she saw us kissing, if she saw me in a man's arms, she might finally cease her mocking."

It was not a complete lie. She *had* wanted someone to see them, and Edita's boasts did make her feel awful and insecure. Torsten did not need to know that the two were unrelated. And now that she thought of it, she wished Edita had truly seen them kiss. It might put an end to the hurtful taunts about her inability to ensnare a man.

Heart beating hard, breathing labored, Aife waited. Torsten was still looking at her, jaw clenched, eyes glowing, as if trying to decide what to make of her explanation. Would he think her ridiculous? Think she was lying? Demand they went to confront Edita there and then? She had no idea how she would react in his place. Anger seemed a safe guess.

"You should have told me why you kissed me," he said eventually, an odd expression on his face. Was he...disappointed? At least he didn't appear angry, which was a relief. "Instead, you made me believe that you... Forget it, it doesn't matter."

Make him believe what? For the first time Aife considered the possibility that she might not have been the only one affected by their unexpected kiss. What if, like her, Torsten had been overwhelmed by the heat flaring between them? What if he'd hoped she had kissed him because she'd been moved by an excess of desire for him? If this were the case, it would be a blow to find out she had only meant to placate a bothersome cousin. But she could not change her version of the story now.

The truth would hurt him even worse.

Suddenly the tension between them became unbearable. Torsten was looking at her with naked, masculine hunger. He was no longer the trusted, harmless friend who knew her inside out—he was an impossibly alluring, potent male, able to unlock her deepest yearnings and make her body quiver with desire. Aife had no idea how to deal with that man.

"I see that it was stupid of me," she blurted out, ashamed, and angry at herself for ruining everything between them. "I'm sorry. I swear it won't happen again. Please, forgive me."

Before Torsten could say anything, she turned around and fled.

"WULFRIC WANTS TO plant a plum tree next to our house when we get married, because he knows the fruit is my favorite," Edita announced, with the air of someone who'd just been told she would be the next queen of Mercia. "He says he wants to pick a plum every day for me to break my fast."

"I'm not sure how he's going to manage that in winter," Aife mumbled under her breath—and in Norse, like her father often did in his niece's presence. Though in reality, she could probably not have bothered switching languages. There was little risk her cousin would hear her while she was extolling the man's qualities, so at least she could safely let out some of her frustration.

As the days progressed, it was becoming harder and harder to hide her irritation. Really, was her future husband's supposed fascination for her all Edita could talk about? Didn't she have a life outside of him? The two women had gone mushroom gathering that afternoon, and inevitably, after a bland start involving the differences in weather between here and Mercia, the conversation had turned to her cousin's future husband.

Wulfric says my eyes are the color of the sea. Wulfric has bought me the most beautiful ring, look. Wulfric loves to hear me sing, he says I have the voice of an angel. Wulfric, Wulfric, Wulfric.

Aife didn't know how long she was going to stand it, today less than ever. Since her conversation with Torsten two days ago, she'd been unusually tense, which was little wonder. She had hurt a friend's feelings, all because she couldn't accept that she didn't have what it took to capture a man's attention, never mind his heart. She was not even sure Sven had seen the kiss. He probably hadn't, because if he had, she had a suspicion he would have delighted in mentioning it to her. This was precisely the sort of things he would delight in doing.

Yes, she had used Torsten, for her sole benefit, and in vain. As if that were not enough, she had then lied to him, claiming she had done so to put Edita back in her place. The whole thing sat ill with her and she didn't know how to make amends. What if Torsten was too hurt to consider forgiving her? What would she do then?

"What about you?" Edita asked, as they came to a halt near the bridge.

"What about me? You want to know if I like plums? Yes, I do."

Edita's laugh crawled under Aife's skin. Did Wulfric like the irritating sound as much as he liked the angelic singing, she wondered? It had not yet been mentioned, which might be a clue.

"No, silly! I mean, have you found someone like I have found Wulfric?" She nudged her elbow playfully. "I seem to remember you mentioning a Thorfinn last time we met?"

Thorfinn, Knut's brother. Yes. Yet another man who'd caught

her attention, another man who'd paid no heed to her. Aife picked a mushroom from the basket and rolled it between her thumb and forefinger. Was her cousin determined to make her feel bad by reminding her of her past failures? Apparently so.

"Thorfinn got married last year, to Rowena," she said eventually. The woman he'd been in love with all along. How had Aife not realized he'd already found the woman of his dreams? From the start, she'd been fighting a losing battle.

"Oh, dear, yet another man who could not see what a gem you are. Who was the other one you were interested in? Was it Haakon? Or Ralph? I forget. Well, not to worry. I'm sure eventually someone will see that a woman doesn't have to dazzle to be a good wife. I actually think most men would prefer to marry a plainer woman, who will not stir the lust of all the passing men and cause them endless worry. It makes for an easier life."

The mushroom was reduced to a pulp when Aife bunched her hand into a fist. How had her cousin turned into such a viper?

"How did you and Wulfric meet, by the way? You never told me and I cannot deny that I'm curious."

Though she was loath to hear more about the man, she would, if the alternative was having to explain that she feared no one would ever see what "a gem she was."

"Oh, you're right. I did tell you he was a friend of Eowald's, but I never told you about the day he finally declared his love to me, did I?"

Aife gritted her teeth while Edita launched herself into a detailed—and highly inappropriate—explanation of how the man had pounced on her during the Midsummer celebrations, mere days after his friend's funeral.

By the gods, it was going to be a long afternoon.

I'm sure eventually someone will see that a woman doesn't have to dazzle to be a good wife.

Torsten clenched his jaw. Had the woman truly said such a spiteful thing to her own cousin? Of course she had, he knew he had not misheard. In fact, placed where he was in the communal smoking room, he'd had no choice but to hear the whole excruciating conversation the two women were having by the bridge just behind. He'd even sneaked regular peeks through the door to see how Aife was dealing with the deluge of thinly-veiled insults.

Not well, if the expression on her face was to be believed.

She'd told him the other day that she had wanted to put her cousin from Mercia back in her place because Edita often mocked her supposed lack of appeal. He had not doubted her, there had been too much emotion in her voice when she'd explained what she felt, but this was a lot worse than he had imagined. The woman was going out of her way to make herself look good, and in the process was making Aife feel lower than dirt. There was no mistaking the self-satisfied look on her face or the scathing words. Worse, he could see from the lack of spark in her eyes that Aife thought Edita was right, and no one wanted her.

Well, it would not do, and enough was enough.

He had been angry at the time for the deception she had played on him, but he could see that she had not lied; she really was convinced she could not capture any man's interest. Kissing him to silence her cousin's taunts had not been her best idea, but he understood now that she had genuinely not meant to hurt him. And she was right, they were friends, and he had no feelings for her, or at least he was not *supposed* to have feelings for her. How could she have suspected that he would take it so badly? Only a few days ago he would have laughed the whole thing off and told her she was welcome to kiss him as much as she wanted because it didn't mean a thing.

Yes, but a few days ago, he'd not stroked himself to release while listening to her laughing. A few days ago, she'd not been the woman responsible for the best, most wicked moment of his life.

Still, none of this was her fault. He should apologize to her for barking at her, find a way to make amends. And he knew just how.

Just then he spotted his brother Sven exiting his hut in the distance. Perfect. Any other man would have done, but he knew he would easily goad his hot-headed brother into action. This was the perfect opportunity to put Edita back in her place and let out his frustration at the same time.

Making sure the two women could not see him, he exited the smoke room and signalled to his brother to hurry to his side. Worried by the urgency of the gesture, Sven almost ran to him. "What is it?"

"Hit me."

Sven arched a brow at the admittedly odd request. "I'm sorry?"

"Hit me. Now. Don't think about why, just do it. Or will I have to tell you exactly what a bastard you can be sometimes to motivate you?"

A scoff. "That won't be necessary, I already know that. And I can definitely hit you if that's what you want. The question is, can you take it?"

With those words, Sven threw the first punch. But because he did not really put his heart into it and Torsten had been prepared for the blow, he did not find it hard to block it.

"Come, is that all you have? Perhaps I should have gone to Ulf," he teased, using their thirteen-year-old nephew as bait. "He would have done a better job of it."

Grinning, he pushed at Sven's chest. His brother stumbled backward and cursed between his teeth. His next punch was in earnest, and this time, he did make contact with his chin.

Torsten's head snapped to the side and he groaned. By the gods, but that hurt. This might not have been the best idea he'd ever had. Suddenly he sympathized with Aife. It seemed that it was all too easy to make wrong decisions while in the heat of the moment.

Just as he was straightening his back and preparing himself to receive another hit, he heard a cry coming from the bridge. The two women had seen him and Sven fight and they were wondering what was happening. Finally! He didn't want this to go on for longer than necessary. His little brother was no weakling, and now that he'd been baited, he would not relent. But Torsten could not allow him to come out as the victor. *He* had to win, that was the whole point.

"Yield," he told Sven under his breath, crouching into a defensive position.

"Never. You wanted a fight, you're getting a fight."

Another punch. Torsten barely managed to sidestep it. Not a man used to getting himself into trouble, he was already getting tired. They had better put an end to this quickly, before he got hurt.

"This isn't about you, or even me," he said, aiming a kick at Sven's shin. "Yield. I'll explain later why. This is important and I'm sure you'll agree with me when you know what it is."

There was a pause. Then a sigh. "I'll yield if you at least make it look like you know how to throw a punch. I have a reputation to maintain, you know."

"If that's what you want."

Putting all his strength behind the blow, Torsten hit him square on the jaw. Sven went reeling backward, arms flailing, before collapsing flat on his back, his head thrown to the side. Torsten wiped his mouth, hiding his smile. This would do very nicely. His little brother had always had a flair for the dramatic.

Panting, he made his way to the two women, who were

looking at him with wide eyes. Edita seemed impressed by his performance, but Aife's blue eyes were veiled with worry and incomprehension. Before she could ask why on earth he was fighting with his brother, he put the basket she was holding on the ground and took her hand in his.

"Aife. That's the fourth of your suitors I've sent to the ground now. What more can I do to prove to you that I can take care of you? Please say you'll consider having me."

The air around them seemed to still.

"Men are fighting over you?" Edita asked Aife, blinking hard. The sheer disbelief in her voice was an insult in itself. Torsten's stomach twisted. The woman was vile and that blasted Wulfric was welcome to her.

"Men are *losing* over her," he growled, not even looking at her. His attention was wholly focused on Aife, who had gone a bright red color. He found himself thinking that it was rather adorable. "It's not the same thing at all. But I'll make sure I'm the one she chooses. Please, Aife, say you'll at least consider me."

Aife's throat went dry when she understood what Torsten was doing. He was making it look as if she were as popular in their village as Edita was claiming to be in hers. Even though she had hurt him, he'd come to her aid, he wanted to help her put her cousin in her place. Her heart wobbled, a most unusual sensation.

But what should she answer? Torsten was still holding her hand, looking at her with eyes full of hope. Though he'd only asked the question for her cousin's benefit, after the kiss they'd shared, she couldn't help but wonder if she should consider him as a suitor. When she'd seen him fight with Sven she'd worried about the outcome, but oddly enough, she'd been more worried about the damage he would do to himself than to the man she was interested in. It was all very disconcerting.

"I, too, have had men fighting over me," Edita piped up,

unable to bear not being the center of attention for once. "And I told them I would not—"

"I care not what you told them," Torsten snapped, not even looking at her. "In fact, you can leave. I need a word with Aife, alone."

Could a silence be loud? Apparently. Aife could practically hear Edita's outrage, and it took all her inner strength not to burst out laughing. At last, someone who had the courage to speak to her cousin the way she deserved, someone who took her side. She had never seen this uncompromising side to Torsten before and she rather liked it.

"You did that for me?" she asked, once they were alone.

"Yes. And no." He shrugged. "I did have a score to settle with Sven anyway, so this was as good an opportunity as any."

Why did she have the impression that he was lying? She was touched, all the more so that they had not parted in the best of terms and she had feared he wouldn't want to have anything to do with her.

"You'll have a bruise, I fear." She brushed his left cheek-bone. It was red, testimony to the violence of the blows he'd received for her. She could only imagine how much a hit from a man of Sven's bulk would hurt. "Here and likely all over your body."

"Bruises are nothing," he answered roundly, as if annoyed she thought him too weak to bear a little pain. She didn't, but she hated the idea of him suffering on her account. "Listen, Aife, I'm sorry for snapping at you the other day. I didn't know what to think of what you told me, but after what I just heard, I understand why you would have wanted to put the woman back in her place. She is vile."

"Yes, she is but that is no reason for you to get hurt. It was my issue to deal with, not yours," she said quickly. "And I too am sorry for what I did. It was inconsiderate of me. I should have at least asked your permission before I kissed you. Or at least explained afterward why I had done it and not let you—"

Torsten cut her off by covering the hand she was still holding at his cheek. "Hush. It's all in the past now. Or...perhaps it doesn't have to be."

"What do you mean?" With his body so close to her, his gaze planted into hers and his hand cradling hers, she was finding it very hard to think.

"We could carry on pretending. For Edita's sake. I mean."

Aife blinked, afraid to have misunderstood, hoping she had not. "You want to pretend we're involved?"

"Why not?" He shrugged again. The gesture made it appear as if he cared not one way or the other, but the light in his eyes belied that first impression. That was the good thing about warm, brown eyes, she decided. They had the ability to catch fire when a thought crossed their owner's mind. Blue eyes could only shine brighter, a much less devastating effect. "If I can help you survive your cousin's visit, isn't it my duty to do so?"

Well, no, it wasn't. It wasn't anyone's duty. Aife knew she should say no. This was all wrong. She slid her hand from under his and took a step back.

"Yes. Please," she said, before she could do the wise thing and refuse his offer. "That would be most helpful."

Helpful. What a dreadful word to describe what she had felt when she had kissed Torsten. It had been incredible... She had enjoyed their kiss, more than she had expected, more than she had the right to.

"Well, then it is decided." He gave her a lopsided grin. "Feel free to kiss me whenever you see Edita watching us."

The suggestion had her heart wobble anew. What *was* that? Nothing or no one had made her heart wobble before. Her cheeks heat, yes, many a time, her loins burn, on occasion, but her chest squeeze and what was inside quiver? Never.

"Very well," she breathed, grateful beyond measure.

"How is your thumb, by the way?" Torsten asked, nodding towards her hand.

"My thumb?" Oh, the bee sting. Aife had completely forgotten about that. "It's fine, thank you. But you never told me why it is that you got stung so many times?"

She'd thought she knew all there was to know about him. Apparently she did not, because she'd had no idea he was prone to bee stings—or that he could kiss like she imagined only the gods kissed.

"Growing up, I was usually the one helping my father gather honey in the forest. My other brothers never had the patience for it, especially Sven. And as you can imagine, collecting what the poor creatures have painstakingly created is not without risks. But the rewards are worth it." He cocked his head, considering. "I think 'tis a good lesson to teach children. If you want to eat something sweet, you have to earn it first."

Why was Aife under the impression that Torsten was talking about something other than honey? Something like their kiss outside the forge? As soon as the thought crossed her mind, her tongue darted out of her mouth to lick her lips, as if to try and recapture the memory of it.

"I never eat honey," she said, before she could blurt out that she was craving more of his sweet taste and was prepared to do what was needed to earn the right to it.

"You don't?" Torsten sounded shocked.

"No. I used to love it as a child, like everyone else, but one evening, when I was about eight summers, I forgot to close the honey pot after helping myself. The following morning, I dipped my finger in the jar and brought it to my lips before realizing it was crawling with ants." She made a face, remembering the awful sensation on her tongue. It had still been dark in the hut and it had taken her a moment to understand that she was actually eating ants. By then it had been too late. "Since then, I haven't been able to eat it."

"Mm. I'm not surprised, but I think you should give it another try. I'll take you into the forest and show you how good it really is."

It was then that Aife understood she would not be able to resist the urge to kiss him a third time. This man had fought his brother for her, he wanted to help her, he'd promised to feed her honey, he made her heart wobble, he looked impossibly compelling. It was more than she could handle.

Amazed at her own daring, she seized him by the hand. "Oh no, Edita's right here, coming this w—"

She was in his arms before she could finish the sentence. Torsten kissed her with fierce intent, as if he'd been waiting for the permission all along. Unlike the last time, he'd not been taken by surprise. On the contrary, he had been the one initiating the kiss, if admittedly in answer to her request.

And the difference was staggering.

Torsten had been accepting, he was now in charge. The kiss had been heated before, now it was scorching. He smelled of delicious, resiny woodsmoke and salt, as if he'd just come out of the smokehouse, and Aife already knew she would never eat smoked meat again without thinking of this moment. While his tongue, sweeter than the most delicious honey, plundered her mouth, his hands closed possessively around her waist—and *everything* within her wobbled.

By the gods, but the man could kiss.

And she was not sure she would ever get enough of it. She moaned into his mouth, too overwhelmed to be ashamed. After what seemed like an eternity of bliss, he drew away.

"Still here?"

What? Who? Still where? What was he talking about? Oh, yes, Edita, the whole reason for this shattering kiss. Holding on to him for fear she would waver if she let go, Aife pretended to check behind him. "No. She's gone."

"Good."

She could only agree. "Yes." Very good indeed.

All too quickly, Torsten released her and winked. "Until next time, then? I'll make you taste the best honey."

I think you already have.

As she watched Torsten walk away, Aife wondered if he'd guessed Edita hadn't been anywhere to be seen.

4

———

"Here, let me help you fold this."

Aife smiled her thanks to her mother and handed her one end of the sheet she'd put to dry in the field earlier that day. "Did you want to see me?" she asked, once they had gathered the rest of the clothes that now smelled of lush grass.

"Yes, to tell you that Thorfinn and Rowena are moving into their new house tomorrow. A group of us are going to help. Will you come too?"

"Of course."

She wanted to help and besides, it would give her something to do besides obsessing about Torsten, the kisses they had shared, and even more pointedly, the kisses she hoped to share in the future. As they had agreed to keep on pretending he was interested in her, there would no doubt be more to come. The mere idea had been enough to keep her awake long into the night, and she already predicted it would be no better tonight.

Shortly after dawn the next day, half the village had assembled outside Thorfinn and Rowena's new hut. Inevitably, since she was staying in their house, Edita had come with Sigurd and

Frigyth. Aife braced herself for the moment when her cousin would see her, and indeed, a moment later, she was by her side. This time, though, Aife didn't mind, as it might give her an excuse to go to Torsten.

The two of them were folding pieces of linen and placing them into a chest when Thorfinn joined them, a smile on his face. Every time she saw him, even if she no longer entertained ideas about him, Aife could not help but reflect that it was no wonder she had fallen under his charm. He really was very handsome and personable.

"Thank you for your help," he said, nodding both at her and Edita. "Thanks to everyone's contribution we'll be able to sleep in the new hut tonight."

"You're welcome, 'tis only normal."

"I hope to repay the favor one day."

Repay the favor? Aife's heart missed a beat. Did he mean that he would help when she moved into a new house with her husband because their family was expanding? At the moment such a thing seemed like an unattainable dream.

An image suddenly popped into her mind. She was standing in front of the firepit at night, looking at the glowing embers, cradling her stomach that was swollen with child. A man was holding her from behind, his hands on top of hers, his mouth at the crook of her neck. With no small amount of shock, she realized that the man's long hair was brown and he bore Torsten's features, not Sven's. This was rather unexpected. Or perhaps it was not, since she had seen Torsten earlier that morning, whereas Sven, who was in town with his father, had been unable to come.

Yes, she decided, that had to be the reason for this disconcerting image, because as she knew, she was only pretending to be interested in Torsten, whereas she truly intended to seduce Sven.

Before she could answer Thorfinn, Oddvarr, one of his friends, called out to him.

"You're a lucky bastard, do you know that?"

Thorfinn smiled. "I know I am. Rowena is everything I could have—"

"Come, I'm not talking about that!" Oddvarr guffawed. "She's a woman like any other. I'm talking about the fact that people are making a home for you. I'm a year older than you and I still live with my parents."

"Well, go get married, father a child or two, and people might build a house for you too," was the spirited reply.

"Humpf, I'm not that desperate, thank you very much. I quite like to dip my cock in different waters each night."

The men around him laughed at the crude jest and Thorfinn rubbed the back of his head in embarrassment. It was an endearing gesture coming from someone so virile. He really was a good man, she thought, considerate and helpful. Rowena was lucky to have found him. Not that she had found him, exactly. He had always been part of her life. With their fathers working together at the forge, they had grown up together. Just then her gaze flicked to Torsten, who was suspending a chain over the fireplace, ready to hang the cooking pot. *He* had always been in *her* life...

As had Sven, of course, she reminded herself sternly—and too late for comfort. Damnation, what was this? Why did her mind automatically fly to the wrong brother, the one she was not trying to seduce, the one she was only pretending to be interested in?

The one who kissed like a god.

"Forgive him," Thorfinn was telling Edita. "He can be quite crude, I'm afraid."

She noticed that he was not trying to justify Oddvarr's crudeness to her, with reason. She already knew the man was a lecher.

Like Sven.

This time she did think of him first but her mind instantly rebelled, because it was not fair. Despite appearances, Oddvarr was not like Sven. Sven was not a lecher, he enjoyed the company of women, and made them feel good, which was not quite the same. He never disparaged the ones he was sleeping with to get a laugh out of his friends, talked about "dipping his cock," or boasted about not being ready to settle.

Yes, it was completely different.

"Don't worry, it's already forgotten," Edita told Thorfinn with what could only have been described as a simper. Then she tilted her head in consideration. "So *you're* the famous Thorfinn. Now I understand."

"What do you mean?" A frown. "What do you understand?"

Aife's stomach fell, because she had a very good idea of what her wretched cousin was talking about.

"Now that I've met you, I understand why Aife would have—"

To Aife's profound relief, Thorfinn interrupted Edita mid-declaration. He didn't seem interested in the least by what she had to say. A small miracle. "If you'll excuse me, I see that the twins have woken up. If they're hungry, Rowena will need my help."

He left after one last nod in their direction. As soon as he was out of hearing range, Aife turned to Edita, fury making her voice crackle. "Just what do you think you're doing?"

"What do you mean?"

"You know very well what I mean." Telling Thorfinn about the feelings she'd once entertained about him, making her look like a fool.

Again.

The expression on Edita's face was one of pure innocence. "But surely there's no need for such coyness. Surely Thorfinn is aware that you once wanted him for yourself? Oh! But I see... Perhaps his wife is not, and you'd rather she didn't get to hear of it. Yes, I understand. It can be awkward. Forgive me, I never intended to put you ill at ease."

Could she hit her cousin, Aife wondered? In that moment she was sorely tempted. Far from being sorry, Edita was enjoying herself, pursing her lips like someone who'd just eaten a sweet delicacy. As if all that weren't enough, at that moment, her gaze crossed Torsten's, who had finished what he'd been doing with the chain. It was clear from the anger swirling in his eyes that he had overheard what Edita had told Thorfinn and guessed what they'd been whispering about just now. Well, at least this latest humiliation wouldn't have been in vain. He would see that she'd had good cause to want to put her cousin in her place. After overhearing a second insulting conversation, Torsten would not doubt her sincerity any longer.

It was some consolation she supposed.

Feeling more dejected than ever, Aife averted her gaze. Then she looked up again when Torsten made a brusque gesture. Her heart leaped in her throat. He had put the chain down and he was walking directly over to her, all smoldering intent.

"Aife. Please. I don't know what else to do." He sounded so fierce, so truly determined to have her that her breath caught. "Put me out of my misery. Say you will have me. I cannot wait another day."

Overwhelmed with gratitude for yet another timely intervention, she took the hand he was holding out to her. He was offering her a way out of this conversation with her head held high. When she spoke, she heard the wobble in her voice.

"Yes, Torsten. I will have you."

"So. Here we are. Do you think you will be brave enough?"

A smile came to tease Aife's lips at the question, because of course she would be brave enough. Besides, even if she hadn't been, after what he had done for her, she owed it to Torsten to at least try.

Thanks to him, Edita had stopped teasing her. Indeed, this morning she had looked at her with, not respect exactly, but something resembling...was it envy? Aife thought it might be. Her cousin, who supposedly attracted all the men, had looked a little bit jealous to see her being wooed so forcefully. It seemed that Wulfric had never beaten anyone to a pulp for her or begged her to have him in front of near strangers.

"I think I will be brave," she said, lifting her chin. "Who do you take me for?"

"A fearless warrior?"

Aife laughed, throwing her head to the skies. Fearless warrior? They were talking about tasting honey, something everyone loved to eat. Surely even someone like her, who'd never held a sword, could manage that? True to his word, Torsten had taken her into the forest that morning, in search of a hive. She suspected he wanted to make her feel better after Edita's attempt to embarrass her in front of Thorfinn the day before, and she was grateful for the intention.

"Yes, I'm a fearless warrior," she said with decision.

A smile curled up the corner of Torsten's lips. "You are. Ready then?"

"Ready." As if she would back down now that he had likened her to a warrior. "But wait," she called, when he made to put his hand into the tree hollow. "Won't you get stung?" Remembering the pain the bee had caused her the other day she didn't want him to suffer.

Torsten shrugged the question away. "I've been stung so many times that another sting or three will hardly matter. It's all in good cause anyway. A life without honey is not worth living in my opinion. I will not have this on my conscience."

Aife melted. What had she done to deserve such a good friend? "Well, then, if you're sure."

"I am."

With careful gestures, Torsten inserted his hand into the hive. He had rolled his sleeve up to the elbow and Aife was fascinated by the way the muscles rippled under his skin. She held her breath when she imagined the bees crawling over his naked arm. If they decided to defend themselves against the intruder, he would suffer. But if the expression on his face was to be believed, the bees had decided not to bother him. Seeing that he'd not been stung on her account, she allowed herself to relax. A moment later, he lifted his hand back up just as carefully as before and she saw that his index and middle finger were coated in sticky, golden honey. He lifted the hand above his mouth and allowed some of it to dribble onto his tongue.

Realization hit.

If she wanted to taste the honey—and she dearly wanted to —she was going to have to lick his fingers clean. Not once since she had agreed to follow him into the woods had she considered that such a lewd act would be required.

Aife's gaze met Torsten's and heat bloomed between her legs. This was a lot more evocative than she had counted on. Where was the fearless warrior now, she wondered? Reduced to a puddle on the forest floor, it would seem.

Not waiting for her to change her mind, Torsten slowly brought his hand to her mouth.

"Open."

Utterly under the spell of the moment, Aife did as instructed, and welcomed the two fingers he was holding out between her lips. Refusing was not an option, even if accepting felt positively scandalous. She sucked at the thick substance he'd gathered for her. Everything within her exploded when divine taste hit her tongue. Her eyes fluttered shut and a groan escaped her lips. This was truly delicious, even sweeter than she remembered. How had she deprived herself of that treat for so long? Greedy for more, she licked and licked, swirling her tongue until, at last, he was clean. Still, Torsten seemed reluctant to move and take his fingers out of her mouth.

Eventually, he did.

Crossing his arms over his chest he leaned back against the tree, looking rather satisfied with himself. "That good, huh?"

"That good," she whispered back. "Better." Was it because he'd made her suck the honey from his own fingers that she had enjoyed the wonderful flavor so much, Aife wondered? Had it somehow added to the experience? Would it have been the same if he'd handed her a wooden spoon? Somehow she didn't think so.

Very conscious of the fact that, this time, she couldn't pretend Edita was looking and that Sven wasn't anywhere to be seen, Aife lifted her head to Torsten, readying herself for a kiss. It seemed the perfect conclusion to the moment they had shared, the only appropriate way to thank him for taking her to the woods and ensuring she would not deprive herself of a delicacy any longer. Would he respond to the silent invitation?

To her relief and delight, he did.

Their first kiss by the forge had been shocking. The second one, after she'd been stung by the bee, had been chaste, little more than a friendly peck. The third one, when she'd pretended Edita was watching, had scorched her insides. This fourth one was heart-stoppingly sweet, and she was certain it was not due to the honey they had both just eaten. Granted, Torsten's tongue was slick with its floral taste, but it was the way he was holding her, careful, reverent, that gave it a special flavor. It was as if he thought her beautiful and precious. And in that moment, she did feel beautiful, precious—and desirable. It was not just in her mind either. Against her stomach was the proof that Torsten was reacting like a man would at the proximity of a woman he found attractive. It was exactly what she had hoped to see for years, the proof that men could want her in their bed.

It was enough, for now.

Torsten wanted her, and yet he was not trying to take advantage of her. They were alone, they were kissing, he could have been forgiven for thinking he could try to coax her into offering more. But he had not even tried to deepen the kiss. He was savoring her, behaving as if holding her into his arms was a pleasure in itself, as if the kiss were enough to satisfy him.

She drew away, one hand on his chest, the other around his trim waist, both touched by his restraint and grateful that he'd shown her there was nothing wrong with her. And for the first time she wondered if she had not been dazzled by the wrong brother.

"So?" Torsten's voice had become impossibly low and husky. "Have you changed you mind?"

"Changed my m-mind?" she stammered. Did he know she had been reconsidering what she thought of Sven? How? Could he read her mind?

"About honey."

Oh, honey... Of course. "Yes. I think it—"

"What the *fuck*?"

The voice booming from behind her caused Aife's insides to curdle. No!

The last thing she wanted right now was to be interrupted and the last person she wanted to see was the one standing by the tree, no doubt glaring at her.

"Moon."

Disentangling herself from Torsten's embrace as naturally as she could, she turned to face her brother. Her very irate brother.

Had he seen the kiss? Or had he merely happened upon them locked in an intimate embrace and drawn his own conclusions? Either way, it was clear he didn't approve.

"What is this?" he growled, taking a step forward. "Never mind, I can see what it is for myself. Sister, move away so I can throttle the traitor."

"Calm yourself. No one is going to throttle anyone," she said, placing herself squarely in front of him, knowing he would never risk hurting her by trying to barge past her, no matter how furious he was. Behind her, Torsten was wisely keeping silent, letting her handle her brother how she thought best. A protest from him now would not help. "We weren't doing anything wrong."

That was true, at least, the kiss they'd shared had felt anything but wrong.

"You mean that you weren't kissing? Because it sure as hell looked as if you were about to—"

"Even if we were, it would be nothing to do with you." Another truth. She was old enough to decide whom she kissed or didn't kiss. It had nothing to do with her brother.

Moon's eyes narrowed but he didn't try to push past her. "You mean that you two are not involved? He's not lain with—"

This time she and Torsten spoke at the same time, before he could finish the sentence. "No!"

There was such conviction in their voices, such shock on their faces that Moon's shoulders visibly relaxed. Disaster had been averted.

"Well then, there's no harm done." He gestured to Aife, his gaze still on his friend. "Come. Let me escort you back to the village."

"I don't need your—"

This time he did look at her. His blue eyes were sending shards. "Aife, either you come with me now or you watch as I have a man-to-man discussion with our friend about what is the acceptable way to hold my little sister."

She sighed, knowing she would never win this battle. It was already a miracle Moon had chosen to give them the benefit of the doubt and had not pounced on Torsten.

"I'm coming."

After one last look at Torsten, she followed her brother.

5

Oh, this was not good, not good at all.

Still panting from the strength of another spectacular release, Torsten stared at the ceiling. Just above him dust motes floated in and out of the golden sunray piercing through a hole in the wood of the shutter. He watched them dance while he waited for his heartbeat to come back to normal. It was not just the intensity of the moment that had stolen his breath away. It was the cause for it. Aife's face had been on his mind while he'd coaxed himself to release, her name had been on his lips when he'd erupted in pleasure. He'd thought of her all the way. With every stroke, he'd relived details of their decadent kisses and their time together.

Stroke. Her wicked tongue swirling in his mouth.

Stroke. Her eyes fluttering in delight as she'd sucked at his fingers in the forest.

Stroke. The little moans she gave when he pressed himself tight against her.

He shook his head. Things were quickly spiraling out of control.

It had started a week ago, the day her laugh had catapulted

him into a new realm of sensations. Then he'd taken illicit plea-sure in kissing her even though they both knew they were only just pretending. Now here he was, stroking himself while imag-ining all he could do to her and all she could do to him. Where would it stop? It *had* to stop—they were just friends, he was just helping her feel better, this wouldn't lead anywhere. That she should stir such desires in him felt wrong. He didn't want to create problems between them or fall out with his best friend over it.

And yet, despite all that, he couldn't deny that he was attracted to her. The proof of his desire was cooling down on his naked stomach right now. How would she feel if she knew what he had just done? How would Moon react if he found out his friend pleasured himself while imagining his sister in bed with him?

The answer was obvious. He would kill him, *had* almost killed him the other day in the forest, for doing nothing more than hold her in his arms. What he would do if he knew what he'd done to her in his imagination didn't bear thinking about.

But all of this begged another question. Why had his desire suddenly awoken with such fierceness? Why did he feel, for the first time in what felt like forever, tempted at the idea of bedding a woman?

Hope surged through Torsten. Perhaps he had finally over-come the obstacle that had blocked him for years? There was only one way to find out if his body had at long last started to behave like other men's. He would have to try to bed a woman, something he had never managed to do since the day he'd first tried. His first thought went to Aife, before he dismissed it. He could not use her for this experiment—she had come to him for no other reason than to protect herself against her vile cousin's attacks. She would be understandably shocked, and possibly horrified if he suggested they lie together, thinking he was taking advantage of the situation to get under her skirts, or that he thought himself entitled to a reward for his help. Neither possibility appealed. He would not have her taking him for a lecher who was not above exploiting her for his sensual gratification. Besides, if he failed to bed her, he would not bear the humiliation.

No, he needed someone else, someone he wouldn't have to see afterward if it all went awry.

Bera.

The name popped into his mind before he could even start to wonder who might be suited to the task. Torsten opened his eyes, wondering where the suggestion had come from. But the more he thought of it, the more he had to agree that Magnus's niece would be perfect. She lived in the village beyond the valley, but had just come for a short visit to her uncle. The last time Torsten had visited the forge she had accidentally walked into him while exiting the door. They would both have fallen to the floor had he not been strong enough to steady her. He had not missed the way she'd looked at him while thanking him, staying in his arms for longer than necessary.

Well, Bera was a comely girl, aged about twenty summers or so, and she would be gone in a few days' time. Perhaps he should kiss her and see what happened. Would he get aroused, like he did when he kissed Aife? Would he want to go further? Would he be able to if she responded to his advances? It was worth a try. Aife had used him to prove something to her cousin —and herself—why could he not use a willing woman to verify if the curse plaguing his life had finally been lifted? There was little risk. If his intuition was correct, Bera would be amenable to seduction, which would allow him to finally know where things stood. If she wasn't, then he would simply not touch her and be no worse off.

He got up, had a quick wash and put his clothes on with

decision. Then he walked over to the forge before he could change his mind. On the way, he couldn't help glancing over to Aife's hut. He knew she was an early riser so chances were she might have already gone into the woods in search of food or wood for the fire. What would she think if she knew what he was planning to do? How would she feel about him going to another woman?

Nothing, he told himself sternly. She wouldn't think anything. She wouldn't be interested or feel betrayed in any way, because they were only pretending to be involved and he was free to act the way he wanted. Yes, except he wasn't sure that going to Bera was quite what he wanted. It was what he needed to do.

He averted his gaze from the hut and carried on, a man on a mission. He could not afford to get distracted by thoughts of Aife, not when he had a goal in mind.

Before he could get too near the forge, the door opened, letting out a waft of warm air scented with smoke and metal—and a tall, blonde woman who blushed as soon as she saw him in front of her. Bera. Two things immediately became clear. She had recognized him and she was most definitely interested in a tryst.

Good. That was just what he needed, or rather, *wanted*, he amended quickly.

"Good morning." Torsten said, coming to a halt a little closer than he would have with a woman he did not intend to seduce. But he might as well make his intentions clear from the start.

"Good morning. Torsten, is it not?"

"Indeed, it is. I'm the one who almost landed on top of you the day you arrived in the village. I apologize for that." He was not truly sorry, as there had been no harm done. He simply wanted to put an evocative image in her mind and see how she reacted. Just as he'd hoped, her blush deepened further.

"It was nothing. And I'm sure I wouldn't have minded ending up under you."

Torsten barely repressed a scoff at this bold answer. He could forget whatever scruples he'd had about seducing her. Just as he'd suspected, she was more than willing, so much so that he found himself at a loss. What could he say to that?

Shall we go into the woods now and see now how you'd feel under me?

No, that was something Sven would say, not him. Fortunately, at that moment the door to the forge opened, preventing him from answering in any way.

"Ah, Bera, there you are. Would you do me a favor?" Magnus asked, walking toward them. Spotting Torsten, he wiped his hand on his apron and gave his hand a shake. "Could you take this axe back to Elwyn, with my thanks? I've finished with it and I know he needs it."

"I will take it," Torsten told Magnus. "It looks heavy."

It didn't, not particularly, but it was the opportunity he'd been waiting for to spend some time with Bera. Magnus arched a brow but didn't comment. Instead, he handed him the axe and went back to his anvil.

"I thank you," Bera said when they were alone once more. "I will admit the axe looks awfully heavy. But you're so strong it shouldn't be a problem for you..."

With this comment she placed a hand over his chest and looked at him from under her lashes. Well. It seemed that they were going to kiss as soon as he had delivered the axe, whether he liked it or not. Not sure what to make of that, he nodded toward Elwyn's hut and started walking. Bera followed, making sure to stay close and throwing heated glances his way.

By the time the two of them had reached their destination, Torsten was having second thoughts. The idea of kissing this woman who was nothing to him and too forward for his taste suddenly seemed not only absurd but also pointless. He already sensed it wouldn't achieve anything, save make him feel wretched, because her attitude was exactly the one guaranteed to make him recoil when the moment came to tumble her onto the floor. What had possessed him to think it would be so simple? He should have thought instead of rushing out of the door while still recovering from his explosive release. Everyone knew men were not at their best in such moments. But rushed he had.

And now, here he was, with a woman about to pounce on him.

That she was so desperate surprised him, for he wasn't even sure what he'd done to attract her. What was certain was that he didn't know how to handle this situation. Unlike his rogue of a brother, he'd never been skilled in the art of wooing women. With Aife, it had been easy, natural even. There had been no need to do anything to provoke her desire. No, indeed, because he had not exactly wooed her, had he? Their kiss had not been provoked by desire, or anything of the sort. It was not the same and he should not compare the two situations—or the two women.

Yes, enough about Aife. He was here with Bera, for a reason, and he should not lose sight of it.

With decision, he raised his hand and knocked on his friend's door.

"Ah, thank you." Elwyn took the axe he was handing him. "Sorry, I would have offered you a drink but Bee and I were about to leave for town," he added, glancing back to where his wife was fastening a cloak over her shoulders.

"It's all right," Torsten assured him. Evidently fate had decided that he would have to face Bera alone and live with the consequences of his rash decision. "We'll leave you to it."

"How can I thank you for coming to my rescue, Torsten?"

Bera whispered, as soon as the two of them started heading back toward the forge.

Her rescue! Really, not only was she bold, but she was not afraid of sounding ridiculous. "There's no need to thank me. I carried an axe, nothing more," he could not help but point out. Surely the feat deserved little praise. But, far from being put out, she placed herself in front of him, forcing him to come to a halt.

"Yes, you did carry the axe for me. Allow me to show you my gratitude."

There it was, the moment of truth. Better get it over with. After all, it was what she wanted, and what he wanted too, he reminded himself. But as soon as he drew Bera into his arms, Torsten knew he would not bed her. He could probably have kissed her, given her this satisfaction, at least, but the problem was, he didn't even want to do that.

She smelled all wrong, she looked all wrong, she felt all wrong against him. Too tall, too soft, nothing like—

He clenched his jaw before he started comparing her to Aife again. This was *not* what it was about, he told himself. It was not his attraction to Aife that made it impossible for him to contemplate kissing Bera; he simply disliked the brash and silly way she behaved.

"I'm sorry," he said, loosening his hold on her. Going to her had been a mistake, he saw that now.

"What are you sorry for?" she whispered, grinding herself against his groin, her intent obvious.

"I think you want something from me..." he started, unsure how to extricate himself from the trap he'd created for himself without hurting her feelings. She had done nothing wrong, this was his issue, not hers. "Something I cannot give you."

Her face underwent a transformation when she sneered. Suddenly she looked almost ugly, much older than her twenty summers and almost mean. "I see. Not only are you incapable of bedding women, but you also lack the balls to kiss the ones who want you." To his shock, she cupped him intimately, the gesture rough rather than seductive, and brought her mouth to his ear. "I'd heard as much and I refused to believe it, considering how manly you look. I can see now that it was no exaggeration. You're as limp as a worm when a real man would be hard as rock with a woman in his arms, touching him thus."

Torsten gritted his teeth. There was no wondering whom the rumors had come from, but he was still shocked to see that Bera, who had only just arrived in the village, had heard them. Either they were spreading fast or she knew Sigrid's friend personally. It was just his luck. But no wonder he was, in the woman's words, limp as a worm. This time it was no cause for concern, as he knew exactly why his body had refused to stir. He felt no real desire for her, to the point that he had not even been able to kiss her, and she was holding him in a grip that was anything but sensual.

All in her bid to humiliate him.

By the gods. Now he knew why she had been so eager, why it had been so easy to woo her. She had not felt real desire for him either, she had just wanted to see if what she'd heard about him was true. And, unfortunately, it was.

"Well, let me go and see if I can find another man to see to my needs," she hissed. "Surely not everyone is as useless in this village."

With those words she finally let him go and headed in the direction of the bridge. He was about to call back to her when a roar from behind him caused his blood to freeze into his veins.

"You bastard!"

Fuck.

When Torsten finally dared to turn around, he found Moon glaring at him from the corner of his hut. His heart fell because there was no wondering what the reason behind his friend's ire was. He would have seen him holding a woman tight, their faces inches apart, and her murmuring words in his ear while she cupped him intimately. It would look damning, as he'd not heard that she was actually disparaging him for his lack of interest in her.

Before he could do anything, Moon had launched himself at him.

"No!" Torsten cried out, blocking the blow aimed at his jaw. "It's not what you think!"

"Oh? You mean I didn't catch you kissing Bera the day after I caught you with Aife in your arms in the forest, when the two of you did your best to convince me you had done nothing wrong? Well, I'm done listening to your lies. You will not treat my sister with such disrespect!"

This time the punch to the gut could not be stopped.

"Yes, you did catch me, but it doesn't mean a thing," Torsten gasped, doubling over. *Sorðinn*, but the man could hit!

"That's what men always say. I'm not sure Bera would agree with you. She seemed—"

"Not with Bera, I meant with Aife."

For a moment Moon looked as if he was about to choke on his own tongue. "You *bastard!*"

By the gods, he was not explaining himself very well. Torsten groaned. He'd just all but told Moon that his sister didn't mean anything to him. Which was not quite the truth, at least not in the way his friend would understand, at least not in the way he'd meant, at least not—

Blast it all, this was precisely why he had gone to Bera, to understand where he stood where Aife was concerned, to make sense of the new development between them and to see if he could function like a man. Look what a mess his stupid idea had landed him in. He was more confused than ever about his feelings for Aife, he'd made an enemy of Bera and he'd made his best friend hate him.

Guilt and shame sliced through him.

Three years ago when Moon and Eyja had come back from war together and he'd seen something had changed between them, Torsten had taken it badly. Though he was not proud of his reaction now that the two of them were married and blissfully happy, at the time it had been an unwelcome shock for him and his two brothers to imagine their friend in bed with their little sister.

No doubt Moon would be feeling the same when he thought of him and Aife together, which explained the blow to the stomach. Except that it was completely different. Torsten had not slept with Aife, nor was he likely to. Unfortunately.

The thought caused him to inhale sharply. He wasn't supposed to entertain such notions about his longtime friend!

"Listen," he said, before his thoughts got tangled any further —and Moon could hit him again. "Please, go and speak to Aife. This was her idea, she'll be able to explain it better than I can."

For the longest moment Moon stared at him, as if trying to see to the bottom of his soul. Apparently what he saw there satisfied him, at least for now.

"Very well, I will," he said darkly, "because you're my friend and I want to give you the benefit of the doubt. But make no mistake. If she tells me that she is serious about you and I see that you're just toying with her, I will make sure you wish you had kept your hands to yourself."

"I saw Torsten kissing Bera this morning."

The unexpected words, or rather the pain they provoked inside her, were a shock to Aife. Torsten was kissing other women? But, of course, he was. She chided herself for her first, instinctive jealous reaction, a reaction she was not entitled to. Why would he not kiss other women? It was not as if they were really involved; he didn't owe anything to her.

She stared at her brother, careful to not betray any dismay because it was obvious that Moon was trying to find out what was between her and Torsten and would not take it too well to be told that they had done things they were not supposed to do. The day before, he had caught them in each other's arms, and they had done their best to convince him nothing untoward had happened. He had allowed them to get away with it, but apparently he still had his doubts and he wanted to make sure he'd not been made a fool out of. It was therefore vital she convinced Moon he didn't need to beat Torsten to a pulp for taking advantage of her.

"Did you?" she asked, doing her best to sound unconcerned. For good measure, she shrugged, even though her chest was strangely hollow at the idea of him kissing Bera. The woman was tall and curvy, everything she was not. The fact played with her insecurities in the worst way. Was Edita right, then? Were men incapable of seeing past her lack of womanly curves? "What of it? He can do whatever he wants, kiss whomever he wants. I care not."

"How am I supposed to believe that, when only yesterday the two of you were—"

"We told you, Torsten and I are nothing to one another," she cut in, before he reminded her of the delicious kiss they had shared. "It is no lie. We are only friends, he can do what he wants. He hasn't promised anything to me, and I certainly didn't promise anything to him."

Her brother appeared more confused than ever, which was perhaps understandable. "Then why the hell did you kiss him?"

Damnation, she had wondered if he had seen the kiss, but it

seemed that he had, after all. There was only one thing she could think of to placate her brother and protect Torsten. She would have to tell him the truth.

"If you must know, I wanted him to help me get the man I truly want."

"And who might that be?"

"Sven," she answered reluctantly. If Moon objected to her and Torsten being involved because he was his friend, then he would object to Sven, for the same reason.

But instead of a roar of outrage, an incredulous scoff answered her. "How on earth is kissing Torsten going to help you woo Sven, or any other man for that matter?"

Yes. That was the question. She had already concluded herself that her plan was a poor one. Still, she had no choice but to answer and expose the whole ludicrousness of it. "I thought that if Sven saw that other men found me desirable, he would start to take an interest in me." It sounded rather ridiculous, now that she was saying it out loud and she dreaded to consider what Moon must think.

"Yesterday you and Torsten were in the middle of the forest, where no one could see you. I only happened upon you by accident, and Sven was nowhere to be seen!" Moon exclaimed. "What good could that possibly do?"

"Yes, well, yesterday we were in the forest but generally we... I try to—"

She stopped, unable to explain herself in a way that would make sense to her brother. Because none of it made sense, she saw that now. Fortunately, Moon took pity on her.

"Has it worked?" he asked more gently.

"No," she admitted, falling on the stool behind her. "Sven still sees me as a friend, nothing more. And I'm starting to think he will never see me in any other way."

And yet... Yet, she didn't feel half as dejected as she'd imagined she would feel. Her pride had been hurt when she'd had to admit out loud that Sven cared nothing about whom she kissed, but her heart had not missed any beat.

"Oh, I've been such a fool! 'Tis like Edita says, no one will ever take any interest in me."

"Wait, what does our unbearable cousin have to do with this?"

Aife made a gesture of helplessness. "She is about to get married for the second time, while I'm alone. She says no man will ever be interested in a plain, scrawny woman such as I am. And she's right. I have never—"

"Hush. Edita is a fool, we all know that." Moon lifted her up and drew her into his arms. "Sister, you know I love Sven. But he is..."

"Yes. I know."

Though he didn't finish his sentence, unfortunately, she knew exactly what he meant. Sven was not ready to settle, might never be. She stayed cradled in her brother's embrace a long moment, relishing his warmth and unconditional support. Then Moon drew away and placed a kiss on her forehead.

"Go tell Torsten you don't need his help any longer."

This time her heartbeat did increase in alarm. Interesting, she observed in a detached corner of her mind... Acknowledging out loud that she had not managed to attract Sven's attention had provoked no reaction inside of her, but the idea of putting an end to what she and Torsten were doing was causing her whole body to lurch in protest.

"Why would I do that?" she asked Moon, doing her best not to betray her consternation.

"Because there's no point in two people kissing if it doesn't lead anywhere."

"No, no point," she agreed weakly. Still, she'd found that she had rather liked it. More than liked it. Torsten kissed exceptionally well, nothing like the other men she had kissed. It was as if he were awed by her, as if he wanted to become part of her soul. The feeling was intoxicating.

"Besides, he clearly is interested in another woman and he should be free to pursue her. It is only fair."

"Yes." The word barely passed Aife's lips. He should be allowed to do what he wanted with Bera.

And she to go back to her inspiring life.

"TORSTEN. I'M SORRY." Moon ran a hand down the back of his head like a man suffering a deep embarrassment. "You were right. I spoke to Aife. She told me everything, and I thank you for doing your best to help her, even though I fear it is a lost cause."

Torsten could not help a snort. A lost cause. Definitely. Edita was so steeped in her own malice he wasn't sure she would ever see—or care—that she was hurting people.

"It's not a problem."

No, it hadn't been. Kissing Aife had been anything but a chore. With her, he had rediscovered the simple pleasure of kissing, something he had enjoyed as a younger man but that had become fraught with complications of late. He'd been too worried about the possible consequences to let himself go.

With Aife it had been different. There had been no fear that the kisses would lead anywhere he didn't want to go. Not once had she demanded more, tried to entice him into bed like the other women had, or used him for her own amusement like Bera had. He had started to relax around her, enjoy her company and their kisses for what they were. He'd noticed they sometimes kissed even when they were alone, as if they could not help themselves, as if they enjoyed the kisses they shared for what they were.

If truth be told, he had started to wonder if he should ask Aife if she really wanted to stop what they were doing once her cousin had gone back home. Perhaps the two of them could see where this might lead.

Every time he made her laugh, which was often, because every time they met he did his best to provoke her evocative laughter, he reacted in the same way. His body ignited in desire, his heart started beating with purpose, and his mind sparked back to life. He had started to notice that his feeling of dejection was beginning to fade. Aife had reawakened his lust for life.

"Anyway," Moon was saying. "What do you think? Do you think Sven has even noticed you two together?"

Sven? Probably not. But what did it matter?

"I would be surprised if he had," Torsten answered. "He has enough conquests of his own to worry about any of mine."

"Yes. As I thought." Moon nodded. "I told Aife as much, as gently as I could, but you know..."

What did he know? This conversation was becoming rather odd and Torsten wasn't sure he quite followed it. "Mm." He gave a non-committal grunt, hoping it would be enough.

"It is probably for the best, because as you can imagine, the idea of my little sister in bed with a man who will never give her what she deserves is not one to please me."

What in the name of Odin was Moon talking about now? Did he believe they were involved, or did he not? Nothing he was saying made any sense.

And then he understood. The day Aife had first kissed him, by the forge, Sven had been with her, talking about what Emma had done. She had been laughing her new, sultry, evocative laugh for him. She had only thrown herself into Torsten's arms when Sven had left to see Freydis. She had wanted *Sven* to see them, not her cousin.

She had used him to make his brother jealous.

And then when he had asked her why she had kissed him, she had lied.

"Excuse me," he said through gritted teeth, feeling like a prized fool. To think he'd been about to ask her if they could see where their new relationship could go... What a naïve idiot he really was, one who didn't know anything about women. "I need to go see Aife."

"Don't worry about it," Moon called out. "I already explained that you wouldn't need to help her any longer. You're free to see Bera. Aife doesn't mind."

6

———

A*ife doesn't mind.*

In other words, she didn't care about him, didn't care whom he kissed or whom he bedded, and no wonder. She cared nothing for him, because the man she actually wanted was his brother.

Thank the gods Moon had come to talk to him when he had. Torsten had been about to make a fool of himself and ask Aife if they could be more than friends, oblivious to the fact that she was trying to attract another man, unaware that this game they had started to play and that had taken over his life meant nothing to her. He'd taken a gamble, and he had lost. For the first time in years he'd considered giving a woman a chance, only to discover that she was lusting after someone else.

To add to his humiliation, that someone else was his own brother. But of course it had been about bloody Sven all along. How had he not seen that? Hadn't he noticed she was laughing in that unusual, sultry way on that day outside the forge, while she was talking to his brother? Hadn't their first kiss, the inexplicable one, happened moments after Sven had gone to join a woman he intended to bed?

Torsten's feet pounded the ground as he hurried in the direction of the forest. Aife's mother, Frigyth, had told him he would find her in the field on the other side of the river where the villagers kept their horses, getting Moon's horse ready for him. Even better. Away from the village there was no chance anyone would overhear their conversation.

He found her tightening the girth on Grendel's saddle. Next to the massive stallion, she looked so petite, so fragile... He did not let the sight affect him. While he was mad at her, the last thing he needed was to admire the contrast between the horse's powerful rump and her delicate hands, or to observe how her golden hair shone against the shiny black coat of—

Enough of this! He was angry, not entranced. He stormed through the gate and called out to her.

"Aife."

She turned her head toward him and instantly flushed. Had she seen the look of thunder in his eyes? Probably. It would be hard to miss.

"Torsten. What are you doing here?"

"Why shouldn't I be here?"

"I-I don't know."

He planted himself in front of her and had the satisfaction of seeing her swallow. Yes, she was definitely nervous. Perhaps she was wondering why his attitude had changed. Perhaps she was feeling guilty for misleading him—as she should. Perhaps she feared his reaction if he ever found out why she was using him.

Well, he *had* found out. And he felt furious and humiliated. Because of it, he decided to get straight to the point.

"I was wondering," he started, crossing his arms on his chest. "How is it going with Edita? Has she seen any of our kisses yet? What has she to say about them? Has she changed her mind about you being unable to attract men? Or perhaps she doesn't see me as man enough to count. Perhaps seeing you with one of my brothers would impress her more."

If he were honest, that she had fallen for one of his brothers was what bothered him the most. Steinar was the eldest, Sven the youngest, he was "the other one." The two of them were both as strong as their father, he was a lot leaner and not as tall. He'd always been the odd one out, in looks and temperament, the one not at ease with women, and he was currently the only one unhappy with his situation. It wasn't even the lies and the betrayal of trust he hated, even if he did, it was the cruelty of choosing him for her petty schemes. If she had to do it, couldn't she at least have chosen someone less insecure in their power of attraction? Haakon, Arne, Oddvarr, none of them would have minded.

Imagining her in another man's arms sent his stomach roiling. He had better get to the point.

"Tell me. Does your cousin even know about us?"

Aife had the honesty to appear flustered at the question. But her answer was far from satisfactory. "You know she does. You pretended to fight for me."

Yes, with Sven of all people. How ironic. "You must have been mightily disappointed to see that I ended up to be the one begging for your favors. Because I am not the one you wanted to win, am I?"

She took a step backward, looking worried. "Please, Torsten."

"Please what? How can I serve now? What do you want me to do? Kiss you? What would be the point? There's no one here to see us." He leaned forward, bristling with intent, closing the gap between them once more. "Tell me, what do you want me to do? Lift your skirts and pin you to the nearest tree?"

With those words, Torsten grabbed her by the waist. The contact of her slender body made his loins flare in ways Bera's lush curves had failed to do. This was most unfortunate—and unexpected. Wasn't he angry at her? Wasn't he supposed to be, if not immune to desire, at least hard to arouse? Yes, and up until then, he had always been. His own inadequacies, coupled with the resentment he felt for desiring this woman who had make a fool out of him, caused him to react a lot more strongly than he would have otherwise, be a lot cruder. His hold around Aife tightened at the same time as his resolve hardened. She wasn't to know he was about to issue an empty threat, that he would never be able to follow through on it, she just needed to see that it was dangerous to play with fire. *He* might not burn, but another man would.

"Do you want me to fuck you where you stand? Make you scream my name?"

"No!" she rasped, trying to push him away. Her eyes had gone wide as cart wheels and no wonder. This was a side of him she had never seen before, a side he hadn't known he possessed, a side he wasn't sure he liked at all.

"No," he said bitterly, releasing her and taking a step back. "There would be no point in us doing anything, would there, since Sven isn't here to see."

"S-Sven?"

"Don't even start pretending that he is not the reason you wanted to act as if you and I were involved." His brother Steinar's horse, Fáfnir, raised his head when he started to snarl at her, but Torsten was too incensed to pay attention. "Seducing Sven was your intention all along, was it not? You don't really care what Edita thinks, and you most certainly don't care about me."

"But I do care."

Aife had never felt so wretched because say what Torsten might, she did care. In the last few days, she had come to care for him more than she would ever have thought possible. Their moments spent together had been perfect, and shown her that there was nothing wrong with her.

And now the moment she had dreaded for days had come. Torsten had found out what she had been desperate to hide from him, that she had kissed him to attract his brother's attention. His reaction was even worse than what she'd feared it would be. Facing his anger would have been bad enough, but the hurt in his eyes was what truly gutted her. How he had found out the truth? Who had told him? Not Cwenthryth, surely? But who else knew about her feelings for Sven?

"Moon told me, in case you were wondering," he said, as if he'd read her mind.

Of course. She had told her brother the truth earlier that morning, thinking to protect Torsten from retaliation. Well, she might have protected him from physical harm, but she had not protected him from what he saw as the worst humiliation.

Tears fell down her cheeks. How could she explain that she wasn't sure what she felt about Sven any longer? Since Torsten had held her in his arms and given her a kiss that had turned her world upside down and her body inside out, she had been forced to reconsider what she felt. Nothing had happened the way she had imagined. He'd helped her willingly, he'd kissed her with exquisite skill, passion even, and yet he'd never once tried to take advantage of her stratagem, never once demanded more than what she was ready to give.

And somewhere along the way she had come to feel things for him.

"I'm sorry. I did want Sven to think we were involved with each other," she admitted in a low voice, feeling both ashamed and ridiculous but wanting to be honest. He deserved that much.

How had she not thought this would end in disaster? Not only had she not attracted the attention of the man she'd set out to attract, but she had wounded a dear friend. Torsten had every reason to be mad at her. She had lied to him, not just one, but twice.

"I wanted to tell you, but I didn't think you'd understand."

The glare he threw her made it clear that it was the wrong thing to say. "Oh. First, you assume that I won't mind being lied to and used, then you don't credit me with the intelligence needed to understand a foolish woman's plan. I'm flattered."

"That's not what I mean... Of course you're not a—"

Aife knew she would never manage to put her thoughts in order while her emotions were in such disarray. All she could seem to do was blurt out the first things that came to her mind and hurt Torsten further. It was best to put some distance between them for now, give herself time to think of a better way of making him understand what it had really been about—and what it had evolved into.

Her brother's horse was grazing just behind her, already saddled and ready to go. Torsten had been so upset earlier that he'd not closed the gate properly. It was wide open, offering her a way out of this mess. She would never outrun Torsten on foot, but Grendel would whisk her away and give her the respite she needed.

She placed a foot in the stirrup and hoisted herself into the saddle before Torsten could stop her. As soon as the horse passed the gate and bounded toward the forest, she felt her heart go lighter. She wouldn't have to continue the painful confrontation right now.

Before disappearing under the cover of the trees, Aife couldn't help stealing one last glance at the field behind her. Torsten, who'd always been a much better rider than she was, had vaulted onto Fáfnir's bare back and was making his way toward her.

Damnation, he was coming after her.

7

———————

Torsten had never ridden a horse without a saddle or bridle before, but he did not let that bother him. He and his brother's mount knew each other well, and Aife had never been the most confident rider. Cantering on Grendel, she would not outrun him on Fáfnir galloping at full speed. Except that she was not merely cantering. When she had seen him vault onto Fáfnir she had kicked Grendel into a frenzied, uncontrolled gallop.

Was she so desperate to avoid him that she was risking breaking her neck? Had he been too harsh, too crude, too frightening?

"Aife, stop!" he called out, cursing her impetuosity and his lack of restraint. This was going to end badly, he could sense it.

Barely a moment later, he was proven right.

As they rounded a clump of trees, Grendel spooked, surprised by the unexpected sight of four men camping by the rocks. Chaos erupted. One of the Saxons' horses, which was being tethered to a tree, took fright and reared, sending his handler to the ground. The men shouted. Grendel bucked in turn, and Aife was tossed cleanly off the saddle. Before Torsten could blink, both panicked horses were racing back to the village.

"*Pour l'amour de Dieu!*" one of the men shouted, running after his friend's mount. "Tonnerre, come back!"

Unsurprisingly, the horse ignored the call and soon disappeared around the bend with Grendel.

Once everything had quietened, the Saxons turned to glare at Torsten who was still in on Fáfnir's back. He expected insults for the way he and Aife had burst into the meadow, shattering their peace and causing their horse to bold away, but to his surprise, the man closest to the rocks smiled when he spotted Aife on the ground next to him.

"Look at that!" he told his friends. He was tall and had dark ginger hair cut in a very distinctive style, shaved very high at the back of the head. This, combined with his and his friend's accent, caused Torsten to reassess his first impression. These men were not Saxons, like he had assumed, but Normans. "A Norsewoman *and* a Norseman. Just our luck," Ginger finished.

He didn't seem overly affected by the loss of Tonnerre the horse, or worried about his friend's injury. All he seemed interested in was having two Norse people unexpectedly brought to him. Torsten could not understand why that might be, and he didn't like it one bit.

He nudged Fáfnir closer to the place where Aife was lying, still as a corpse. His heart picked up speed. Why was she not getting up? It had been a while since Grendel had sent her flying. Was she more hurt than he'd feared? He jumped down and made to go to her but the three men still able to move placed themselves in front of him, blocking his way.

"*Is* he a Norseman, though?" the oldest one asked, taking in his dark eyes and hair that was most definitely not golden. "He doesn't look it. Not blond enough."

Torsten bristled. How dare the men question his identity, and what was it to them anyway?

"Of course I'm a Norseman, though why you should care is beyond me," he growled in Norse. The best way to convince them was to talk his father's language. Besides, he didn't want to enter in a negotiation with them. He just wanted to get to Aife, and see that she was all right. "Now, out of my way!" he added in English.

He tried to elbow his way between the men, but the ginger-haired man, who appeared to lead this pack of obtuse men, moved forward.

"Not so fast, Norseman," he said, pointing a short blade to his heart. "The woman is ours now, and so are you."

Torsten cursed himself for being taken unawares. Too focused on Aife, he had not even seen the man draw the knife out. He stilled. No sense in getting injured straight away. "What do you want with us?"

Instead of answering, Ginger asked his companions. "Are you thinking what I'm thinking, *mes amis*?" Grunts answered him. Evidently, they were. "That's right. I'm thinking that Ranulf will have no choice but to eat his foul words. He thinks that we Normans are pampered weaklings hiding behind King Guillaume's authority and cannot fend for ourselves. He bet me only last night that I could never defeat a Norseman in single combat. Well, I'll bring him this one on a plate, along with a pretty Norsewoman to take his pleasure with. After that he will never dare question my ability or my loyalty. I will finally be allowed my rightful place and be accepted into the clan."

Whatever clan he was talking about wasn't clear, but one thing was certain. The men were freshly arrived from Normandy, and eager to find recognition amongst the local Saxon lords by playing on their contempt for the Norse community. Torsten swallowed. There was nothing like having a common enemy to unite two people. If Ginger wanted to prove his loyalty to this Ranulf by handing him a Norseman and woman, then they were in serious trouble.

He might be killed in some cruel ritual while Aife would be allowed to live, but only for as long as the man needed her for his amusement.

Before the three men joined forces to immobilize him, which he felt sure was coming, he threw a branch at Fáfnir's rump. The animal had to flee before he could be captured also. Not only that, but with luck, his arrival in the village so shortly after a riderless Grendel would signal there was a problem and a search party would be sent. The slap had the desired effect—the surprised horse bolted off, narrowly missing stomping over one of the Normans.

In the next heartbeat, Torsten was seized by both arms and a second, longer blade dug into the base of his spine, preventing him from moving. Had he been alone, he would still have tried to disentangle himself, headbutted one of the men while kicking back at the one holding the knife, but he wasn't alone, which was the problem. He had Aife to consider. He could not risk a debilitating injury now. If he was killed, or even only maimed, she would be alone to face the men when she woke up, and there were four of them, even if one seemed incapable of standing up at present. His fleeing horse had broken his ankle in his panic, at least that was what Torsten hoped.

If he wanted to protect Aife, he'd have to use his brains, not his fists, so he forced himself to stillness.

"Now, what say you we sample the woman's charms before Ranulf gets his hands on her?" the man holding his right arm asked, nodding toward the unconscious Aife. "He'll never know, will he, if we make sure not to damage her?"

"No," Ginger decreed, to Torsten's immense relief. "She's

senseless, in case you hadn't noticed. What is the point of fucking someone who doesn't even know what you're doing?"

A jarring laugh answered this question. "She doesn't need to know. This would be for me, not for her. Senseless or not, she still has a cunt, does she not? That's enough for me."

"You really are an animal!"

The man guffawed again. "That I am, and I've never heard any complaints. Well, not many anyway."

The four men laughed as if that was the wittiest thing they'd ever heard for weeks. Torsten bunched his fingers into fists. Why did they have the misfortune of riding into this group of miscreants?

Just then Aife's eyes fluttered open. Panic flooded his chest at the same time as relief. No! She couldn't wake up now, while the men were debating whether to rape her or not. If they saw her come to, they would not hesitate. Her being senseless was the only reason Ginger had refused to let his friend touch her. Guessing that the men didn't understand Norse, he shouted a warning to her.

"Whatever you do, Aife, don't move. Pretend you're still unconscious. The men are—"

"Silence!" Ginger barked, punctuating the order with a jab of his dagger. This time the tip of the blade went all the way to his skin and he clearly felt the sting of the cut. Torsten wouldn't be surprised if the man had drawn blood. "I don't want to hear another word out of your mouth, Norseman."

"Well, you will hear this: you're not taking her to any of your—"

Another jab, even more forceful. Another painful nick. "I'll do what needs doing, and *you* will shut up, understood?"

Torsten looked at his chest. Blood had started to seep through the wool of his tunic. He didn't let it worry him. His priority was protecting Aife from the men's lust. "I will, if your men leave her alone."

"They will. We only mean to hand her over to Ranulf. Now, how are we going to do this?" he asked no one in particular. "We've lost a horse and Girard's ankle is likely broken. That means he will have to ride double with Enguerrand. The Norseman is too heavy to be bundled up behind one of us and the woman..."

He was talking to himself, trying to find a way to get them back to this Ranulf, whoever he was. Torsten stopped listening, instead focusing on his and Aife's predicament. He only had the eating knife at his belt to use as a weapon. But even if he'd been armed with his father's mighty sword, alone against three able men and one who could still help by threatening to cut Aife's throat should he hurt his friends, Torsten didn't stand a chance.

"So, what have you decided?" the man still lying on the ground—Girard—asked. He seemed in pain and eager to leave to seek assistance.

"We can't take the two captives with us, so we'll tie up them up and leave them here while we go to Ranulf. He can decide what to do with them," Ginger declared. "After all, all he needs to see is that I have defeated a Norseman in combat and taken his woman at the same time as a gift to him. We don't have to deal with the aftermath. Enguerrand, will you do the honors?"

At his nod, the man holding his left arm released him to go to his saddlebag. With the blade still poking him in the back, Torsten didn't dare move. Besides, there was no need. If he and Aife really were to be left on their own, he was sure they could find a way to escape.

"Shouldn't someone stay behind with them?" The question came from the man who'd said he didn't mind raping unconscious women earlier, the one holding the knife against his spine, the one Torsten had started to call Vermin in his mind. It wasn't hard to guess what he was thinking. If he was selected to keep watch, as soon as his friends were gone, he would release Aife from the ropes and rape her, leaving Torsten tied up to watch, powerless. It didn't bear thinking about. "You know, just to make sure they don't—"

"No," Ginger snapped, evidently agreeing this was what his vile friend had in mind. "We'll all go to Ranulf together. Now, let us tie them nice and tight, before placing them between those rocks so no one can see them before I come back with Ranulf and his men."

Torsten didn't miss the shift from "we" to "I." The man intended to attribute the capture of two people to himself alone. He meant to pretend he'd defeated a warrior in single combat and abducted a beauty from her bed, reaping all the benefit and giving his friends none of the credit. Torsten didn't care what happened, even if he wondered how the idiot hoped the captives would not give their version of the story, a version that would contradict the heroic tale. But perhaps Ranulf wouldn't care how the two of them had been captured, as long as they had.

"Move. Over there. You heard him, you *fils de putain*." The words were not ones Torsten recognized. Probably a scathing insult in the Norman tongue. The order was followed by a jab to the base of the spine that Torsten felt all the way to the base of his skull.

"Yes, I heard him. And I will be the one carrying the woman," he growled, ignoring the pain in his back.

"I will do that, I think. She seems—"

"No. You promised your men would leave her alone," he reminded the ginger-haired Norman whose name he still didn't know. "They are not to touch a hair on her head."

"Enough of this! Carry her if you insist, Norseman, but do it now. I'm in a hurry." Ginger shrugged, his mind clearly already on the conversation he planned to have with Ranulf.

Not waiting for anyone else to protest, Torsten bent down to lift Aife, who still hadn't shown any signs of waking up. Was she pretending to be unconscious, as she'd been instructed to, or was she genuinely hurt? He whispered soothing words into her ear, not knowing if they were destined to reassure her or himself. What would he do if he found out that she had died from the fall? All his life he would remember that the last thing he'd done was threaten to fuck her against a tree in retaliation for the humiliation she had inflicted on him. How could he bear to know that they had parted on a disagreement, before they could set things right?

It would be horrible.

"Lie her down here and kneel by her side," Vermin ordered, making sure to keep his blade at the ready. It was clear he didn't trust him. Torsten couldn't blame him. At the first opportunity, he would pounce and they both knew it. "No sudden movements or I'll gut you, do you hear?"

"*Non.* You're not to kill him just yet. Ranulf will be the one deciding on his fate," Ginger interposed. "'Tis most important. Just keep an eye on him."

"I don't see why we can't kill him. It would save us some time and still prove—"

"I will handle this as I see fit, thank you." The rest of the comment was uttered in a language Torsten didn't understand.

Ignoring the bickering Normans, he did as he'd been told and settled Aife on the mossy ground, taking care not to jostle her further. He wanted to believe she was awake and only heeding his instructions, but in truth, he was getting very worried by her lack of reaction.

"I could only find enough rope for one of them," the man called Enguerrand called out a moment later, showing the coil of thin rope he was holding. "This is all I have. The rest is in Tonnerre's saddlebag."

"*Mordiable!*" Ginger seemed to consider this a moment. "They're both rather slender so we'll bundle them together. It's even better that way, as they won't be able to move an inch if they are stuck together. There will be less chance of them escaping until Ranulf and I come for them." He let out a small laugh. "The Norseman wanted to hold her? I'll be glad to grant his wish."

Torsten clenched his jaw. He didn't have any objection to being tied to Aife, but it was true that it would make escaping a whole lot more difficult. He had hoped she would be able to grab the eating knife the men had somehow forgotten to remove from his person once they were alone. But if she was stuck to him, she would be unable to. Still, he knew it was pointless to beg, it would only earn him another poke in the back. Better tied up than killed outright when Vermin lost his temper. Besides, he wanted the men gone, so he could finally ascertain how Aife was faring.

"Lie down. And don't try and be clever. I cannot kill you but I can certainly poke your eyes out." Having been denied his pleasure, the dark-haired man sounded gruffer than ever.

Moments later Torsten was lying on his side, with Aife in front of him. She was cradled in his warmth, her back plastered to his chest, his arms encircling hers, her wrists and ankles tied up to his. In such a position they were well and truly helpless. She had done her best to stay limp through the whole ordeal, as he'd instructed her earlier, but he was now convinced that she was only feigning unconsciousness, not an easy task when the men made sure to grope her breasts and hips while they moved her about. His own blood was boiling at the treatment.

At long last it was over. For good measure, the Normans had removed all the sharp rocks within reaching distance and finally remembered to search him for weapons. His eating knife was found and taken away. Even if he could have reached his belt, there would be no slicing through the ropes. Damnation.

"We ride," Torsten heard Ginger instruct his friends from somewhere behind the boulders concealing them from view of any passerby.

The company set off immediately, leaving him and Aife alone at last.

As soon as the noise of the horses' hooves pounding the ground had receded in the distance, he whispered in her ear. "Aife. Are you awake?"

"Yes."

That one little word allowed the blood to flow back into his veins. "Are you hurt?"

"No. Just...my shoulder is likely a bit bruised after the fall."

Yes, it would be, but at least nothing appeared to be broken. Torsten let out a sigh of relief. When he had seen her tumble off Grendel, for a dreadful moment he had feared never to see her rise again.

"Are you still mad at me?" she asked after a while, her voice betraying her anguish.

Was he? In view of what had happened since their conversation and their current predicament, he wasn't sure what to think.

"Probably. Only it is of no importance right now."

She didn't seem to agree and spoke again. "I'm sorry, for everything. For lying to you, for using you, for thinking I—"

"Hush. We have a bigger problem than that on our hands for now. Did you hear what the men said?"

"Yes."

Her voice was little more than a breath. She knew what was in store for them, and she dreaded it. Not that he could blame her, since she was to be handed to a stranger to be used for his pleasure, and he most likely tortured and killed.

It was a dreadful prospect.

"Don't worry. People will see Grendel coming back to the village, with a saddle and no rider, then Fáfnir and another, unknown horse in tow. They will understand something has happened to you and come investigate," he told her, bringing his forehead closer to her head. In the position they were in, it was as close to a kiss he could give her. Why he should want to kiss her right now, he wasn't sure, but the urge was definitely there and he didn't think to resist it.

Predictably, Aife wasn't fooled by the empty reassurance. "Even if they do set out in search for me, it will take them forever to reach us, as they won't know in which direction to start looking, and we are hidden out of sight among those rocks."

"Yes. But we can shout if we hear anything."

She didn't answer. Indeed, there was no guarantee anyone would find them before Ranulf and Ginger came back.

"Can you move?" he asked, already guessing the answer.

She tried to wiggle and turn to face him, in vain. "No," she said in a sob. "Oh, I'm so sorry, this is all my fault. If I hadn't tried to flee, we wouldn't have ended up—"

"It's done now," he cut in firmly. No point wasting strength bemoaning what could not be changed when they should focus on trying to escape. "We have to find a way to free ourselves. There is nothing else to do."

Anything rather than lie there and wait patiently for Ranulf.

They tried everything, shuffling on the forest floor in unison, testing the bonds around their wrists, twisting their bodies as much as they could. Nothing worked. Eventually, out of breath, they ceased moving and Torsten just held Aife tight. He wished he could at least brush the hair away from her face and look at her, but even those small comforts were denied them. It was odd to be so intimately close to someone when he knew it would not lead to lovemaking, and he felt sure Aife would feel the same.

Above them, the sun had started its slow descent toward the

horizon. It would not be too long before dusk stole whatever light was left.

A moment later they heard the sound of a horse approaching. Hope spiked through Torsten. Aife's disappearance had been discovered and riders sent out. Then he forced himself to reason. Too little time had passed and whoever was out there sounded too sure of where they were heading to be one of their friends. The villagers would likely have traveled in groups and called out to Aife as they rode. Before Torsten could decide whether to risk calling out or not, one of the Normans appeared through the rocks.

Vermin, the dark-haired one who'd offered to stay behind to guard them.

Everything within Torsten tensed. Obviously, he'd come back as soon as he'd left Ginger in Ranulf's company, in the hope he would have enough time to put his evil deed into action.

He took one look at Aife and gave a sinister smile. "So. You're awake. Not that I would have minded either way, as I said. But I do like a responsive lover."

Responsive. He meant struggling, he meant suffering. Ice froze what little blood was left in Torsten's veins and he tightened his hold on Aife protectively. The man would have to kill him before he touched her.

"You're not to—"

"Shut up, Norseman, I'm not talking to you," Vermin said, taking hold of his dagger. "And I won't need you for what I have in mind. Go to sleep."

He raised his fist and stars exploded in Torsten's skull. The hilt of the dagger had hit his temple with the force of a battering ram. For a moment he feared he would pass out from the pain, which was no doubt the intention. By pure force of will, he fought the oblivion beckoning and allowed his whole body to slacken to give the impression that his attacker had succeeded in putting him out of action. Thinking himself safe, the bastard would untie them at last. It would give him the chance Torsten had been desperate for.

"No! Look what you've done, you've killed him, you beast!"

Aife's panicked voice almost put paid to his resolve to remain still. But he had to resist the temptation. If the man thought him unconscious, he would free Aife and once he was busy, Torsten would jump, stopping him before he could hurt her.

"No!" she cried again when the man sliced the rope binding them together and yanked her to her feet.

The dull noise Torsten heard next told him that the foolish Norman had thrown the useless dagger to the ground. This was unhoped for, and just what he needed. As soon as his enemy's back was turned, Torsten would slice the rope keeping his ankles bound together.

"I'll likely get a beating from Geoffroi for getting between your thighs before Ranulf has had the chance to have you, but it will be worth it," Vermin was saying. The satisfaction in his voice was nauseating. "Those titties have my mouth watering— I'll be sure to fill my mouth with them first. Then it'll be your turn to suck something of mine."

Torsten wished he didn't understand the man's awful threats, or hear Aife's struggle but he did, all too well. Despite his anguish, he didn't dare open his eyes even a fraction for fear that seeing her in the brute's arms would spur him to act too rashly. He could not afford to make the slightest mistake because there would only be one chance. Before he could do anything useful, he needed to free his feet. Which meant he had to reach the dagger Vermin had dropped. But he could not move while the bastard was still standing, and no doubt looking at him for signs of movement.

"Let us tie your friend's hands back, in case he wakes up

when things become interesting," the Norman said, clearly convinced he had succeeded in rendering him senseless. "We wouldn't want to be disturbed, do we? Then he can watch us and see how it's done."

As if she was going to let him take her without protest!

Aife thought quickly. The man could not restrain her and tie the rope around Torsten's wrists at the same time and she would not wait patiently until he was done. When he released her to reach to the rope lying on the ground, she bent down to grab the heavy piece of rock at her feet. She didn't dare hope she would actually manage to put the man out of action—he was massive, almost as big as a Norseman—but she would do her best. And maybe the noise of a fight would wake Torsten, and then he could finish freeing himself and come to her rescue.

Filled with hatred and determination, she swung her arm, but just as the rock was about to connect with the back of his head, the man turned around, as if alerted by a warrior's instinct. Aife only managed a glancing blow to the temple, not enough to inconvenience him in any way.

"You bitch!" he snarled, imprisoning her wrist in a hold so tight it forced her to drop her makeshift weapon. Blood was trickling from his wound but he paid it no heed. "You'll pay for that! Don't think your pathetic attempt will stop me from having you. I was planning on being gentle, but now you'll take it as roughly as I want and like it."

Gentle. The man likely didn't know the meaning of the word. He proved it by backhanding her and throwing her to the ground. Though she should panic about what was about to happen, Aife could only think of Torsten. Was he still alive? The blow he'd received to the head had been severe. For a dreadful moment she'd thought the man would use the blade to slice his throat, not the hilt to stun him. That he had not had only marginally reassured her.

Unable to look at the man only to see triumph on his face, she closed her eyes and started to sob. "Please..."

"No need to beg, *ma beauté*. I'm ready for you."

There was fumbling, grunting, squirming. All too soon a heavy body settled between her legs, the hem of her dress was lifted up to expose her thighs, her right breast was smothered by a scalding hand. *No.* A tear escaped Aife's eyes. This was going to kill her.

"Torsten," she said in a whisper.

Then, as if in answer to her plea, the weight crushing her was lifted, allowing her to breathe. When she opened her eyes, it was to see Torsten crouching on the floor next to the prone Norman, the blade of the dagger digging into the side of his throat just along his jaw bone. Too stunned to move, too relieved to protest, she let him decide whether to cut their enemy or not. He was alive, it was all that mattered to her.

"Aife! Are you all right?" he asked, glancing at her in a flash of amber. "Talk to me."

"Y-yes, I'm all right."

She was now. But she had been so afraid. For him. For herself.

Torsten bent down to bring his face an inch away from the man's ear. There was an expression on his face Aife had never seen before, and when he spoke through gritted teeth, his voice was as cold as the icicles hanging from trees in winter. "Now listen, you vermin, I was never planning to be gentle with you," he said, allowing his knife to slide down the man's neck, leaving a crimson trail in his wake. "You'll take your punishment exactly as I want to give it to you and like it."

He was repeating the foul words the Norman had told her earlier. Something inside Aife melted. But when blood started to pool under the man, she was shocked into action. Was Torsten really about to cut his throat open? She couldn't let him do so.

"Torsten, stop!" she told him in Norse. "You can't do this."

"Why not?"

"Because you're not a killer. Please. Just, let's use the ropes, tie him up. It will be enough. His friend Geoffroi will deal with him later, no doubt." The man would understand what had happened and make his friend pay for disobeying his orders and allowing his prey to escape. That way her attacker would still be punished, mayhap killed, but she would never know about it, and more importantly, Torsten's hands would be clean. "Please."

For a long, tension-filled moment, Torsten seemed to hesitate. The dagger was still poised under the man's jaw, and the muscles in his arm flexed. It was clear that the temptation to plunge it into the soft neck was gnawing at his gut. Finally, he let out a shaky breath, like a man drawn from an abyss where he'd almost fallen, and he relaxed the pressure of the blade.

"You're right. Of course, you're right. Get what we need to tie the bastard up." He nodded at the ropes he'd discarded by the rocks. "Ginger will find him later and decide what is to be done to him."

"Yes," Aife agreed. That was a much better solution.

"As for you," Torsten told the man, reverting back to English. "Should you and I ever cross paths again, I *will* slice your throat. But not before I've cut off your balls and stuffed them into your rotting mouth. You've been warned."

With those words, he slammed the butt of his knife into the Norman's temple.

While he was unconscious, they worked efficiently together, tying the man up much in the same way they had been bundled up earlier. Overhead, ominous clouds had gathered in the purple evening sky and the temperature had dropped rather dramatically.

"Come," Torsten told her, taking her by the hand. "It's time to go."

8

———

Aife and Torsten didn't even need to talk to agree they should steal the Norman's gelding to get back home. After what he'd done, the man deserved no less. Hand in hand, they made their way to the horse tethered to a nearby tree. As soon as they were settled in the saddle, heavy drops of rain started to fall. Cursing under his breath, Torsten nudged the animal into a canter to try and cover as much ground as possible before the deluge started, but it soon became clear that they would not escape a thorough soaking.

Cradled in his arms, Aife was shivering, both from cold and from shock. She had come too close to being raped not to feel unsettled, and Torsten had almost been killed. All this because she'd been unable to face his legitimate anger at what she'd done and galloped off without thinking, when everyone knew she was not the best rider. Would he forgive her? He had refused to talk about it while they were tied up, which made sense. There had been more pressing matters to attend to. But now that they had escaped, she would have to address the issue as soon as possible.

They could not have something like this hanging over them.

"We'll need to find shelter," she heard Torsten say in her ear. Thunder was rumbling overhead and several skeletal bolts of lightning had already split the dark skies.

She nodded. The village was not too far, and they had hoped to reach it before nightfall, but they would have to stop to find cover. The storm had stolen what little daylight had been left and night was falling fast, impeding their view further. The driving rain had reduced the ground to a mire. On such dangerous terrain, cantering was out of the question. The horse could slip or break a leg, and Torsten had no choice but to bring him back down to a walk. As if that was not enough, there was also the risk of being struck by lightning, now that they were out in the open. There was only one thing to do. They had to stop for the night. Aife shook her head. That was all very well, but where could they go?

And then she remembered.

"The Roman ruins," she told Torsten, raising her voice against the deluge. "Over there, to our right."

As children, they had often gone to the abandoned pile of stones with their friends. No one knew quite what it was supposed to be, but it was a vast structure. It had clearly once been a building of some importance. Some of it still stood, meaning that there were various corners where they would be out of the wind and rain. Aife had not gone to the ruins for years, but it was only at the bottom of the hill, much closer than any other shelter.

Without a word, Torsten urged the gelding in the direction she had indicated.

Relief flooded through Aife when they reached the place that would provide them and the poor horse with even better protection than she had dared to hope. Apparently someone, perhaps a shepherd or a group of children, like they had once been, made regular use of the place, because a large area had been weeded and smoothed out. A few furs had been scattered over soft straw in one of the smallest, most sheltered corners, offering a comfortable nest in which to spend the night. After inspection, they found a blanket, a wineskin filled with ale and some dried meat in the Norman's saddlebags, a veritable treasure. It was as if after having put them in mortal danger, fate had decided to make amends and offer them a comfortable night to compensate.

Reassured they were now safe and would not go hungry, they sat down next to one another, huddling together for warmth. The evening was not as cold as it would have been in winter, but still cold enough to make them wish their clothes were dry.

"I think..." Torsten started. Around them the darkness was almost complete, so Aife could not see him very well but she thought he sounded hesitant. "I think we should take our clothes off and wrap ourselves in the blankets and furs to dry. There is no way of starting a fire in this weather and we'll catch a chill if we sleep in cold, wet clothes."

He was right, and only a month ago she would not have given it another thought. But now...now everything was different between them. Could they sleep next to one another, naked, and not think anything of it like they would have before they'd shared scandalous kisses? It was dark, admittedly, but not so dark that she would not see his body—and he hers—and she wasn't sure she would be able to resist the temptation of running her hands all over his chest if she did, because she suspected that it, like the rest of him, was a work of art. The problem was, after what she'd done to him, she feared touching him would only make things worse.

"I'm not—"

"I promise I won't look," he said, turning his back to her.

"Just cover yourself with the blanket when you're finished. I will make do with the furs."

Aife swallowed. It would seem that he was not going to allow her the option to refuse. And she was dreadfully cold, she had to admit. What would be the point of surviving tonight's ordeal only to fall ill because of false modesty? She stood up with decision and started tugging at her dress. It was so wet it took her a while to remove it but eventually, she managed it. A sigh of relief escaped her when she wrapped herself in the surprisingly soft blanket. Yes. This was much better.

"Your turn," she told Torsten, sitting back down and facing the wall. Then, for more safety, she closed her eyes. "I promise I won't look."

She couldn't see, but having to listen while he removed his clothes only feet away from her was torture. She tried not to imagine how he would look naked, but she could not stop herself. His legs would be long and his waist trim, his stomach taut and sculpted, his chest chiseled without being overly muscular. He would be mouthwatering.

"All done," Torsten said after a while, his voice gruff. "Now we should have something to eat before we go to sleep."

Aife turned around. By now her eyes had adjusted to the darkness, enough for her to see him reach into the saddlebag.

Enough to see that, unlike her, who was decently covered, he was bare chested, with only a small piece of fur wrapped around his loins.

Blood rushed all the way to her skull, flooding her cheeks, her chest and her own loins as it did. A moan tried to escaped her mouth, but she ruthlessly bit it back. This was just as bad she had feared. Just as wonderful. He looked just...perfect.

She forced herself to avert her gaze and reached out to the wineskin. Hopefully the ale would help with the dryness in her throat.

Torsten sat down, placing the saddlebag between them.

"Are you not cold?" she asked him, worried. He would have wiped his chest down and it was not windy in their corner, but he was still a lot more exposed than he should be in this weather.

"No." The curt tone made it clear she had better not insist. She didn't. If he was anything like her in this instant, he would indeed not be cold. "Are you hungry?" he asked, getting the dried meat out of the saddlebags. "I'm afraid it looks a bit tough."

"It doesn't matter. Thank you, I'm ravenous," she murmured, accepting the strip he handed her.

They started to eat. Aife had no idea what the meat could be, neither did she care. She was concentrating on chewing and looking anywhere but at Torsten's perfect chest.

Finally, having done all they could to delay the moment they would have to lie side by side, they settled down next to one another, covering themselves with the extra furs. Now all they had to do was pretend this situation was perfectly normal.

"I think this might have been a palace once," Aife mused, looking at the stone arching over their heads. She had never really wondered about the building's past as a child, but it seemed obvious to her now. It was too grand, too ornate to be anything else.

"Yes, you're right, it might have been a palace," Torsten answered in a flat voice. He seemed to say that he cared not one way or the other, not when they had something much more significant to discuss.

"I wonder what those Romans ate, what they wore, and what they did all day? What they thought? Probably the same as us, all things considering. We always seem to think that people who lived many centuries before have nothing in common with us, that they looked and behaved vastly differently. But I doubt that is the case. People are people, they have the same needs and hopes, don't you think, no matter where or when they were born? They crave recognition, tenderness, they need to be loved."

There she was, rambling on again because she couldn't face what she felt, couldn't find the courage to do what she really wanted to do or say what she wanted to say. She took in a sharp inhale. Would she ever be brave enough not to hide behind a stream of nonsensical words...to confront what she felt?

"Aife. Why don't you just tell me what's on your mind instead of asking me questions about Roman people you don't care about?" Torsten suggested, his voice slightly more animated now that he'd had the confirmation she was not unaware of what they needed to do, but merely uncomfortable. Having known her all her life, he knew about her propensity to ramble on when she was nervous.

She closed her eyes and decided to speak at last. If she could be brave and honest with anyone, it was with him.

"I guess what I'm trying to say is I'm sorry. I'm sorry for what I did. For everything. For kissing you without warning or permission, for lying to you about the reason, for landing you into trouble with my brother, for getting you almost killed today, for making you consider killing a man, for—"

A warm hand landed on hers before panic could overwhelm her.

"I understand. You're sorry. Now, would you like to explain to me why you really kissed me? And please, be honest this time."

Torsten didn't sound angry as much as dejected. And because she had made him feel so bad, she decided to bare her soul and her worst insecurities. If it made her feel bad, then so be it. It would only be a fair punishment for what she had made him go through.

"I will do my best." She screwed her eyes shut, unable to look at him for embarrassment. "But I must warn you, it's pathetic. I did want to attract Sven's attention, like Moon told you, which is bad enough, but I fear it's even worse than that."

When she'd noticed that the failure of her plans to provoke Sven's jealousy had not devastated her overmuch, she had come to the conclusion that the problem was a deeper one. Kissing Torsten had been about her, no one else. She had no faith in herself and did not trust her ability to seduce men.

"What do you mean?"

"I wanted to make myself feel better, give others and myself the illusion that I, too, could be with someone, could attract a man. I wanted to be like the others, for once."

"I see nothing pathetic in that."

"Are you listening to what I'm saying?" Aife asked, daring to look at Torsten at last. Lying on his side, his head propped in his left hand, he was scrutinizing her intently. His right arm rested atop the furs covering his chest. The naked skin appeared smooth and flawless, the muscles underneath sculpted to perfection. Her fingers itched to touch him. Why had she thought that she preferred overly muscular men? This was more than strength, it was grace.

So beautiful.

"I am listening," he said earnestly. "And I'm telling you I see nothing pathetic in wanting to be like the others."

She made a gesture of exasperation. Couldn't he see? "I kissed you because no one else will kiss me, because deep down I know my cousin is right. No one has ever taken a real interest in me. I'm nine-and-twenty and I've never been with a man."

"So? Me neither."

A snort of incredulous laughter was wrenched out of her. Really, was that all he had to say? She'd noticed how he seemed to go out of his way to make her laugh of late, but this time it felt out of place.

"Torsten, please be serious." This was the bane of her life. She didn't know what to make of the fact that he didn't seem to take her seriously.

"I am being serious. I've never been with a man." All the mirth disappeared from his face and he clenched his jaw, as if wondering whether to carry on. "Or a woman."

The world stilled around Aife. Torsten, never been with a woman? Impossible.

"But..."

"But what?" His brown eyes, so unusually compelling, glimmered in the darkness. "Did you think all men rut with every willing woman they can find?"

Like Sven?

"Well..."

In truth, she had rather believed that. But now that she thought of it, she was forced to reassess her first impression. Her eldest brother, Elwyn, had only ever been with his wife, Bee. Her other brother, Eirik, though older than her as well, had never been seen with a woman. That was not to say he was without experience, but he certainly didn't bed his way around the village. Torsten's brother, Steinar, had married at aged twenty and remained faithful to his wife despite her denying him access to her bed. Thorfinn had not taken any interest in her advances because he'd been in love with Rowena all his life. Torsten had just admitted to being a virgin. So, perhaps he was right. Perhaps Sven was the exception rather than the rule. She wasn't sure how that made her feel.

Well, she would have to examine this later. For now, she was talking to Torsten and he'd just revealed something surprising. He was worried about not being like the others, just like her—a virgin, just like her. But how could he be? Sigrid had mentioned that he'd been with her friend, at least, and surely he looked too good for women not to have tried to seduce him?

"You've never been with a woman? Why?"

Something flared in his eyes before he lay back down on the furs. Annoyance? Shame? Anger? "Do I need a reason?"

She hadn't meant to make him feel bad, but he sounded too dejected for her not to suspect something was not as it should be. "No. But I think you have one," she said more gently.

For the longest moment he didn't talk, just stared at the ceiling, arms crossed behind his head. Aife wondered if he was going to give her an answer. Then finally, he spoke.

"You're right. I haven't been with a woman because I...can't. My body will not let me."

Now this was the last thing she had expected to hear, even more shocking than what he had revealed earlier. "What do you mean?" Surely there was nothing wrong with him? She'd seen only a moment ago how magnificent his body was.

Heart in her throat, Aife waited for Torsten to carry on.

"When I turned seventeen summers, one of the fishermen's sons, Njal, declared it was time he became a man, in his own words. To give himself courage, I imagine, he talked someone into going to town with him. Why he chose me of all people, I have no idea. We had never really been friends. But perhaps that was the reason he took me, because he didn't want to look ridiculous in front of a friend."

"Perhaps," Aife agreed. "I remember Njal. A rather unpleasant boy."

"Mm. That's the least you could say. But I will admit that when he suggested we find a willing woman, the idea tempted me. Part of me agreed it was time I knew what transpired between men and women. Steinar had just gotten married to Astrid and I was only three years younger than him, plenty old enough in my opinion." He scoffed as if he had since come to change his mind about that. "Anyway, the point is that I agreed to go with Njal. He took me to town that very night, to visit a

Saxon widow who, he assured me, had agreed to welcome us both in her bed."

"Had he lied?" Aife whispered when Torsten twisted his mouth in what she interpreted as disgust. Was that what the problem was? Had he been forced to watch while the fisherman's son raped an innocent woman, then been made to do it also? Please, let it not be the case. She could not imagine the horror of it.

"Oh no, he hadn't lied. The widow was more than eager to be bedded by the two 'strapping warriors,' as she called us. She was also well into her fifth decade and the dirtiest woman I had seen at the time, or have seen since. Njal started to rut with her as soon as we arrived, clearly too desperate for release to care about what I thought. As for me, what little desire I'd felt vanished at the sight of the two of them kissing. I should have run there and then, but I was rooted to the spot." Aife waited while he ran a hand over his short beard. "The whole thing didn't last long enough for me to make any decision or gather up the courage to leave. Moments after having tumbled the widow on the pallet, Njal was roaring in pleasure. He rolled off her, panting, telling me it was my turn. I had better make it quick because he fully intended to have another go at her. Again, his own words."

This was not what Aife had dreaded to hear, but horrid nonetheless.

Torsten swallowed, reliving the awful moment when the widow had laughed at his friend's eagerness and told him she hoped for more stamina on his part.

What had possessed him to confide his moment of shame in Aife? Would she be disgusted? He wouldn't blame her if she was. Everything about that evening had been grim. From the moment the Saxon had opened her door, he'd known he wouldn't be able to bed her, or even touch her. He was not ready to "become a man" if it had to happen with that woman. Being forced to watch as she'd undressed had been bad. Watching her kneel at Njal's feet to put his already erect shaft into her mouth had been worse. Seeing him tumble her to the pallet and plunge inside her had been the worst of all.

And then, as if all that had not been enough, she'd smiled at him through rotten teeth and gestured at her spread legs in clear invitation. Torsten could see Njal's seed dripping out of her, coating her hairy thighs. To this day, he had no idea how he had not retched.

"When the widow asked me to join her in bed, I could not. I was petrified. It was all so..."

Horrifying.

Though he didn't finish the sentence, he saw in Aife's eyes that she understood.

"I fled the house, not looking back once. The following day Njal came to see me, boasting that he'd spent the whole night rutting away, mocking me for my lack of virility, but I didn't care. I've never once regretted not bedding the woman. He left the village shortly after, and I tried to put the whole ordeal behind me. It was not easy, and it took me years to even attempt anything. Then one evening I accompanied my father on one of his missions to another of the Norsemen villages. There, while he met with the men, I started talking to one of his friend's nieces. Soon it became obvious that she liked me and might welcome my advances. It seemed to be the perfect opportunity to see if I had finally overcome my disgust of lovemaking."

He swallowed. Would Aife not think less of him for going to someone he didn't have any feelings toward just to see if he could perform? To his relief, she didn't seem to.

"It was the ideal solution," she said, nodding.

"I thought so at the time. Away from the village, no one would know what happened either way."

Of course it hadn't quite worked that way, as the girl happened to be a good friend of Sigrid's, the miller's daughter. And apparently, after months of silence, she had finally shared what had happened that night in the meadow. In turn, Sigrid had delighted in spreading the word through the village. Gudrun, the baker's wife, had winked at him only the other day, when he'd bought his bread, and given him an extra flat cake for free, telling him he needed to build his strength. The woman behind him had smirked, as if she knew exactly what they were talking about. Torsten found that he was not strong enough to not care. Because it was not malice but the painful truth.

He *was* a failure of a man—and soon everyone would know it.

Bera had delighted in proving it and would no doubt relish telling anyone who would listen that he had been unable to get hard for her.

"It didn't work, then," Aife said, drawing him back to the conversation. She had made it sound as if no one, himself included, should have expected a different outcome, and he was grateful. This lack of judgment gave him the strength to carry on, even if what he was about to reveal was humiliating.

"No. We went to the meadow together and at first everything was as it should be. But as soon as she lay down and offered herself up, legs spread, like that woman, I... My body refused to obey. Even though I had felt desire for her during the evening and had enjoyed our kissing, at the crucial moment, I could not get hard, I could not do what was expected of a man. That was more than a year ago. I haven't dared try to renew the experience."

What would be the point, except more humiliation? Torsten shook his head, utterly disgusted with himself.

"So you see. It is even worse for me. You haven't known a man's touch, but you at least know that when the time comes, you will be able to act on your desire and behave like any other woman. Your body will welcome your lover as it's supposed to."

The thought of Aife bedding a man sent a sudden and very unwelcome shard of displeasure up his spine. But was it any wonder? In just a few days, what he thought of her had undergone a drastic change. From friend she had become... He wasn't quite sure what she had become, but he knew things would never be the same between them.

"Forgive me," she started, her voice hesitant, "but I know that you can feel desire for a woman, and that your body responds accordingly. I have felt you go hard when you kissed me."

Yes. His body definitely responded to her proximity. He was a young man, after all, and there was nothing broken within him. But it was not the same. With Aife there had been no expectations of performance. He had been able to enjoy their decadent kisses without worrying about what would come next.

"It does respond to a woman's touch. But I fear, no, I *know* that any desire I initially feel will vanish as soon as I see a naked woman in front of me." He would always be reminded of the filthy widow offering herself so wantonly, her dirty body filled with another man's seed. The issue was not with his body but in his mind. "In any case, it doesn't matter. We should try to get some rest."

Torsten sighed and turned his back to Aife, already knowing he wouldn't be able to sleep tonight.

This conversation had been a mistake. He'd thought to make her feel better but not only was he not sure it had worked, but he had made himself feel worse, exposed his failings to her, the last person he wanted to think ill of him. Though, come to think of it, if she was to hear about his lack of virility, it was perhaps better that she'd heard about it from him rather than Gudrun or some other villager. At least she would know where it originated.

Aife watched Torsten's back a long moment. He was not moving, but she knew he was still awake, probably musing on the confession he'd made.

Her heart went out to him. He had wanted to make her feel better about being a virgin, but it wasn't hard to guess that it would have been deeply humiliating for a man to admit to such a thing as being unable to bed a woman. She guessed that Sigrid's friend had been the one he had tried to bed in the meadow, the one Gudrun had been told about. Had he heard the rumors starting to circulate about him? Probably. How awful for him to have his insecurities exposed for the whole village to comment on. It would only make it harder for him to overcome his doubts about his ability to perform. He was convinced he was unable to bed a woman, and hearing that everyone else thought the same would only comfort him in that belief.

But she could not help but think he was wrong.

His body was capable of responding and feeling desire, regardless of what he thought. She had felt him harden every time they'd kissed, as she'd just said, aroused and ready against her stomach. It had been wonderful, the proof that she was just as desirable as any other woman despite her lack of curves. Could she help him in turn? Make him see that it was all in his head, and that with a woman who didn't demand anything, but only gave, who didn't expose herself to him but saw to his plea-sure, who didn't expect him to do all the work and did not put pressure on him, he could perform?

She couldn't be sure that was the case, of course, as she was even less experienced than he was in the art of lovemaking, but she thought it was worth a try. After all he'd done for her, it was the least she could do. He had helped her with Sven, with Edita, with her own insecurities, and today he had even saved her life. With his wonderful kisses he had given her back some of her confidence, and she ought to do the same.

Now she understood why he had never tried to push his advantage when they had kissed. Because he'd thought it could lead nowhere except to more disappointment.

Aife nestled close to Torsten, and wrapped an arm over his waist. He stiffened in surprise at the intimate gesture, but to her relief, he didn't ask her to leave. For a moment she just let the warmth of their bodies mingle. When she felt him relax in acceptance of the embrace, she started to talk.

"I think it is perfectly normal that you could not bed the widow in town. The scene you described was horrendous. Any normal man would have reacted in the same way." Of this she was certain. "And as to the other woman you tried to bed, unfortunately, she behaved in a way that reminded you of that night. You saw her offering herself in the same position, you had an image in your mind of what you had to accomplish and it was all too much."

"Mm."

Torsten didn't sound so sure, but at least he didn't contradict her. Aife let her words sink in a moment, then bit her lip, giving herself the courage to utter her next sentence.

"But you do know that lying between her legs is not the only way you could have your pleasure with a woman."

Torsten turned his face to her, not enough to meet her gaze but enough to signal his interest. "What do you mean?"

What did she mean, Aife wondered? She wasn't quite sure, having little to no experience of men herself. But she had heard of different positions and, of course, there were intimate caresses lovers could share.

"Have you ever brought yourself to release?"

"I... Yes."

His voice was strangled, as if the admission was costing him. Or perhaps it was the way her hand had slid under the furs to land over his naked stomach that had rendered him speechless.

A good sign. He was not indifferent to a woman's touch. *Her* touch.

Blood heated in her veins at the thought. Yes, if she was brave enough, this would be beneficial for both of them.

"Well, if you have managed to feel pleasure, then we can agree that your body is functioning properly. There is nothing wrong with you, only your mind will take you to dark places when it sees something that brings you back to that horrid night."

Torsten made a sound she chose to take as an agreement and she felt the muscles under her palm bunch. Another good sign. Aife smiled in the darkness. This might work.

Emboldened by his reaction, she stroked him lightly, waiting for a sign of protest. When none came, she slid her hand lower. Mm, he was so warm, so smooth, so taut... Before he could stop her, she brought her mouth to his ear.

"But what if your eyes didn't see anything? What if your mind didn't dictate what happens? What if it did not worry about trusting the woman in bed with you? What if it allowed your body to just feel for once, and enjoy?"

"I... It—" The two words were little more than ragged breaths. He sounded like a man on the edge of his control. "I don't think—"

"Don't think. Just feel."

Aife pushed her hand under the fur he'd wrapped around his loins earlier. The knot loosened and the fur fell open. A moment later her hand landed on Torsten's pulsing shaft. Her breath caught in her throat. He was hard. As hard as any man would ever be. Her body went as limp as his was taut.

She smiled and squeezed her fingers.

"Show me what you do to bring yourself pleasure."

9

———

S *how me what you do to bring yourself pleasure.*

Torsten almost erupted from the wicked order pronounced in the sultry voice that so closely resembled the laugh he'd been obsessing about—and the feel of the bold fingers pressing around his manhood. What was the wretched woman doing to him?

"Why would you want to see that?" he rasped, knowing he should instead ask Aife to let go of him and go to sleep. But he could not have uttered the words if his life depended on it. He could barely move or breathe. Her hand around him felt too good, her voice in his ear too seductive. Never had he been more aroused or desperate to see what would happen next. He was utterly at her mercy.

"I don't want to see it," she answered, in the same maddening, hoarse voice that caused the hairs at the back of his neck to stand on end. "I just want to know how you do it, so I can do it for you."

Fuck.

His cock gave an almighty jerk, signaling its agreement to the scheme. In that moment it certainly didn't feel as if it were about to deflate any time soon. Torsten closed his eyes. He could not allow it to control him, or allow Aife to do what she was offering to do.

Or... He paused. Was her idea so crazy? Here in the dark, with a woman he trusted to be understanding—and clean—it would be nothing like it had been with the widow, or even the woman from the other village. With a friend who wanted to help and did not expect anything, who was not after some manly performance, perhaps he could find out if there really was something wrong with him. The experiment with Bera didn't count, as he had not felt any real desire for her. Surely even Sven would not get hard with a woman he did not truly desire in his arms?

He shook his head, trying to be reasonable. "I don't want to take advantage of—"

"You're not. I asked. I want to do this for you. I'm a fearless warrior, remember?" she said, alluding to what she had told him in the forest when he had fed her the honey. "You haven't forgotten the kiss we shared that day?"

Forgotten! It was haunting him. It had been carnality itself, and he had thought about it more often than he should.

"No, I haven't forgotten."

"Well, I felt you go hard when you held me in your arms and it helped me see that I could be desired, made me happier than I'd been in years. Now it is my turn to help you." Her fingers started to slide up and down his shaft in slow, unpracticed movements that somehow scalded his body all the way to his scalp. "I could make you see that there is nothing wrong with you."

Could he do it? The last of his scruples lingered, making him hesitate. But then Aife groaned in his ear, and everything disappeared. He rolled over onto his back. With swift, jerky movements, he sent the furs flying into the air, exposing his erection.

Damn, he was so hard he could not remember why he was worried his body would not obey him.

"Close your fingers around me and stroke," he rasped. He was going to explode if she didn't do anything to alleviate some of the pressure boiling in his shaft. "Up and down. Harder than you did before. Like this." He wrapped his bigger, stronger hand over her dainty one and showed her what he meant. He wanted to urge her to go even faster, but at the last moment sanity prevailed. "That is, if you—"

"I do. Keep your eyes closed," Aife instructed. "Don't think, remember. Just feel."

"Yes, like this. Keep talking to me."

This time he sensed her hesitation. Clearly, she had no idea what she could say, and it was hard to blame her. This was all new, and he guessed that she had never been asked to talk a man into release. Could he ask her to laugh? No, of course not, and no matter. Her husky voice was enticement enough and might push him over the edge.

"You feel so strong in my hand, so good. I never imagined a man's member would be so smooth, so warm... I wish I could see it better. It looks beautiful, unlike anything I've ever seen, just perfect." A sigh of pure longing escaped her throat. She wasn't lying... She thought this part of him beautiful. As if to acknowledge the compliment, his shaft jerked again. "I've often thought about it when I touch myself at night, how it would look, how it would feel in my hand."

Bloody hell! Torsten almost swore out loud. Aife thought about his erect cock when she pleasured herself at night, just like he thought of her when he stroked himself? This was the most arousing thing he had ever heard in his life, and the best thing she could have told him in that moment. Because it meant that she saw him as potent and hard.

As more than a friend.

"What else do you think about?" he whispered. Imagining her in her bed, naked, with her hand between her thighs, writhing with the pleasure she coaxed from her body by thinking of him, was enough to steal his breath and what little was left of his control.

"I also imagine how it would taste if you allowed me lick it."

And without waiting for his permission, she did just that. Bending her head, she gave a slow, languorous lick along the underside of his shaft. The move utterly undid him and for a moment Torsten feared that he'd unmanned himself. Then Aife moaned her appreciation and he understood that, thankfully, he'd been spared that humiliation. She wouldn't be moaning if he'd suddenly drenched her with his seed, he was sure of it. Of their own accord, his fingers coiled themselves in her hair, keeping her in place. Responding to the silent command, she engulfed the pulsing head into her mouth, plunging it into the most decadent softness he had ever felt. He groaned, unable to believe the sensation.

Bloody, bloody bleeding hell.

In that moment there was no question of not being able to reach his pleasure, no reason to doubt his virility or ability to function like other men. The very opposite would happen. He was going to explode with unprecedented force, far more quickly than he would have liked—and straight into Aife's mouth.

His fingers tightened their hold around her head. "Aife, please."

Whether he was asking her to stop before he flooded her mouth or begging her to bring him to completion, he wasn't sure. What was certain was that she chose to believe he wanted her to allow him to experience his pleasure to the full. She took him all the way to the back of her throat. That was all it took to push him over the edge.

The last thing Torsten thought before his seed shot out of him in bolts of searing heat was that if Moon ever heard about that moment, he would definitely kill him.

Aife was beyond shame, beyond doubt, beyond anything.

The feel of Torsten's manhood hard in her hand, the masculine scent of him, the way he groaned and writhed under her caresses, everything about that moment was pure bliss. Stroking him had been the most wickedly satisfying thing she had ever done. It had rendered her incapable of thinking, so much so that she'd admitted out loud to her most secret thoughts and desires. And it was true that these last few nights she had pleasured herself imagining not Sven kissing her, as she had of late, but Torsten, and how she wanted their heated kisses to evolve into something more.

Well, here was the chance to make it happen.

Unable to resist the temptation, she'd placed the flat of her tongue at the base of Torsten's shaft and slowly licked her way up, marveling at the sensation. There was such power contained under the velvety skin... Acting on instinct, she'd closed her lips around the smooth head, and sucked on it, gently at first, then harder when Torsten had closed his fingers in her hair and begged her in a raspy voice. What he'd been begging for exactly, she wasn't sure but she'd wanted to give it.

He felt too good in her mouth for her to stop anyway.

In one bold move, she took him all the way to the root.

A heartbeat later she felt a jerk and a warm, sticky substance landed on her tongue. Another, even more powerful jerk followed, then another. Unsure what to do, Aife waited, cradling the tip of Torsten's manhood against her tongue while he emptied himself into her waiting mouth. The strangled cry he gave when he finally finished twitching was the most erotic she had ever heard. Satisfaction washed over her. *She* had done that, she had pushed him over the edge. He'd thought something was broken within him and she'd proved that wasn't the case by bringing him pleasure in no time.

Not that he had been the only one benefiting from this.

She'd feared no man would find her desirable, and he'd shown her that she'd been wrong. He'd been hard for her, he'd welcomed her caresses, he'd liked her ministrations. It was clear that the problem was not her, but the men who had been too entranced by others to notice her. Apparently, she could be more than enough.

Gratitude filled her and she took a good look at Torsten who was still panting on the furs, with his neck arched and his arms outstretched. She wished the scene had been drenched in sunlight instead of wrapped in darkness. What a glorious sight he would be, recovering from the pleasure she had given him.

After a while he opened his eyes and raised himself on his elbows, looking barely strong enough to support himself, and utterly dazed.

"I'm sorry. I couldn't—" He had to allude to the releasing of his seed into her mouth, for he had definitely been able to perform like a man. "I couldn't stop myself. It was too good."

"It's all right."

Eager to live this first experience with a man to the full, she had quickly swallowed the salty liquid flooding her mouth, and she could tell that it had been the right thing to do. Torsten seemed awed by her generosity.

"Aife. You really are a woman like no other." His hand landed on her cheek, the gesture so tender she felt tears sting her eyes. In that moment she was glad for the shadows engulfing the ruins, as it helped conceal her emotion. "Thank you."

"It's not a problem." That was a ridiculous thing to say, but she couldn't think of anything else. Sucking on his most masculine part had been delicious, both wicked and sensual, and she had loved every moment. It had reminded her of the day she had licked honey from his fingers in the forest. At the time, she had thought it the most scandalous thing imaginable. She now knew that it had been nothing in comparison.

There was only one problem. Torsten had reached his release, but she had not. And her body was on fire, demanding she do something about it.

Aife lay back down on her side of the furs, arms wrapped around her middle, wondering how to appease the need boiling in her veins. This had been for Torsten, a way to prove to him that he could enjoy what other men enjoyed. She could not start making demands on him now, even if her blood had been stirred by the sheer wickedness of the experience. She closed her eyes and willed herself to calm. Eventually her desire for more would go away.

There was a rustle from her right and a heartbeat later she was trapped under a deliciously hot masculine body. Torsten was caging her in, his hands cradling her head, his legs imprisoning hers, his face inches away from hers.

"What are you—"

"Are you aroused?" he purred in her ear, much in the same way she had spoken to him earlier. All the nerves endings in her body ignited at the same time.

She had been aroused, and now that he was covering her with his naked body, she was desperate. Could she admit to it? Would he be pleased to know that sucking on him had set the place between her legs throbbing, or disgusted by this proof of her wantonness? She decided to be honest. There had been too many lies between them already.

"Yes," she breathed, hiding her face in the crook of his neck. "I fear I'm too aroused to go to sleep."

Could she ask him if he minded if she touched herself? Her

body was so taut it wouldn't take long for her to erupt. Would she dare do such a thing with him so close?

In the end there was no need to say anything.

"Well then, we cannot have that. It's your turn to show me what you do to pleasure yourself," Torsten said, his voice huskier than ever. Fingers landed on her hip, squeezing lightly. "And my turn to help."

Oh. Aife smiled. Even better.

In the distance, thunder started rumbling again.

10

Aife looked through what might have once been a window to the line of trees on the horizon. The storm had cleared at last. It was safe to go, even if it was still raining steadily. In this weather the journey would not be pleasant, but they had to reach the village as soon as possible. People would be worried about their absence, they had to reassure them.

"I suppose the good news is, we're already soaked anyway," Torsten said from behind her, clearly thinking the same thing.

She nodded. Leaving the nest of furs—and the warmth of Torsten's embrace—this morning to put on her wet, cold clothes had been one of the hardest things she'd ever had to do.

"Shall we?" he offered, nodding toward the horse grazing in what might have been the palace's banqueting hall. "Your family will be worried by your disappearance. We need to reassure them. Though what they will say when they see your bruise, I dare not think."

Yes, she could well imagine she had a bruise below her eye, where the man had struck her before pouncing on her. Her brothers would draw her into a bear hug, her mother would fuss and take care of her, and her father would swear to hunt the bastard down. Torsten brought his hand to her cheek and brushed it lightly, thunder in his eyes.

"Is it that bad?" she asked, worried at his reaction.

"Yes. You should never have had to endure this."

"Neither should you," she whispered. He sported an impressive bruise over the temple, courtesy of the Norman's dagger hilt, as well as a cut on the chin. She almost reached out to stroke it but resisted the impulse. If she touched him now, she wasn't sure what she would do next. Pushing him back onto the furs was not out of the question.

As if agreeing with her touching was unwise, Torsten let go of her face and took a step backward. "We should go," he said quietly.

"Yes."

Still, Aife made no move to go to the horse. Not only had the caress on her cheek caused her core to tighten, but before they left there was something she needed to say.

"I think it might be better if we forget what we…"

Though she didn't finish her sentence Torsten nodded, looking as embarrassed as she felt. He seemed to have understood what she hadn't found the courage to say, that they should forget their wild night together. It had been incredible, but it was better if they went back to being just friends. Her feelings were getting too confused to her liking.

What about him? What would he think about her now? Would he remember all they had done every time he met with her? Her cheeks heated at the thought. He had stroked her intimate folds, which was scandalous enough, but she had taken him into her mouth, which was ten times more shocking, and swallowed his seed. Would they ever be able to get past that? Was it even possible?

They stared at one another, emotions swirling in the gray pre-dawn light.

"You will be pleased to know that Edita is gone, by the way. I never got the chance to tell you yesterday."

Yesterday. In other words, when he had come to find her in the field to demand she tell him the truth about her scheming and she had fled, putting both their lives in danger. How clumsy of her to allude to the painful moment! And how silly to mention Edita, which would only remind Torsten that she had lied about the real purpose of the deception she had played on him. Really, what was wrong with her? Next she would ask him if he thought Sven would ever take an interest in her...

"You must be relieved," Torsten said carefully. The light in his eyes had gone stormy at the mention of her cousin.

"I would, if only she hadn't stolen my comb," Aife answered in an effort to alleviate the tension. Would the diversion work?

"She stole your comb?" He sounded incensed, much more than the declaration warranted.

"Well. I can't be sure she did, but I certainly cannot find it anymore."

It wouldn't be the first time the woman had stolen something from her. Once, when Aife was about twelve, she had gone to Mercia with her mother, her aunt Dunne and her cousin Bee, to see her aunt Birgit to celebrate the summer solstice. At that occasion, all three cousins had been given the gift of a silver coin. Aife had been delighted, having never seen such bounty before. The following morning, however, the coin had not been in the place she had left it. Birgit's hut had been thoroughly searched but the coin had never been found. No one had been able to prove anything but both Aife and her mother were convinced Edita had been the one to steal it.

It seemed she had not lost the habit.

"Well, I have a comb you can have, if that would serve. I

finished it the other day and was thinking that I have no one to give it to. I considered Sanna, but I have time to make another one for her."

Aife beamed at the offer of the precious gift.

"Really, you made a comb?" These were especially difficult to make but she shouldn't be surprised. Torsten had always been gifted in that way, rather like her father, Sigurd, who wove the most intricate baskets without even thinking. "You've always been nimble with your fingers, have you not?"

"I... Erm, so I have been told, yes."

Oh, what had she said? Now he would be reminded of the scandalous caresses he had given her the night before, of how quickly he had learned how and where to stroke her. Nimble indeed. It hadn't taken him long to understand what she liked and how to make her erupt, not only once, but twice in quick succession, something she had never managed on her own.

"Anyway, if you don't know what to do with the comb, I will gladly accept it," she hurried to say.

"It's yours." The intensity with which he said the words took Aife's breath away. It sounded almost like a pledge.

"I thank you."

She almost closed the gap between them and reached up to kiss him, but then at the last moment stopped herself. What was she doing? Only a moment ago she had told him they should forget about their night together and revert to a friendly relationship, and he'd agreed it was for the best. They had to go, before she made a mistake that ruined everything.

Torsten seemed to think the same thing because he cleared his throat. "Let's go. The rain will not stop anytime soon, so there's no sense in delaying any further."

Without waiting for her answer, he headed out into the rain and straight toward the horse he had tethered to a crumbling pillar the evening before. While he saddled the animal, Aife went to retrieve the saddlebags. A moment later, they were ready to depart.

The journey was spent in silence and soon they arrived in view of the familiar thatched roofs. Because of the rain, no one was about and they made their way to Aife's parents' hut without encountering anyone.

"Aife!" Her mother gasped when she opened the door and saw her and Torsten soaked to the bone but alive and well. Dropping the spoon she was holding, she threw herself into her arms. "Thank God! We saw Grendel and Fáfnir trot back home yesterday evening and immediately understood something had gone wrong. Because of the weather, we decided to wait until the morning to send a search party. But we were so worried! What happened? Did you get stuck in the storm? But...wait, what's this? Are you hurt?" She drew back and brushed the bruise on her cheek, concern swirling in her eyes.

"Worry not. I will explain everything later."

Frigyth's gaze darted from her to Torsten and her eyes widened further when she saw the bruise on his temple. "Lord, Torsten, look at you, are you all right?"

"Yes, thank you," he answered, staying by the door so as not to drip water all over the floor. "But I'll have to go speak to my father."

Aife nodded. She knew Wolf would want to know about the Normans' actions. Being the one in charge of the relations between the Norse settlement and the local people, he had to be told what had happened without delay and try to locate this Ranulf's clan. If they were really intent on getting rid of Norsemen and raping their women, they had to be stopped.

"Thank you," she told Torsten before he could leave. "We'll speak later."

After one last nod, he headed back out, closing the door behind him. Aife's chest constricted when he disappeared from view. It seemed odd to be without him. But of course, there was nothing more normal. She had better get used to the idea. After two weeks of madness, they would be back to just being friends.

"Here, get yourself warm," her mother said, herding her to the firepit where a pot of stew was bubbling away. The smell of onions reminded Aife that she had eaten little the day before and nothing at all this morning. "Are you hungry?"

"I am, thank you," she said, accepting a bowl of the fragrant stew.

"You will also need a change of clothes."

"Yes, and a rest." After all the events of the day she had found it hard to fall asleep, and now that she was home and safe, she was feeling the effects of her sleepless night. She just wanted to get fed, get warm, get to bed, and fall into oblivion. "Then I promise I will tell you everything."

THE EXPRESSION ON HIS PARENTS' face when they saw him was one Torsten wished never to see again. But it was little wonder they would worry. With his chin cut and his face bruised he would look as if he'd been in a fight. Which, of course, he had.

"What happened?"

His parents knew he was not the kind to get himself embroiled in pointless brawls, so they would have understood this was serious.

"Aife and I were abducted, or rather tried to be, by a group of Normans."

His mother gasped. His father arched a brow. "Normans?"

"Yes. Four of them. A ginger-haired man named Geoffroi, who seemed to be their leader, another one named Girard, who will likely have a twisted ankle, and a third, older one named Enguerrand, who spoke with a strong foreign accent. The fourth one was tall with dark hair. I don't know his name." At the mention of the man who had hit Aife and almost raped her, Torsten felt his body tense. He sincerely hoped the bastard had met his demise by now. "We happened upon them at the edge of the forest, not far from the Roman ruins, while we were out riding yesterday."

Could men blush? Torsten hoped not, but he felt his heartbeat increase at the mention of the place where he and Aife had spent a scandalous night in each other's arms.

"We saw Fáfnir trot back into the village alone with Grendel which is why, now that the storm has passed, I was about to send out a search party." His father sounded suspicious. "I certainly never thought you'd gone riding without any saddle or bridle."

Torsten shrugged, trying to appear natural. "I sometimes do. It's good practice for balance, I find. I take it you got both horses safely, then. That's good. But wasn't there a third one with them? A black gelding?" he asked, eager to change the topic.

"There was. One of the Normans' beasts, I take it?"

Torsten nodded. "He almost trampled his rider to the ground, which caused the man to twist or perhaps even break his ankle. The animal did go after Grendel when he spooked, so I guessed he would have followed him all the way to the village. Tonnerre, his name is."

"Ah. Thunder." After the recent invasion, his father had started learning the Norman tongue. Having to deal with the people who had arrived from Normandy with the new king had become increasingly commonplace. Unfortunately, the exchanges were not always cordial, which was why he asked his next question. "Is there anything else you can tell us about those men?"

"They mentioned a Saxon called Ranulf who had a clan they wanted to be part of. In fact, that is why they captured us. They wanted to impress him, which is why I'm guessing the man hates Norse people."

Though clearly, he was not above raping the women, if they were beautiful enough. Torsten's gut roiled anew at the thought of what had almost happened to Aife.

"Ranulf. The name is not familiar," his father was saying. "I will go see the reeve in town right now. He's a reliable man and we've built a good relationship since he helped us when Steinar was wrongly accused of murder. If you'll excuse me, little one?"

"Of course."

After placing a kiss on his wife's temple, Wolf exited the hut, a man on a mission. Torsten didn't doubt for a moment he would get results, and sooner rather than later. Not many men could stand in the way of the formidable Icelander, especially when it was a family matter.

Once they were alone, his mother took a step forward, a reassuring smile on her lips. "You can trust your father to get to the bottom of this."

"Yes." He always did. "Now, if you'll excuse me, I'll get back home." He'd changed into dry clothes before going to his parents' hut but he was feeling rather tired and he longed to lie down.

"Of course. But before you go, I have one last question. What exactly is between you and Aife?"

Torsten swallowed. Trust his mother to leave the practical aspect of the questioning to her husband and focus on the personal side of the adventure.

"What do you mean? We've been friends since we were born."

He was sidestepping the question but what else could he say? That they had kissed many times over the last few days, each with increasing urgency? That the reason they had been captured was that they'd argued about her motives for kissing him? That he fantasized about her when he stroked himself in the morning? That last night, for the first time, he'd been intimate with a woman and it had been her? That he'd allowed her to pleasure him and had been so lost to decency that he'd filled her mouth with his seed? That he'd teased her softness with his fingers and could still feel the spasms he'd wrenched out of her in his soul?

That he wanted to feel those spasms again, this time on his tongue?

"Well, my hair was auburn from the day I was born. Until it started turning gray," his mother told him with a side smile. "From then on, there was no going back."

Torsten shuffled on his feet, unsure what she was trying to say. Of the four siblings, he was the one who had the closest relationship with his mother, perhaps because he was the one who resembled her the most physically. Most of the time they understood one another without words, but she was being unusually cryptic today.

"Things we take for granted can change," she added when he remained silent. "Sometimes it is for the best."

"You do look good with the sliver streaks in your hair," he agreed slowly, because he was starting to have an inkling of where this conversation was going, and he didn't like it. Better to focus on her hair since she had started it. "I'm sure *Faðir* has told you many times."

She made a cutting gesture, indicating she was not fooled by his pretence at evasion, as he should have guessed. She never was.

"The night Aife was born I was with Frigyth, assisting her instead of Helga, who was in bed with a high fever. It was her fourth child and we were confident all would be well. You were only a year old then, as you know, and you found it hard to be without me. So I took you with me, knowing you would sleep most of the time anyway." She gave a fond smile of remembrance. "When you woke up just after dawn, the baby was born. You took your first real steps that day, waddling toward her as if drawn by an invisible force and took her hand in yours. She gripped your little finger and refused to let go. You didn't say anything, you just looked and let her hold on to you."

By the time she had finished her story, Torsten's throat had gone dry. How was he finding out about this only today? It appeared hugely significant somehow, even if he could not fathom why.

"You share the day of your birth with Aife, but I think you share much more than that, have from the start. Only, neither of you were aware of it."

Yes, perhaps. And perhaps now they were all too aware of it.

He took his mother's hand in his and kissed the knuckles lightly. "Forgive me, I have to go. I didn't sleep well last night. I mean not enough. I mean—"

A squeeze on his hand stopped the fumbled declaration. "I know what you mean, son. Go and get some rest."

AIFE STARED AT THE CEILING, panting with the strength of her release. Her body had spasmed out of control for long moments, draining her of all her strength. This had been unprecedented, almost as good as what she had felt in Torsten's arms. She had not even taken the conscious decision to touch herself, the caresses had been brought on by the dream she'd had. A dream in which she had revisited what she and Torsten had done two nights ago in the Roman ruins. As she lay down, still fighting sleep's hold over her, her fingers had found their way to the place between her legs. It was throbbing, slick and hot from the very naughty images her mind had conjured up, and before she'd known what she was doing, she'd been stroking herself to a storm of release that bore no resemblance to her usually tamer explorations.

It was as if something had been unlocked in her body, allowing her to access its full potential.

Though no one could see her or know what she had done, she blushed to the roots of her hair. It was not the first time she had thought of Torsten as she brought herself pleasure. As she'd told him the other night, over the last few days she had imagined him while she stroked herself. But never had it been so wicked, so...precise. And no wonder. This time she had not imagined what they could do, she had remembered what they had done, in all its scandalous glory.

Once she'd gotten her breath back, Aife left the pallet filled with a sense of purpose. Today she would set things right. She couldn't let Torsten be maligned any longer, not when she knew there was nothing wrong with him.

As soon as she was ready, she exited the hut and headed straight for the baker's shop. The morning was chilly and a light drizzle was falling from the skies but she didn't bother with a cloak. Resolve would be enough to warm her. Sitting next to her stall in front of the hut, at her usual place, Gudrun welcomed her with a smile.

"Aife. How are you this morning?" The baker's wife eyed the bruise on her cheek with ill-concealed curiosity.

"I'm exhausted, if you must know." That was no lie. Between images of the man's assault and lewd memories of the moments she had shared with Torsten, the last two nights had not been as restful as she'd hoped.

"You will be, poor thing. I heard all about your ordeal at the hands of the Normans."

Of course, she would have, the woman made it her business to know—and comment on—everything that went on in the village. Which was precisely the reason Aife had come to her. She wanted to make sure Torsten's name was mentioned in the next few days, and that what was said contradicted the current rumors. But she had to be clever about it. It would not do to just announce that Sigrid's friend was lying about Torsten not having been able to bed her because, well, he had indeed been unable to. But that didn't mean he was the impotent lover he was purported to be.

The best thing to do was to let Gudrun know that, with her, he had definitely been able to perform and let her draw her own conclusion. Once in possession of this juicy piece of information, she would make sure to tell everyone about it.

"Yes, it was rather horrible. But thanks to Torsten, nothing happened in the end." The baker's wife didn't need to know how close they had come to disaster. That she had almost been raped and Torsten almost killed was not the point of the story. Gudrun only needed to understand that he was not as impotent as she believed him to be. "And, well, it was not all bad, considering what it led to later that night, while we sought shelter from the storm."

"What do you mean?" Gudrun's eyes had sparked with interest, just as Aife had hoped. It was almost too easy.

She smiled to herself and picked up a pale loaf from the back of the display. Wheat bread, nothing like the rye loaves she usually bought. But why should she not treat herself today? It had stopped raining at last, and she was enjoying taking her time choosing what to buy.

"Do you know, I think I'll have a wheat loaf for a change," she said, purposefully acting as if she had not just let slip a vital piece of information and was only interested in purchasing bread. "How much is it?"

The baker's wife wasn't so easily distracted. "Wait. Are you saying that you and Torsten...?"

Revealed our most painful secrets to one another? Shared the most amazing, most wicked moment under the cover of darkness? Gave each other sinful pleasure? Yes, all this happened.

Instead of answering, Aife blushed, which was not difficult to do when she remembered what she'd had the audacity to do to Torsten. It had been most daring, most delicious, and she could still taste him on her tongue. It seemed that this response told Gudrun what she wanted to do more efficiently than if she had started to detail everything they had done.

"But I d-don't understand," she stammered.

"What don't you understand?" Aife asked innocently, eyeing up a golden hazelnut flatbread. Should she buy it as well? The wheat bread was already an indulgence she rarely afforded herself.

"Well, it just so happens that Sigrid told me the other day that he could not bed women. Apparently a friend of hers tried to seduce him a few months back and he could not...well, you know..."

Yes, she did know.

"Torsten?" Aife infused all the disbelief she was capable of in her voice. "Torsten, Wolf's son? One of the strongest, most virile men in the village? Sven's brother, the man who's bedded all the women who want him? *That* Torsten you mean? You think he would be incapable of bedding a woman?"

"Well...that's what Sigrid said." But Gudrun didn't sound so sure anymore.

"Why on earth would she say that? You must have misunderstood. Or else..." Aife twisted her lips in mock consideration and leaned in conspiratorially. "Or else the problem is not so much with him as with Sigrid's friend. Perhaps she was so put out that he refused her advances that she started to spread rumors about him. There is no telling what people will do for spite. In any case, let me tell you that there is nothing wrong with his ability to perform."

Another blush, impossible to stop.

"Apparently not... You at least seem quite satisfied with his—"

"I will take the wheat loaf and the flatbread as well," Aife decided, thinking it best not to insist. She had said enough. Within the week, everyone would know what to think of Torsten.

She handed the coins to a dumbfounded Gudrun and made her way back home, already biting into the warm flatbread. Delicious. As she rounded the baker's hut, she came to an abrupt halt.

Standing by the fence was Torsten, looking at her with intense brown eyes.

"You heard," was all she said, swallowing the mouthful of bread with difficulty.

"I heard."

She had expected anger, resentment at her interference perhaps, but his lips were twitching in what looked like a mixture of amusement and gratitude. Oh dear, he looked utterly striking in the morning sun, the golden light making his eyes glow and his bronzed skin shine. With the bruise at his temple, he looked like a warrior back from battle. A battle he had fought for her. Why had she decided it was better to revert back to being friends and forget about kissing, exactly?

Right now she couldn't remember.

"Thank you."

Aife tried a carefree shrug, ended up coughing when she choked on the last crumbs of flat bread. Eventually she was able to answer. "After the way you helped me with Edita, I could not let you be maligned throughout the village. It wasn't fair.

Besides, what I said was no lie," she added in a lower voice. "You are capable of the same as any other man."

His eyes, aglow with gratitude a moment before, now sent sparks of pure lust. "Mm, apparently. And now thanks to you I might find myself having to fend off women's advances instead of trying to convince them I can perform."

Oh. She hadn't thought of that. He might indeed attract more female attention from now on. The thought tore at her guts.

"Will you make the most of it?" she asked with commendable effort at breeziness. Why should he not? And why should she care? Hadn't they decided to forget the madness? Yes, only it was hard to convince herself that was what she wanted when her body was still humming from her earlier release and he was standing in front of her like a mighty warrior.

Torsten seemed to hesitate for a moment, and Aife was certain he was only doing it to tease her. It worked, damn him, because she did hate the idea of him going to other women. Her heartbeat picked up when he gave her a slanted smile.

"I would perhaps try to make the most of it if I found someone who stirred my interest half as much as you do."

Her heartbeat went from a trot to a gallop in the blink of an eye. She already knew that she could stir his lust. Now he was saying that she stirred his interest as well? That was wonderful news. Or rather it would be, if they had not agreed to put an end to what had blossomed between them during the two weeks spent pretending to be a couple.

"Good luck with that," she answered, deciding it was better to jest.

"Yes. Good luck indeed." He winked.

By the gods, was he saying that it would be impossible to find a woman who interested him as much as she did? And if that was the case, what would they do about it? Unsure what to reply, she waited. This conversation was not going the way she had anticipated.

"Your father came yesterday to thank me for saving you from the Normans," he told her, crossing his arms over his chest.

Could she feel any worse, Aife wondered? She had only needed rescuing because of her own folly. Had she not fled, neither of them would have been in any danger.

"Yes. I guessed he would have." The Dane had been incensed when he'd heard of the attack, even though she had been careful to keep the most frightening details to herself. "But did you tell him why we—"

"No one knows why we were in that meadow," he cut in. "And no one needs to know. I'm sure you'll agree."

Relief flooded through her. "I do, Thank you."

"Now, how do you think Moon will react if he hears about the night we spent together? He was told only the other day that there was nothing between us. Will he not think he's been taken for a fool? Again?"

Oh. Aife's insides shriveled further. How hadn't she thought of that? But, of a certainty, her brother would kill Torsten if he thought they had lied to him and then found out what they had done. It would not matter that she had been the one initiating the seduction, that Torsten had reciprocated the favor instead of simply taking advantage of her, and that they had agreed it would lead nowhere. All he would see was that his friend had done what only selfish men did, and that—well, that it would lead nowhere. He might have made his peace with a tryst that would lead to marriage, like Torsten himself had done when he had understood that what was between his best friend and his sister was serious, but he would balk at the notion that he had used her so shockingly for his pleasure.

She forced herself to calm.

"I don't think there's any cause for concern. Moon is not in the habit of listening to women's prattle. If there is any issue, I will talk to Eyja. She will make him see that Gudrun only jumped to conclusions, as she often does. Besides, he knows we are not really..." Her voice trailed when she realized that, once again, she was reminding him that she had only gone to him because she'd hoped to provoke his brother into action. Why was she so clumsy around him? Hadn't she hurt him enough?

"Yes, you're right," Torsten agreed slowly. "We're just pretending. You are only trying to attract Sven's attention and Moon knows it. You told him yourself. In such circumstances, he will never believe you are interested in me or that you wanted to give me pleasure."

The flatbread she had just eaten sat like a burning piece of coal in her stomach, the sweet hazelnut taste suddenly sickly.

But I did want to give you pleasure and I am *interested in you, in who you are, not just in how you look,* she wanted to scream. It was different than it had been with all the other men she had taken an interest in over the years. It was better, inexplicable. And yet it was destined to disappear. Because they had agreed it was for the best.

"Here." She shoved the almost complete flatbread in Torsten's hand. "I won't be able to eat any more. You can have it."

Clutching her wheat loaf as tightly as if it had been made of gold, Aife ran back to her hut.

11

———————

"Going anywhere?"

Aife started when the familiar voice caught her off guard. When she turned around, Sven was walking over to her, one thumb stuck in the belt hanging low at his waist. By the gods, but he did look good, if slightly too arrogant for his own good. His lips were the same shape as his brother's, she noticed for the first time, but perhaps because his beard was blond, rather than light brown, the effect was less striking somehow.

She blinked. What did the color of his beard have to do with the appeal his lips exerted over her? And since when did she think him anything less than striking, or too arrogant for his good?

"Yes. It being such a nice day I thought I would go to the coast to gather cockles," she answered, gesturing at the bag slung over her shoulder. For three days after the thunderstorm that had forced her and Torsten to take refuge in the ruins, it had rained more or less constantly. But today the sun was shining and she had decided she would make the most of it.

"Cockles, really?"

Sven laughed, and she didn't understand why that might be. She shrugged. He could think what he wanted.

"Yes. They're my favorite." Didn't he know? They had grown together, and she'd thought he would remember something like that. Didn't she know he only liked goat's cheese when it was very fresh?

"If you say so." He placed a shoulder against the wall of the hut, a roguish smile playing on his lips. That smile put her in mind of a wolf on the hunt, something Torsten's smile never did. "Want some company?" he asked, leaning in toward her.

Aife's heartbeat increased, an automatic response to his proximity and the offer she had been hoping for for weeks. She opened her mouth to accept—and then she realized that, no, she didn't particularly want him to come with her. Or at least, not in the hope that he would take advantage of the privacy of the beach to steal a kiss. This was odd. Only a few days ago she would have jumped at the chance of spending some time alone with him. Today, the question did not cause any flutter in her chest, or any stirring lower down. Why? Surely what had happened with Torsten in the Roman ruins had not turned everything on its head? Her heart sank.

But of course it had.

How could she share such an intimate moment with a man and not have it change anything? How could she forget what he had confided in her? What they had done under the cover of darkness? She knew how his most intimate part tasted, he knew how her body felt when she spasmed in pleasure, they'd heard each other's lewdest moans. She wasn't sure anything would ever be the same between them again, or even that she wanted it.

Aife cleared her throat. Lost in shameful musings for a moment, she had forgotten that Sven was waiting for an answer.

"I'll be fine, thank you. You're probably busy anyway," she

answered, barely believing what she was saying. Was she really turning him down? Yes, apparently. "Weren't you and Freydis—"

"Freydis is gone." Sven's jaw clenched, his displeasure evident. "She's gone back to her village to prepare."

"Prepare?" For what? Not her wedding to another man, surely? Was that why he looked so angry? Had he found out that the woman he'd been bedding was set to marry another?

"She intends to leave this country, go and live in Denmark, in the village where her parents were born," he told her in a burst of anger. "Just like Hedda, her decision was made years ago and yet, unlike your sister, she kept it a secret, allowing everyone to believe she intended to settle here. She is leaving in less than a week's time on a ship of Danish merchants who agreed to take her, and she didn't ever think to tell me as much when I started seeing her."

In an uncharacteristic gesture of powerlessness, he ran a hand through his unbraided hair and grimaced. In that moment he didn't look half as self-assured as usual, or arrogant in the least but almost vulnerable. It was rather odd, a side of him she was certain not many people had seen. She certainly had not. He had always been all about confidence.

"I see," she said, feeling rather at a loss. Had he been playing a role all this time?

Sven gave a scoff. "I really liked her. I thought we would have the opportunity to...you know, get to know one another better."

This was turning into the strangest conversation. Aife wasn't sure what to say or think. She had always assumed that Sven would be the one to put an end to his dalliances when it suited him, not the other way around. She had also assumed that he had little or no interest in getting to know the women he bedded. Now she was finding out that he was not immune to doubt, that he, too, could feel the pain of rejection and wish for more than a fiery night or two in a woman's arms. Apparently, he would have liked to see where things could go with Freydis, he had taken their relationship more seriously than she had. From someone who wasn't supposed to want to settle, it was unexpected to say the least.

"I'm sorry," she said sincerely. "She should have been more honest with you."

What was happening? A few weeks ago, she would never have believed she would feel sorry the woman was gone or that she wouldn't jump at the opportunity to make the most of this turn of events. But here she was, feeling sorry that his lover had abandoned him, and refusing his offer of an escort. If that didn't prove that what she had felt for Sven had been nothing more than a shallow infatuation, then nothing did. Arms still crossed over his chest, he was looking at her intently. The position emphasised his impressive strength. His body was decidedly more muscular than his brother's but she found that she actually preferred the leaner—

Stop! She chided herself. She had to stop comparing him to Torsten at every turn. She was not comparing him to Steinar, was she, though everyone would agree he was the brother who looked like him the most? So why was she looking at Sven and thinking only of Torsten?

Her heart sank. Because if she were honest, she would admit that she had thought about Torsten a lot these last three days. In many ways, none of them suitable.

"You know," Sven told her suddenly, "You look different. Have you bought a new gown? Started to braid your hair differently?"

"No."

He cocked his head to one side—the gesture reminiscent of his brother. Aife mentally kicked herself. Here she was again, comparing the two men.

"Well, whatever it is you've done, it suits you. You're glowing."

Glowing? Oh, wonderful. He was finally taking an interest in her, right when she had accepted that nothing would happen between them and didn't even mind.

She gave him a swift smile, not knowing how to deal with this new development. "I'd better go. I don't want to miss the low tide."

Aife headed toward the horses, shaking her head in disbelief. Would she not come to regret refusing this chance to see if she could woo Sven after all? Perhaps. But it would have felt too odd to try.

It had taken time, but she had at last accepted that Sven would only ever be a friend.

She placed her forehead against Imp's shoulder, in search of comfort. The family horse was getting old and for that reason she usually chose another mount, but today she needed his reassuring presence. After one last hug, she headed to the shed at the edge of the field to get the saddle. It was time to go.

"Going anywhere?"

Oh dear. The same question, asked in a rich, deep voice, just as before. Only this time her insides did ripple, her loins did definitely heat up. Everything that should have happened with Sven but hadn't, happened with Torsten. To hide her turmoil, she started to walk faster.

"Yes, if you must know, I woke up this morning in the mood for cock—" Just then she tripped on a root.

Torsten caught her by the elbow before she could fall flat on her face and kept her steady, his gaze planted into her. Then he lowered his head to speak in her ear.

"Could you say that again?" His voice had gone impossibly gravelly. "I think I might have misunderstood."

"—les," she finished the word in a panic, realizing what her sentence would have sounded like. "Cockles. The shellfish. To eat, you know. I mean..."

"Yes. I know perfectly well what you mean. Cock—les," Torsten repeated, stopping half-way through the word like she had. "I see. That makes more sense. They're your favorite, are they not?

He remembered. Sven had not, but Torsten had. Her heart wobbled. She had gotten used to the sensation in the last few days and now found it pleasant.

"Yes. I love cockles."

For a delicious, heady moment, heat sizzled between them. Why did she have the impression she had said something lewd?

"Would you like me to come with you?"

"Yes."

The word shot out of her mouth before she could think. She had refused Sven, but it did not even cross her mind to say no to Torsten. For three days she had feared he would not want to have anything to do with her.

"Let's go then, find some cockles."

THE DAY WAS GLORIOUS. It was good to be out in the sunshine, riding. Aife was mounted on Imp, her father's old gelding, and Torsten had borrowed Fáfnir for the day, this time properly fitted with saddle and bridle. Mayhap it was time he got himself a new horse, he reflected. His faithful stallion, Satan, had died the previous year, and he had not yet found the energy to select a mount suited to his needs. Besides, he'd not been in a mood to leave the village. But he had been full of renewed energy of late.

This was no doubt down to the woman cantering by his side, her fair hair flying in the wind, her face turned up to the sun, her lips curled up in a smile. Gratitude flooded through Torsten.

In just a few days and despite her dubious reasons for coming to him, Aife had given him a purpose and his confidence back. He now felt ready to confront his demons and trust in his ability to perform, if not *with* a woman, at least *for* a woman. It was a first step, more than he could have hoped for, and one that could one day lead to a more fulfilling love life, a life in which he was not afraid to be what he was supposed to be.

Odd how life worked. He and Aife had grown up side by side, and not once had he thought of her as anything other than a friend, someone like his own sister, Eyja. All it had taken for him to see her differently was that wicked laugh. Yes, a laugh she had directed at his brother... He should not forget that. She had not come to him because of the desire he inspired in her, she had not been interested in him as such, only in provoking another man's jealousy. She had thought she could use him to make herself feel better and get what she really wanted—another man.

True, she had since apologized and gone out of her way to help him in turn, but the fact remained. She'd wanted to seduce Sven, maybe she still wanted to, and they had now agreed to put an end to whatever was between them. He should stop seeing her as the answer to his questions.

The only problem was, it was easier said than done. It seemed that the last few weeks had irremediably changed things between them. They would have to find a new way to function, one that was suited to their unique situation. Friends didn't know the taste of one another's pleasure. Lovers didn't usually pretend nothing had happened between them.

Well, that was a problem for another day. For now, he wanted to enjoy the moment.

"I'm going to ask my father to give me Ghost," he told Aife, once they had brought the horses back down to a walk out of consideration for Imp's age. Even if what had been between them was over, she deserved to know that he was now restored to his old self. And it felt good to acknowledge it out loud. "He's already got more horses than he knows what to do with, so he won't begrudge me this one. Devil has already sired five foals this year."

Ghost was a four-year-old colt, full of spirit, ideal for a skilled rider seeking a challenge. Like all his father's horses, he was descended from Demon, the stallion bought upon the Icelander's arrival in his new country more than thirty years ago.

"I'm glad. It was time you replaced Satan," Aife agreed, a smile on her face.

Yes. It was time. Time to start living again.

They soon reached the sea and after a short trot along the edge of the cliff, Aife brought her horse back down to a walk again, indicating a beach down below.

"We'll go there, it's ideal for what we want to do."

They negotiated their way down the path leading to the middle of a small, crescent-shaped bay, flanked on either side by imposing rock formations the color of rust. Under the powdery blue sky, the sea was shimmering as brightly as a tapestry woven with diamonds. Overhead, a handful of seagulls soared and swooped in graceful arcs, sending an occasional squawk, the sharp sound slicing through the distant rumbling of the waves. The beach was completely deserted and the tide was as far out as it could be. Perfect, or so Aife declared in a competent air. Torsten had no idea, having never gone cockles-picking before.

"Don't you want to go for a swim beforehand?" he asked, nodding to the sea in the distance. "It's a lovely day, even if the wind has picked up."

He knew Aife loved to swim. In fact, she was the best swimmer he knew, much better than he was, because although he could swim adequately and perhaps even faster than she could in the lake next to the village, he was nowhere near as comfortable in sea water. Her father, Sigurd, who'd lost his parents and younger brother when their boat had capsized, had made sure to teach his wife to swim as soon as he'd met her, and then taught his children from a young age. As a result, Aife could swim in rough seas without ever getting tired or scared.

"No. Not today." Despite her answer, she was staring at the sea longingly and he guessed that she was foregoing the pleasure of a dip because he was here. Knowing he would not be able to keep up with her in the choppy waters, or indeed willing to go in these conditions, she preferred to stay with him. He was touched, but loath to see her sacrificing herself for him.

"I wouldn't mind waiting for you here," he encouraged.

Indeed he wouldn't. He most especially wouldn't mind seeing her emerge from the water in her wet shift, the transparent fabric clinging to her body like a second skin, highlighting her slight curves. Her hair would cascade over her shoulders in a ripple of gold, her nipples, puckered by the cold, would do their best to pierce through the thin linen. Or it might even be that she went into the sea naked, considering that they were alone.

His throat went dry at the idea—while another part of his body flooded with blood. By the gods, was that why he was trying to convince Aife to go for a swim? So that he could see her naked and see the shape of her breasts, find out the exact shade of her intimate curls? That night in the ruins it had been pitch dark and she had kept her clothes on, even when he had stroked her. He had not thought to bare her breasts and suckle her while he used his fingers on her, which proved what an inadequate lover—and a perfect idiot—he was. Well, he would not make the same mistake again. If he ever had her under him again, he would make sure to look his fill before devouring her. He would take her soft nipples into his mouth and tease them until they grew rock hard. He would then lick every inch of her gorgeous—

"Do you remember the day all of us went to the beach?" he blurted out, in an effort to steer his mind away from the scandalous thoughts.

Aife burst out laughing. Predictably, his groin, already affected by his musings, tightened further at the sound he'd come to love.

"How could I forget? It was a rather memorable moment."

Yes. It had been. That day, his and Aife's siblings, all nine of them, had gone to the nearest beach, a few miles from where they were today. The two families had always been very close, and Wolf and Sigurd's children had spent most of their time together so there was nothing extraordinary in that, but it had been the first time they'd gone to the beach alone, under the supervision of the two eldest boys, Steinar and Elwyn.

Against everyone's advice, Eyja had gone to swim in a shallower pool filled with seaweed. Predictably, she had become entangled in the mess. When she had emerged from the water covered in slimy, brownish strands, a veritable maritime monster reminiscent of the sea god Njǫrd himself, everyone had burst out laughing at the apparition. Her hair had been so tangled with the sticky algae that it had proven almost impossible to comb when she'd reached home that night, and there had been talk of cutting it right back. Torsten had been the one saving the day. Young as he was, he had made a comb with spaced out teeth that had allowed Frigyth to restore the hair to its usual slickness. For days, though, Eyja had smelled of the sea and glowered at any villager who dared remark on it.

"I'd never seen Eyja so vexed," he commented, remembering the expression on their friend's face. To her utter annoyance, the boys had called her Njǫrd for weeks after the incident. Aife had been the only one kind enough not to tease her. "Come to think of it, I don't think I've ever seen her so vexed since."

"No. And even though it's been years, I think anyone who

values their life should avoid mentioning it to her. Even Moon might not get away with it."

Torsten let out a scoff. "Aye. He might well lose a part of his anatomy if he dared remind her of how she slipped on the slimy rocks and, because of the weight and the slipperiness of the seaweed, could not get up until he and Eirik lifted her back to her feet."

"You could have gone to help her," Aife accused, letting out a fresh burst of laughter. This one was joyous and light, nothing like the sultry richness that never failed to rouse him. Instead of stirring his senses, it tugged at his heart, which was perhaps even more worrying. "You were closer."

"I was, and so were Steinar and Sven. But we were laughing too much to move, and being the imp's brothers and used to seeing her get herself into all manner of trouble, we thought it fair to let others deal with her for once."

"Mm. I suppose. She's always been reckless, has she not?"

She sounded rather envious, which surprised him. Surely Aife didn't think herself dull? She was nothing of the sort. "Yes, she has. She wouldn't have done half of what she's done otherwise."

He knew Aife would understand what he was talking about. A few years back, his little sister had taken the rash decision to go to war. Disguising herself as a boy, she had joined the army of Saxons recruited to fight the Norse invaders. Fortunately, Moon, who had gone also, had taken care of her and made sure she came back home unscathed. It was during that adventure that his friend had come to see the imp in a different light and fallen in love with her.

At the time Torsten had wondered how Moon could prefer a woman he'd grown up with to a more exciting stranger, but now he thought he understood. There was something wonderfully soothing in knowing someone so well you didn't have to explain yourself or hide your worst traits. They knew and accepted you the way you were. Aife certainly did. The two of them had shared so many wonderful moments... And now, of course, they would have the memory of their night in the Roman ruins to go back to.

By the gods, but it had been unlike anything he could have imagined. Never in his wildest dreams would he have believed that his childhood friend would be the one to introduce him to the delights a man and a woman could experience together. And there were so many more to be discovered... Would he want to explore them with someone else? Would he be able to? Or was Aife the only woman capable of coaxing a response from his body?

Silence replaced the laughter, and the air suddenly became thick with sensual tension. Torsten could have sworn Aife was thinking of what they had done in the ruins as well. His cock, already stirred by her laugh, was now fully erect, and threatening to poke a hole in his braies. Damnation, his tunic was barely long enough to cover it. Was Aife aware of the state he was in? He hoped not. He didn't dare move for fear of drawing attention to the lower part of his body and making her uncomfortable. For now, she was looking straight into his face and something like lightning was flashing in the blue irises.

"Let's go get the cockles, shall we?"

That word... He would never hear it again without thinking of her and what she'd unwittingly told him earlier.

I woke up this morning in the mood for cock.

Though she hadn't meant it like that, the shocking words had been uttered, and he would never forget them.

"Yes," he agreed. "Let's go get these cockles."

Before he tumbled her to the ground and begged her to let him prove that he had really overcome his fear of lovemaking.

Aife handed him one of the two leather pouches and gave

him her rake, saying that he could use it, since he was new to it. It would be easier that way. She would use a stick for once. "And tomorrow, when the cockles have had time to purge themselves, you can come to my house and we'll eat them together."

"With pleasure."

He could watch her eat something she enjoyed all day, be it cockles, or...well, other things that sounded similar. Damn it all. He had to stop thinking such things, or his erection would never go down. For someone who had doubted his virility for so long, it was disconcerting to see his body respond so readily. But with this woman, he seemed to be in a constant state of arousal. He didn't know whether to be relieved or horrified.

After giving him one last smile, Aife took her pouch and headed toward the rocks to the left of the beach in search of a piece of driftwood with which to dig up the cockles. Alone at last, and able to focus on something other than the way his body behaved, Torsten crouched down. He had never been cockles-picking before, and in truth, he was more at home in the forest. What should he look for? He should have asked Aife before she left, but he'd been too distracted.

He watched her, some distance away, bent over, raking the wet sand with a two-pronged stick, her hips swaying with the movement. His groin stirred again and he focused his attention back to the task at hand.

In vain. When she joined him a long moment later, he'd only found five shells, while her pouch was already half full.

"You are made for this. I'm impressed," he said, straightening his back.

By the gods, not only was this hard, but it was back-breaking work as well. How did Aife manage it so easily? She was a wisp of a girl.

"I find that greed is the best motivation, don't you?" she

answered, laughing. "Worry not, I won't let you starve. You can have some of mine tomorrow."

Aife's laughter died in her throat because Torsten was looking at her strangely, much like Sven had earlier that day, as if he saw something different in her. Or rather, as if he'd only just noticed something that had always been there, something he'd been waiting—hoping—to find. Somehow the difference seemed important. Sven had thought her glowing because she had changed, in his opinion. Torsten found her fascinating because he was seeing her for who she truly was.

"What is it?" she breathed.

"I love your laugh," he told her, his voice hoarse.

"I... Thank you."

It was not what she had expected him to say, an unusual compliment, but lovely. Anyone could have told her she was beautiful—well, potentially they could, because in reality, no one had. But very few people would have chosen to praise her laugh instead. And she found that she rather liked that. It sounded more sincere, not something chosen to please her.

To hide her turmoil, she bent down and started to run a hand over the tiny rocks at her feet, wet and mingled with coarse sand, finding the rustling sound soothing.

"I used to bring a piece of rock home every time I went to the beach with my father when I was small," she told Torsten, who'd knelt down next to her, his head only inches away from hers. "I always took ages to find one, which annoyed him, and ended up selecting one of the smallest ones I could find."

"If that's the case, why didn't you just bring grains of sand? It would have saved your poor father a lot of frustration."

"I suppose I could have." She laughed again, and made the mistake of looking at him at the same time. There was a look on his face she would have described as pure lust had she thought herself capable of provoking that emotion in men. But she wasn't, was she? Besides, she hadn't done anything other than laugh and agree with him.

"Fuck, Aife, but I do love your laugh."

Why did it sound as if he'd just told her the most scandalous thing she'd ever heard? The place between her thighs, the place he'd helped her stroke the other night, rippled. By the gods! Had she been a man, her shaft would be hard as rock. But she was a woman, and her insides had gone soft as butter.

"All right, I'll take this one," she said, picking up a pebble at random.

With her mind still reeling from their proximity and his unusual compliments, she could not focus. But she did want a memory of this day, this moment with Torsten. The stone itself was of no import, all that mattered was that every time she looked at it, she would be reminded that, for a heady moment, he had looked as if he wanted her.

And for a heady moment, she'd wanted him.

All of him.

It was then that she realized. Thorfinn, Haakon, Sven even, they had been little more than infatuations. If truth be told, she had never imagined things would work out between them. She had simply been desperate to find someone and they had happened to be there. Her relationship with Torsten, by contrast, had been real, based on mutual liking, not physical attraction, and strong enough to survive the deception she had inflicted on him. She had been dazzled by the other men's appearances but she had fallen in love with Torsten because of who he was. It had crept up on her while she was busy looking at his brother.

In love.

Yes, she had to be in love with Torsten, it was the only explanation for how she felt. She felt stupid, like someone who had been handed a real gem and had not seen it because she'd been too busy sifting through common rocks to notice.

"What do you think of this one?" she asked him, her throat dry. "Should I take it home?"

He let out a scoff, not in the least impressed by the piece of rock she was holding out, with reason. It was misshapen and of an uninspiring gray color.

"That one is a monstrosity and you know it. It's not even that small, so it will look ridiculous in the middle of your collection. I'm sure we can do better than that."

He let his fingers sift through the rocks between them a moment. Aife watched him, fascinated. He really did have the most nimble fingers, long and assured. Another ripple warmed her core when she remembered just how nimble they could be when they touched a woman, when he touched *her*. Was that all she would be able to think of when she watched him from now on? Probably. She did not see how she could not.

All too soon, he ceased his search and placed a small pebble on her open palm. "How about this one?"

It only took Aife one look to understand that this would be the rock she brought back home and cherished forever. It was perfectly round, polished to a smooth finish and almost translucent. The color, of a deep, honeyed amber, reminded her of Torsten's amazing eyes. The misshapen monstrosity was instantly dropped to the ground and forgotten.

"Yes. You're right. This one is perfect," she said, lifting it in air to admire the way the sun pierced through it, revealing the myriad of hues hidden within. Just then a seagull squawked and swooped right above her. Surprised by the jarring noise and the unexpected move, Aife ducked—and dropped the little rock at her feet.

"Oh no!"

She'd meant to keep it as a souvenir, and now it was lost

amidst thousands of almost identical rocks she'd trampled in her surprise. Not daring to move or use her hands in case she unwittingly buried it any further, she searched frantically with her eyes. Torsten helped, but they could not find it.

"Let's go get more cockles," she said, standing back up after a while. No need to cry over what would never be.

Just like the beautiful pebble, Torsten would have to remain a memory treasured in her heart.

12

After what felt like an eternity bending over in an awkward position, Torsten straightened up and stretched his aching back. By the gods, he was definitely more at home in the forest, despite the lovely view. Ahead of him, the sea had advanced quite considerably and was now lapping at the rocks huddled to his left, frothing as it surged and retreated in a rhythmic motion. Where was Aife? Lost to his search, he had not seen her disappear. Was she hiding behind the tallest of the rocks?

He was considering going to check when he heard her cry of —was it delight or dismay?—from behind him. Alarm spiked through him, an instinctive reaction. Had the Normans come back? Was someone else attacking her?

"What is it?" he asked, turning to face her.

She was at the foot of the cliff, waving at him, a huge smile on her lips. His whole body relaxed. Clearly, nothing was wrong.

"Come and see," she called, "someone has arranged the rocks in the shape of a beautiful flower!"

Her enthusiasm was infectious, irresistible for someone who had spent months feeling sorry for himself without quite knowing why. Not for the first time Torsten reflected that Aife had burst into his life at the perfect moment, when he'd needed it the most. Well, not burst, exactly, as she had always been there, but rather...eased herself into his daily routine, become an intricate part of it. She was by his side even more often than before and in his thoughts constantly. Without making any ripples she had claimed her place in his soul, without ever disturbing his days, she somehow made them brighter. It was as if whoever was weaving the tapestry of his life had decided to add a thread of gold to the original, somewhat dull threads they'd selected at first. The design hadn't changed, but suddenly everything shone. Everything was different. Beautiful.

Tucking his find in the purse at his belt, he hurried to join her by the cliff.

"Look," she urged him, gesturing at the ground. "It's so pretty."

At her feet were stones and rocks of various sizes and colors arranged in a swirling pattern. The effect was most impressive, he had to admit, even if he probably wouldn't have given it another thought if she'd not pointed it out to him.

"It is pretty, but it's not a flower," he contradicted, just for the pleasure of seeing her reaction. He'd discovered a fondness for teasing her, as she always responded so beautifully. "It looks more like an overblown cabbage to me."

She didn't disappoint. Her eyebrows shot up to the roots of her hair, betraying her shock and disbelief. "How dare you? I'm very sure it is meant to look like a flower."

"Oh, I'm sure it was *meant* to be a flower. But it ended up looking like a cabbage. And I'm sure that whoever did it agreed with me. They probably stomped home in a foul mood, angered at their inability to distinguish between a flower and a vegetable."

Mock outrage caused Aife's eyes to twinkle. "I'm sure they did not. And it is most definitely a flower."

Torsten swiveled on himself, gesturing at the empty beach. "Well, as there's no one here we could ask, we'll just have to agree to disagree, won't we?"

"I guess we will." Her mouth quivered at the pleasure of their nonsensical conversation. A little bit more and she might actually laugh, that wonderful laugh that never failed to set his loins on fire. He could not resist, knowing he wouldn't stop until the husky sound had burst out of her lips.

"Why don't I try to do a flower? Show you how it's done? I've been told that I had nimble fingers."

As soon as the words had passed his lips, he regretted them. Damnation, why did he have to allude to what they had done in the Roman ruins? Teasing her was one thing, provoking her quite another. He'd meant to coax a laugh out of her, not force another inappropriate erection out of him! And yet, here he was, as hard as the stone of the cliff behind him. Even worse, instead of laughing, Aife had gone as still as a statue and her cheeks had turned a delightful pink.

It was then that Torsten realized how naïve it had been of them to agree to forget everything they had shared. There would be no forgetting it. Even if it had been possible, he wasn't sure he wanted to forget what had been the most intense, the most erotic, the most amazing moment of his life. He didn't want to forget the woman who'd given him pleasure, who'd given him his life back, the first woman he'd stroked to release.

She was too bloody perfect. Perfect for him. Could he be perfect for her as well? There was only one way to know. He would have to ask.

He took her hand in his.

Well, he reflected when she swallowed, as if in readiness for what was to come. It was safe to say that their minds were no longer on the flower at their feet. Aife had made no move to disentangle her fingers from his and she seemed waiting for the kiss he was steeling himself to give her. Or...should he tell her what he felt first? What was the right way to do this?

Having never really wooed any woman, he had no idea.

Aife stood in front of Torsten, panting, wondering what to do. He had just alluded to what they had done in the Roman ruins, as if his mind was so full of the memories that he could not help himself. She understood the feeling all too well. It was all she had thought about for days, but she hadn't dared hope it would be the same for him.

And yet...and yet, perhaps it was. He was holding her hand, looking at her as if he wanted to kiss her and more. There was a glint in his eyes that made them appear as luminous as the pebble he had found earlier and he had—

An ominous rumble interrupted her thoughts. Odd, as the sky was the same vibrant blue as before and there wasn't a cloud in sight. What could it be? Not thunder, surely? Before she could think, she was thrown to the ground and Torsten was lying on top of her, caging her in much the same way he had done before asking her to show him how she pleasured herself. A burst of joy exploded through her chest and a flash of heat seared her loins. She could only think of one reason for which a man would want to lie down on a woman thus, and her heart leaped at the thought. The rumbling she'd just heard must have originated from Torsten's chest. She'd been right. He wanted to do much more than kiss her.

A heartbeat later, however, she understood that their position had nothing to do with seduction.

Torsten was not making love to her, he was saving her life, using his body as a shield.

A shower of rocks and loose earth tumbled over them in a deafening crash. The edge of the cliff, rendered unstable by the recent storm, was falling apart. *That* had been the rumbling she'd heard. Aife screamed when she felt the jolt of a big boulder hitting Torsten in the back and then reverberating all the way to her own pelvis. No! He would never survive this. Unlike her, he didn't have anyone absorbing the shock for him. A moment later, another, slightly smaller rock hit him on the head and he went limp above her, heavy as a corpse.

At long last, silence fell and the dust settled.

Panic sliced through Aife. All danger was past, but Torsten was not moving. Why was he not moving?

"Help!" she cried, doing her best to infuse strength in her voice. Pinned to the floor by his body and the earth heaped over her legs, she couldn't move either. She could barely breathe. "Help!"

Would someone hear her? Would they both die here, alone, half buried under the rubble? The beach had been deserted, despite the good weather, and they hadn't seen anyone from the moment they'd arrived.

Aife started sobbing, tears she couldn't wipe sliding down her cheeks.

"Torsten, please, please wake up! You cannot die, not now, not like this, not because you saved me! I cannot bear it. I need you. I...I love you."

She should have told him earlier, when he had taken her hand and looked at her with such feeling, when he had found the beautiful rock for her, when he had asked her if she needed company, even.

"Help!" she screamed again and again, until her voice grew hoarse. She could not give up. She was still conscious, she still had a voice. She would scream until someone heard her or she passed out from exhaustion. There was no other choice. "Help!"

And then she heard it. A tentative call, from up above. "Anyone here?"

"Yes, here!" Aife shouted, relief scalding her veins. At last! "Over here. Please!"

By the time the group of men reached her, she had stopped crying and was doing her best to free her hands.

"All right," one of the Saxons said, looking at the scene in front of him. "No need to fret. We'll get you out of here."

13

———

till. So still.

Why was Torsten so still? Surely it was not normal for anyone who was not dead to be so still? Aife looked around the hut in despair. She was alone with an unconscious Torsten and her dark thoughts for sole company. There was no one to reassure her. The Saxons who had found them on the beach had brought her and Torsten to their village just down the road, carrying his unconscious form straight to an empty hut. Shortly after, the healer had paid them a visit.

Far from comforting Aife, their discussion had sent her into a state of shock.

"Having been struck in the back like he was, your man might never be able to walk again," the woman had told her after a perfunctory examination. Either she held a grudge against Norse people or she enjoyed upsetting strangers, because there was no attempt at mitigation in her assessment or compassion in her eyes.

"N-never walk again?"

A shrug, as if it hardly mattered, one way or the other. "'Tis a strong possibility. Come to think of it, he might not be able to make love to you either, considering that his cock is below the waist as well." The woman's eyes narrowed on Aife's stomach. "I hope for both your sakes that you're already with child because I doubt it will happen now. Oh well. You could always take a lover, I suppose, if you're desperate for a babe—and other things."

Aife bunched her fists so hard her nails dug into her palms. How dare the woman talk to her in such a cruel way? Didn't she know that the news she was imparting was devastating? She was saying that Torsten might never walk again, might never be able to make love to a woman again...

Oh, the cruel irony of it. After so long worrying about his ability to perform in bed, he might now find himself truly impotent. Mere days after he'd proved to himself that there was nothing wrong with his body, he would see his ability to feel and give pleasure taken from him. How would he bear such a blow?

It was all her fault. Had she not wanted to go to the beach that day, had she not called him to come so near to the cliff, they would both be at the village now, and Torsten would be whole.

"You're wrong," she told the healer, wiping her tears in an angry gesture. Surely her examination had been too brief to be conclusive. Why should anyone set score by it? "He will recover. I'm sure of it."

But night had now fallen and Torsten still had not opened his eyes or even moved. Aife looked at him until her eyes ached. He was so beautiful, his naked chest golden in the firelight, the lean muscles delineated by the shadows dancing in the hut. On his right shoulder was a nasty cut, surrounded by what promised to be a nasty bruise. On his left bicep was the silver arm ring he'd worn since he'd become a man. Each of Wolf's three sons sported a different one, matching their personality. They had been presented to them, as was tradition, the year they had turned sixteen. Aife remembered it vividly, because the year

Torsten had turned sixteen, she had turned fifteen, and she'd fancied herself a woman as well.

The arm ring gleaming in the light of the flames was chiseled and elegant rather than sturdy, just like him. The image of a wolf sitting on his haunches was carved in the middle, his gaze planted directly in the observers' eyes. It denoted wisdom and honesty rather than strength, like Steinar's or vitality, like Sven's. It was perfect, the perfect adornment on a perfect man. Or at least, perfect until now.

Another sob got caught in her throat.

Please wake up, Torsten, she silently begged. *I need to know you're going to be all right.*

The healer had not said anything about him dying from his wounds. In fact, her prediction about him not being able to walk suggested she didn't doubt he that would wake up. That was something at least, something she desperately hung on to.

Eventually Aife decided she had better try to get some rest. There was nothing else to do and she didn't want to be tired when Torsten finally woke up and needed her. Ignoring her aching muscles, she headed toward the chair set by the firepit. Just as she reached it, the door opened with an ominous creak.

"Has he woken up yet?"

The healer walked into the room uninvited, a basket of herbs in hand. Despite the question, she didn't sound particularly interested in her patient's welfare. She was only doing what she was supposed to do, no doubt to maintain her reputation as a reliable healer amongst the village folk. Either that or she had only come to gloat. Aife gritted her teeth. Whatever it was, she didn't need any of it.

"No," she forced herself to say, hoping it would be enough to send the woman on her way.

It wasn't.

"I told you it would be rather complicated. But mind you,

you Norsepeople seem to be made of stronger stuff than us Saxons, so you never know. My cousin married a Norseman a few years ago. She tells me he's rather more...well, let's just say he has enough stamina for two and will not easily be satisfied in bed. She doesn't mind, rather the opposite." The woman let out a giggle, highly unwelcome in the circumstances. "Actually, you might know him. He must be about the same age as you. Njal, a fisherman?"

Everything soured in Aife's stomach because she might indeed know him. It sounded as if the insatiable Norseman was none other than the one who had taken Torsten into town to see the filthy widow all those years ago and left the village shortly after. Njal had been a fisherman's son, it was reasonable to think he had taken up his father's trade. She cursed their bad luck. Of all places, the man had to have come here to live.

"Sorry, no, I don't think I know him," she answered as calmly as she could. "There are many of us, you know, spread over a few villages, so chances are he and I have never crossed paths. Is he here at the moment? Perhaps his face might be more familiar than his name?"

The last thing Torsten needed when he left the hut was for his old "friend" to see him. It would only bring back horrid memories and make him feel ten times worse. If the healer had informed the whole village that the Norseman they'd rescued had lost the use of the lower part of his body, with everything it entailed, Njal might well be unable to resist teasing him.

To her relief, the woman shook her head. "No. They live in the next village and don't visit very often, especially not in the summer."

From the way she sighed it was clear she regretted not seeing her cousin's virile husband more often. Aife didn't share in the disappointment. The longer Njal stayed away, the better.

"Oh," was all she said, eager for the healer to leave. If she'd not brought anything useful and was only going to make her feel bad, she had no reason to be here. Fortunately, she took the hint.

"Well, I'll leave you to it. Try to get some rest while you can. It's not easy to look after an invalid, as you'll soon discover."

The loathsome woman.

"Are there any herbs in your basket I could use to make a tisane to give to Torsten when he wakes up, something to ease his pain?" she asked as calmly as she could. Was that not why the woman had come?

"Oh. Yes, here. Peppermint and willow bark. I suppose it can do no harm. Though it might help you more than it can help him. His headache is bound to be too strong for the remedy to offer much relief. It's probably better if he sleeps the worst of it off. Here, give him this potion when he wakes up. It will help him sleep," the healer said, placing two small leather pouches on the table along with a small vial filled with a brownish liquid. So she had come prepared. Why had she not offered the potion before? That was what she was supposed to do, was it not? Did she care so little for her patient? "Make him drink the whole thing in one go; a strapping man like him can take it."

Aife didn't answer, didn't reach out to the pouches, she merely waited for the door to close on the vile woman.

Alone at last, she remained a long moment standing in the middle of the room, willing her heart to stop hammering. They needed to leave that place as quickly as possible. The people had saved them from the rubble and she was grateful, but it would be better for them to be amongst sympathetic people, and in a place where they were not in danger of running into Njal.

When she had calmed at last, she set the pot of water to boil over the fire and steeped the dried mint leaves and willow bark into the only cup she could find. Then, utterly drained of energy, she lowered herself into the chair. It was hard and too big for her to be comfortable. She brought it close to the table and tried placing her forearms on it before laying her cheek against the top of her hand. Better. She was dozing off when a movement on the pallet in the corner caught her eye. Aife shook herself from the torpor invading her. Had she imagined it? The whisper she heard next made it clear she had not. Torsten had finally woken up.

"Aife."

She fell to her knees by his side, relief making her light-headed, hot and cold at the same time. "Oh, Torsten!"

At first he smiled at her, but then his eyes widened. As if unsure of what he was seeing in the dim light of the fire, he lifted a tentative hand to her left cheek. She knew from the constant throbbing that it was badly bruised, and the healer had cleaned a few cuts on her forehead earlier. She would look a fright, which explained his dismay.

"Who the hell hurt you thus?" he growled. "Not the Normans?"

The Normans? Her heart fell. Was he imagining himself back in the forest with Geoffroi's men? Had he forgotten what had happened at the beach? Surely this was not a good sign. But then again, he had received a severe blow to the head. By the gods, would he have lost his memory as well as the use of his lower body?

"No one hurt me," she said, placing her hand on his unin-jured shoulder. "We got caught in a landslide, remember, while we were gathering cockles?"

He stilled and let his hand drop, taking his warmth away. "Oh. Yes."

She barely repressed the urge to stroke his hair, take his hand in hers, brush his cheek, anything to feel that he was alive and breathing. Instead, she started to explain. "The edge of the cliff collapsed while we were looking at the flower made of stones and we—"

"It was a cabbage, not a flower," Torsten shocked her by saying.

Aife stared at him in disbelief. Really, was that all he had to say? Then she took in a deep breath, feeling some of her anxiety melting away. He could not be in such a bad state if he was jesting with her. For good measure, she decided to play the game.

"Fine, it did look a bit like a cabbage, I will admit." A nod and a side smile were her reward for this concession. "Anyway, while we were looking at the cabbage, the edge of the cliff collapsed. We got half buried under the rubble and could not escape. You had been knocked unconscious. Saxon villagers eventually found us, alerted by my shouts, and brought us here. A messenger has been sent to the village. I expect someone will come soon to get us."

He nodded. "I'm thirsty," he said, glancing over to the table as if in search of ale.

"Of course. I've made a tisane for you. It should still be warm and will help with the pain in your head." She picked up the wooden cup from the table and settled back down by the pallet. "Let me." While he drank, she did her best to behave as if it were normal that she should do that for him.

Once Torsten had emptied the cup he frowned and looked down the length of his body. "I feel odd. As if... I couldn't move."

A sob escaped Aife's lips, anxiety returning fast. No wonder he felt odd. "Some heavy rocks fell on you when you shielded me with your body." Another sob. Was she destined to do nothing but cry? "Without you, I would likely be dead now. You saved my life."

And because of his generosity, he might never be complete

again. Aife fell onto Torsten's chest, sobbing. After a while, a careful hand landed on her back.

"Hush, it's all right. You didn't die."

He was comforting her, when he was the one injured. It was unbearable. "I'm sorry, I'm so sorry. If I hadn't wanted to go to the—"

"You did nothing wrong. I should have been more careful, guessed that the place was dangerous. After the rain we've had, the land was bound to be unstable."

He winced. Yes, the healer had said he would have a terrible headache. It seemed she had been right about that, at least. Would she be proven right about her other prediction?

Swallowing her fears, Aife reached to the potion she had placed on the floor by the pallet earlier. Talking could wait. For now, he needed to rest and get better.

"Here," she said, uncorking the vial. The smell was strong, earthy and not altogether pleasant, reminiscent of leaves rotting on the forest floor after a downpour. "This will help you to sleep and forget the pain in your head. It's the best thing you can do for now, while we wait for people from the village to arrive."

To her relief, though he did grimace when the smell hit his nostrils, Torsten drank the contents of the vial without protest. Moments later he was asleep again, getting the rest he needed. Seeing as there was nothing else to do but to wait, Aife took her place back in the chair and placed her head over her arms like she had done before.

A gray morning light had started to filter around the ill-fitting door when Aife next opened her eyes, indicating that she had slept, at least a little. Carefully, she stretched the stiffness out of her muscles. She had not dared lie next to Torsten in case she caused him pain when she inadvertently rolled over in her sleep, but the night spent on a chair in an awkward position had done little to ease the pain in her own body. Outside, the village was slowly waking up, the noises far more unpleasant than the ones in her village. A man coughed just outside the window, then scolded a child, who started to cry. A cat screeched at the same time as a woman cursed. Had she stepped on its tail by accident? Had she kicked it on purpose? Aife rubbed at her temples, wishing she was back home, in her peaceful environment.

She had just added a log to the dying fire embers when footsteps were heard on the gravel surrounding the hut, too heavy to be those of the healer—at least she hoped so. A moment later, someone pushed the door open and Sigurd, her father, entered.

Aife threw herself into his arms. "*Faðir!*" Never had she been more relieved to see anyone. She had feared seeing the healer, back for more gloomy news.

"Daughter, look at me. Are you well?" He drew back to cradle her face in his hands, looking anxious, and no wonder. This was the second time in less than a week that she'd come back to him hurt.

"Yes, I'm well," she said hurriedly, knowing her bruises and cuts would worry him. But it was nothing, they would heal in no time. "It's Torsten... We were on the beach gathering cockles, everything was going well. And then...the cliff started to crumble away. He was the one caught under the falling rocks because he wanted to protect me and he—"

She shook her head, unable to say any more.

"He will be fine," her father soothed. "He is his true father's son. The man's indestructible, or have you not noticed?"

Though he meant to reassure her, Aife couldn't raise a smile. Yes, the Icelander was strong, but he was still only human, just like his son. They were still susceptible to injury. "I know, but the healer said he would—"

"Yes, I saw her when I arrived. A most dour woman, who clearly isn't used to dealing with Norsemen." Her father placed a kiss on her hair, like he'd done when she'd been a girl. The gesture never failed to soothe her. "But she doesn't know Torsten. Let Helga see him before you despair."

Aife nodded. She had to believe Torsten would be all right because the alternative was too dreadful to contemplate.

"Let's leave, please, as soon as we can." She couldn't bear to stay another moment in this place. But would Torsten be able to travel? Would the journey not pain him or cause his injuries to worsen?

Her father seemed to read her mind. "Stay here with Torsten. Let me go and speak to the villagers to see what they think. We have the means to take him back home. Björn and I came in Magnus's cart as soon as we got your message. Wolf would have come too, but he was in town when we left."

Of course, he would have rushed to his son's side if he'd been able to do so. But her father and uncle would take care of him just as well. Aife bit her bottom lip at the thought of getting back to the village. How would she face Wolf and Merewen? Would they blame her for their son's injury? Even if they did not, she knew she would blame herself. She already did.

Left alone, she poured herself a drink of ale, wishing it were some of her brother Eirik's strong mead. It might help her calm the worst of her anguish.

"What did the healer say?"

She froze, lips on the rim of the cup. Damnation! Contrary to what she'd thought, Torsten was awake and he'd heard what she had told her father. Even if she had not finished her sentence, he would have understood that something was wrong, that he was not just suffering from a headache. When she finally dared to turn around, he was looking at her with burning eyes.

"What did she tell you?" he repeated.

"I... She didn't really s-say anything other than—"

"Don't lie. She told you something that upset you."

Oh, he knew her too well. Not that it was hard to see her turmoil. He also knew she would not refuse to answer and be honest with him, so he waited. Eventually, she relented.

"She said you might not be yourself even after you'd recovered from the bruising on your spine. Various heavy rocks fell on your back and your legs..." Her voice trailed away. There was a difference between being honest and being blunt. At least she was the one telling him what could happen, not the Saxon healer, who would have simply told him he could forget any idea of a normal life from now on. "It might take you a while to..."

He glanced at his mid-section and finished the sentence for her. "To function like a man. In all ways."

Aife fell to her knees once again. "I know she's wrong. You heard my father. You're one of the strongest men I know."

Torsten gave a small smile at her protest. Trust Aife to try and minimize what had happened. He loved her for placing her trust in him, but he knew it was not that simple. And he did feel odd, as if the lower half of his body were still buried under the rubble.

"It has nothing to do with strength and we both know it."

Aife did not pretend it was not the case. "Yes. I'm so sorry."

"Don't be." He stared at the ceiling, not wanting to see sorrow, or worse, pity in her eyes. Not now, not when she had been the one restoring his faith in himself. He didn't want her to start seeing him differently. "At least you proved to me that there was nothing wrong with me before, convinced me the problem was all in my head."

Yes. And now the problem might well be in his body. How cruel. Some ruthless god really did seem intent on having a laugh at his expense. Why? What had he done to deserve it? He had never caused anyone harm.

Before he could add anything, the door opened again, letting in Sigurd and Björn, who nodded their greetings to him. He nodded back, doing his best to behave normally.

"The healer agreed we could take you home on the cart, provided we keep the horse at a walk," Aife's father said. "If you feel strong enough?"

"I do."

He would feel better in his own home, amongst his own people. And he did want to hear Helga's opinion.

It was when the two men unfurled a blanket on the floor next to him that Torsten understood he was going to be carried like a helpless babe. Would there be no end to his humiliation? Apparently not, because there was no way he could have walked to the cart when he could barely move his legs.

"Could I have a moment alone with Torsten?" Sigurd asked before they could lift him up.

Björn nodded and placed a hand on the small of Aife's back to lead her outside. Though she obeyed the silent command, Torsten could see she was reluctant to go and leave him alone with her formidable father, fearing what he would do. In truth, he was nervous himself. The Dane, who had been nicknamed "Beast" in his youth, was not a man to be trifled with. Had he spoken to his mother and guessed what had transpired in the Roman ruins? Was that what this was about? Was he about to warn him to stay away from his daughter, like his own father had done with Moon when his friend had started to see Eyja?

It was not impossible.

What would Torsten answer if Sigurd demanded he stopped seeing his daughter? Would he tell him that he and Aife had already decided to stop whatever was between them so there was no need to worry? Even if they hadn't, in view of what had just happened, he would have put a stop to it. How could he be with Aife now, or any woman? He had at least to wait until he knew for certain what the future held for him before he thought of bringing a woman into it.

"What is it?" he asked, behaving as if he were in control of the situation.

Sigurd crouched down on the floor, his face unusually earnest.

"Once again, I would like to thank you for saving my daughter's life."

Oh. Not a remonstrance then, and nothing to do with what had happened in the Roman ruins. It was when his body relaxed that Torsten realized how tense he'd been. "It's nothing," he said, relieved he would not have to justify his behavior.

"It is not nothing, and you know it. You saved her, for the second time in as many weeks, and you are now paying the price for your bravery." Sigurd's eyes sparkled with intent. "I spoke to the healer's husband. He was the one who found you on the beach, along with a group of friends. He told me what you had done to protect Aife. We both know that had you not shielded her with your body, she might be dead by now."

Dead. Up until then, and rather foolishly, Torsten had not considered the possibility. He had done what he needed to do, acting without thinking. But Sigurd was right. Aife would have been crushed by the rocks had he not been there. She was so much smaller than he was.

"It's nothing. I'm sure you would have done the same in my place."

"Of course, I would have. Because I love her."

There was a pause, as if Sigurd wanted him to understand something he hadn't said. Was he hinting... Torsten shook his head. Had the man suggested that he had saved Aife because he was in love with her? What was going on? His mother, now Aife's father... Had everyone started to suspect that things had changed between them? And was Sigurd right? Had Torsten really saved his friend because of the new, confusing feelings he harbored for her? No. He knew he would have done the same for any other woman, or child. Hell, he would even have done it for his oaf of a brother, Sven. Yes, but he might not have felt that excruciating anguish while doing it...

His heart had jumped in his throat when he'd realized that the cliff was falling apart and they were about to be smothered under a shower of rocks. There had been no time to run to safety. The only option had been to use his body to protect hers. And despite the possible repercussions to his health, he could not regret it.

"I would do the same again in a heartbeat," he whispered.

The reason for it was best ignored for now, irrelevant even. The important thing was that Aife was whole and well.

"So I see, and I'm telling you I'm grateful for it. My wife will no doubt tell you the same when we reach the village. Now, let me call Björn. We'll take you to the cart." A side smile lit up the Dane's face. "Not like a babe, mind, but like a wounded warrior after battle. Does that sound better to you?"

Despite his wretchedness, Torsten couldn't help return the smile.

Yes. That did sound a lot better.

14

The next few days were the longest of Aife's life. She alternated between despair and hope that Torsten would be all right. Despair because she had still not seen him on his feet, hope because, despite the seriousness of the situation, like her father had predicted, Helga's opinion about his chances of recovery had not been as grim as the Saxon healer's.

"The blow to his spine was severe and he might not be himself for a few days, or perhaps even weeks," the healer had conceded, "but he is a strong, determined young man, who will do what is needed to get better. I see no reason to think he will spend the rest of his life bound to his bed."

And so for the next few days Aife had desperately clung to that hope without quite managing to believe all would be well. She didn't dare go visit him and see for herself how he was faring. If she saw him lying down on his pallet she would start sobbing or blurt out what she had understood that day at the beach, that she had fallen in love with him. Neither would be a useful option, or wise. Indeed, why would he want to hear such a declaration from her, the fickle woman who'd once been attracted to his brother, the friend who had told him only days ago that they should forget all that had happened between them, the person responsible for the ruination of his life?

To add to her misery, that week was a series of unfortunate events.

She woke up one morning to the indignant clucking of her chickens. She rushed out, too late to prevent the fox that had managed to jump the high fence from carrying away one of her hens. The next day, lost to her thoughts of Torsten, she over-loaded the wicker basket her father had given her as a present when she had moved out of the family house. The handle broke before she reached the hut, scattering turnips everywhere. For a long moment, unable to think what to do, she just stared at the broken basket. No doubt her father would make her another, equally beautiful one, but she had loved this one, which had marked the start of her independent life. That same morning, still upset by the loss of the beloved gift, she'd burned herself whilst frying a piece of pork.

Fortunately, that afternoon, Cwenthryth visited with baby Sanna, otherwise Aife would have spent the day in bed, crying and hugging herself. Her friend, sensing she needed distraction, sat down and accepted a cup of dried chamomile sweetened with honey. Since she had tasted it on Torsten's fingers, honey had become Aife's favorite treat and she used it everywhere.

While they sipped at their tisane, Cwenthryth shocked her by telling her that Knut the blacksmith's son had been caught kissing Brenna, the butcher's youngest daughter, the previous night, behind the forge.

"Neither seemed particularly sorry to have been seen and there is now talk of them getting married. And yet Steinar tells me the two of them spent their childhood fighting." She laughed, as if amused by the turn of events.

"They did," Aife confirmed. This was what made this particular announcement shocking, not the fact that two young people had been kissing. There was nothing more normal than this. "And now apparently they are in love?"

"Apparently," her friend confirmed, settling her daughter at her breast. "Such unions seem to be a regular occurrence in the village, which I suppose is not so surprising when you consider how close a community it is. Moon and Eyja, Rowena and Thorfinn, Bee and Elwyn... There seem to be many couples here who grew up as friends. Thank God Steinar gave the outsider I was a chance and did not instead choose to marry someone he'd known all his life."

Couples who grew up as friends... Yes, indeed there were many here, and if Aife had her way, there would be another soon.

"Talking of friends who start seeing one another differently," Cwenthryth started cautiously. Aife's heart missed a beat. Was she ready to discuss what was happening between her and Torsten? In truth, she wasn't, not until she had discussed it with him and found out where she stood. "How is it going with Sven?"

Sven? It took Aife a moment to remember that, as far as her friend was concerned, she was still trying to ensnare him. How much had changed since that conversation outside her hut...

Slowly, she shook her head. "It's going nowhere. You were right, he is not the man for me, and I was never truly in love with him. I know that now, so you need not feel sorry for me."

What would be the point in telling her friend that she was now in love with Sven's brother? She would think it another whim, and it would be hard to blame her. It did look as if she was going from one infatuation to the next. Except that she had never felt that way before and she knew it was not the same. Two trees might appear identical at first glance, and only when you felled them could you see which was rotting on the inside and destined to die, and which would make the perfect, solid foundation for your hut.

"I don't feel sorry for you," Cwenthryth said, placing a hand on her baby daughter, who seemed to be falling asleep. "Things happen when they are supposed to happen, not a moment before. Why worry in the meantime about what you think you're missing? You might not have a husband but you have a good life here, surrounded by friends and family who love you. Enjoy it."

Yes, her life was good. Her friend should know. Before meeting Steinar she had been subjected to the cruelty of a man who'd claimed to be her half-brother to come live under her roof. He'd taken advantage of her father's illness and used her body for his pleasure for months. Indeed, compared to that, Aife's life was perfect.

Humbled, she gave her friend's hand a squeeze. "Thank you."

Cwenthryth nodded and swallowed, visibly reliving the nightmare she'd endured until Steinar had put an end to the bastard's life. "You're welcome. Now, if you'll excuse me, I'd better take Sanna home to have a rest."

"Of course."

That evening, thanks to her conversation with her friend, Aife felt better than she had for a while, and the following day even went without any mishap, providing a welcome respite from the succession of alarming incidents. Then she had an unexpected visitor.

Aife was filling a pitcher with the ale from the cask brought by her uncle Björn the evening before, when the door opened on the man she had most dreaded to see. Wolf.

Her whole body tensed. Had he come to berate her for placing his son in danger at the beach? For getting him almost killed again? She forced herself to stay calm. He didn't appear angry, even if his mouth was set in a determined line. She suddenly had an inkling of how Torsten might appear later on in life, strong and dependable.

If he ever regained the use of his legs, of course. His recovery was still not assured.

"Good morning," the Icelander told her, closing the door behind him.

"Good morning." She placed the pitcher back onto the table. Her hands were shaking and after the week she'd had, she didn't trust herself not to drop it.

Heart in her throat, she waited for Wolf to explain why he had come. When he spoke, he said the last thing she had expected him to say.

"Aife. I need you."

THEY SET OFF WITHOUT DELAY, Aife having not entertained the possibility of refusing Torsten's father. Even though he hadn't explained what he wanted from her, she followed him to the field where the horses grazed. Knowing that Moon wouldn't mind, she borrowed Grendel and Wolf took his stallion, Devil, an enormous beast with a coat black as night. As they nudged the horses into a trot in the direction of the town, the Icelander started explaining why he needed her help.

"It took me a while, but I have finally located the Saxon called Ranulf and the Normans who attacked you and Torsten the other day."

"You have?" Aife exclaimed, taken by surprise. She had not thought for a moment that would be what this expedition was about. Not that she had forgotten the attack, of course, or did not want the men punished for what they'd done, but so much had happened since then that it felt like months ago.

"Yes. In fact, that was why I was in town the morning Sigurd and Björn went to get my son from the Saxon village." He sounded grim, as if he regretted not having been there to offer support. "I hope to see the bastards punished, because it is clear from the information I have gathered about their little 'clan,' as they call themselves, that they intend to harm the Norse community."

"They most certainly do." If they had jumped on the opportunity to capture two Norse people who had done nothing to provoke them, there was no telling what they were capable of. Such hate-filled people were not above making up stories to justify their despicable actions.

"This is why I need you. I need someone to identify them for me, and I could not ask Torsten to come with me."

No, he could not, because he was confined to his bed. Her chest squeezed.

"You look scared," Wolf observed, frowning when she didn't respond. "There's nothing to fear. I hope you don't think I would ever allow the Normans to—"

"I'm not scared, not of those men, at least," she whispered, deciding it was time to be honest. She would only spend the day worrying if she didn't speak out now. She hadn't had the courage to go see Wolf and his wife during the week, but since he was here, she would do what she should have done days ago, beg for his forgiveness. "I'm scared of you."

"Me?" He recoiled as if having a woman fear him was the worst thing that could have happened to him.

"Well, not of you, precisely, but of what you must think of m-me," she stammered. "Because of me, your son was almost killed that day by the Normans and I never—"

"Aife." Wolf's firm but paternal tone was the same her own father would have used with her. "You're not responsible for the violence of bad men. Torsten explained what happened that day in the clearing, it is clear neither of you did anything wrong.

That the Normans decided to attack you and hand you over to this Ranulf was not your doing."

Perhaps not, but she was responsible for taking Torsten to the beach and then too close to the cliff. That was definitely her doing. "Because of me, he might never walk again."

Or know pleasure.

"Torsten will walk again," was Wolf's tranquil answer. "Just give him time, it's only been a few days."

There seemed to be no question in his mind that his son would recover. Aife swallowed. It didn't even sound as if he were trying to reassure her. He simply was convinced all would be well.

"Yes," she said, unaccountably comforted by his certainty. "He will."

And she took her first real breath in what felt like months.

"Now, back to the topic at hand. I am confident the two men who've been arrested are amongst the ones who attacked you in the meadow. Girard and Enguerrand. They match my son's description exactly, but the reeve wants conclusive proof of wrongdoing. The problem is, the Normans pretend they can't speak his language, so he's been unable to interrogate them." He let out a groan of frustration. Evidently, he was not used to being thwarted. "I understand the Norman tongue reasonably well and even speak a little, but 'tis not enough to conduct a proper interrogation. Besides, it looks as if I am only translating what suits me."

"Surely if the men refuse to speak English, an interpreter can be found?" Unlike the reeve, she didn't for a moment think that Wolf had arrested the wrong men, innocent Normans who genuinely didn't understand what they were asked and had no idea why they had been apprehended.

A sigh. "Of course, but the reeve happens to be married to this Ranulf's niece. I got the impression that he doesn't particularly like the man but is wary of upsetting his wife's family and making a powerful enemy by accusing him of wrongdoing. If, however, he sees that you identify the men, he will have no choice but to pursue the matter further, at least find an interpreter as you say, and establish the truth."

Aife nodded her head pensively. She could see Wolf's thinking, but there was a flaw in the plan, in her opinion.

"Even if I recognize the men, it will achieve little. It will still not force them to speak to the interpreter, or confirm what happened. For all the reeve and Ranulf know, I could be in league with you, or I could simply be mistaken. No. We need to trick Girard and Enguerrand into revealing that they are in fact pretending not to be able to converse with the reeve, and that they were amongst the men involved in my and Torsten's abduction."

"What do you suggest?"

"Have the reeve free them, on the pretence that their guilt has not been successfully established." When Wolf raised his head in protest, she hurriedly added, "Having been freed, they will think themselves safe and relax their guard. But it will be far from over. As they exit the gaol, I will place myself in their path. You and the reeve will follow discretely, so you can overhear our conversation. When they recognize me for the woman who's caused them so many problems, they will be sure to come speak to me, and their complicity in the abduction will become clear, as will their knowledge of the English tongue. The reeve is reluctant to investigate against his uncle by marriage at the moment, but he will have no scruples in arresting men whose guilt has been proven."

"Mm. It might be dangerous for you to be on your own with them," Wolf said slowly. He didn't seem to think it was a bad idea, but appeared worried all the same.

"I think it will be fine," she assured him, with more confidence than she felt. "We'll be in town, surrounded by people, not in the middle of nowhere. And you and the reeve will be there, ready to intervene if need be. No harm will come to me."

There was a silence, then Wolf gave a low admirative whistle. "You really are your father's daughter," he said slowly. "That Dane is nothing if not resourceful."

The compliment went straight to Aife's heart. No one had called her resourceful before, even if her family had always commented on her practical nature. Even more gratifying was the fact that Wolf did not try to dissuade her or doubt that she could achieve what she'd set off to achieve. He trusted her, he understood that she wanted revenge for what she and Torsten had endured, and he was willing to give her the opportunity to get it.

"Yes, well," she said with a smile, grateful for his understanding. "We women have no choice but to resort to cunning, considering we cannot rely on brute strength."

"Believe me, I do know that, being married to Merewen." His smile was proof that his love for his wife was stronger than ever. "Very well, you just do your part. Then as soon as brute strength is required, I'll take over."

"Thank you."

"No. Thank *you* for allowing me to avenge my son."

Aife sobered, remembering all Torsten had endured these last weeks through her fault. "You can thank me when it is done. Besides, I am grateful you are allowing me to avenge myself also."

She had her own score to settle with the men. It was not all about Torsten, even if he'd almost been killed. She had almost been raped that day, and then handed over to a man who would have used her for his amusement before likely disposing of her. It was not insignificant.

"You're very brave, you know that?" she heard Wolf say.

Aife shook her head. "I don't think I am. Your daughter Eyja is the brave one."

"Eyja is brave to the point of foolishness sometimes." Wolf's mouth quivered, betraying his immense tenderness for her. "But it's not because she is that you can't be as well, in your own, more sensible way. She's not *the* brave one, but *a* brave one, amongst many. You don't think there is only one brave person in each given village, do you? One clever one, one funny one, one determined one, and so forth? Most people are a bit of all this, in different proportions."

Well, Aife felt rather silly because she had thought something along those lines up until not too long ago. She'd been unable to pinpoint what her special achievement was and thought herself unworthy of interest because of it. But perhaps Wolf was right. Perhaps everyone had their own unique set of skills and abilities that made them special, and if they happened not to have one obvious or rare one, it was not a problem. She was brave like Eyja, if an admittedly different way, compassionate, even if perhaps not as much as Bee, sociable, though unlike Rowena, she felt sometimes ill at ease in front of strangers, and just as helpful as Cwenthryth, in the right circumstances. She was also a fearless and accomplished swimmer, good at finding cockles, devoted to her friends and family, and she had been the one proving to Torsten that he was a man like any other, her proudest moment.

Torsten... Despite all he had been through because of her, he certainly had never given her the impression that whatever she was, was not enough.

"Thank you," she told Wolf, moved. This conversation would mark a turning point in her life. It would be a first step toward acceptance of who she was and what she could do.

As if sensing she needed time to absorb what he'd just told her, Wolf launched his horse into a canter, preventing further discussion. She followed, trusting Grendel unconditionally despite her recent fall. At this speed, the city walls soon came into view.

They entered through the south gate and did not stop until they had reached the reeve's residence. To Aife's relief, it wasn't hard to convince him of the validity of her idea. It was as Wolf had said—the man seemed happy enough to pursue the two Normans and go to interrogate Ranulf, but first he needed to be given irrefutable proof of foul play to protect himself from any accusation coming from his wife's family. This was what she would hopefully provide.

"As soon as the men exit the gaol, they will see me in the street, stationed as if waiting for someone. I'm certain they will not resist the temptation of coming to see me."

"We will take John, one of my guards, with us," the reeve decided. "He's one of Ranulf's closest friends. Having him corroborate the story will protect me from his family's ill will. It will be clear this is nothing personal, only a necessary investigation, and he will lend a hand if we need to restrain the men."

Wolf nodded, satisfied. "Go and tell the bastards they are free to leave, then."

The knock was self-assured and masculine, nothing like the tentative and feminine one he'd been waiting to hear. Torsten closed his eyes in disappointment. Over the last few days, he'd received many a visit. His parents, Steinar, Moon, Haakon, even Aife's brothers, Eirik and Elwyn. He'd hoped to see Aife herself but it would seem that she was avoiding him. Since Sigurd and Björn had brought him back to the village, she had not visited him once. Why? Did she feel guilty for causing his injury, as she had hinted at the Saxon village? Or had she lost interest in him, now that he could do naught but lie on his pallet? He dearly hoped not, but unfortunately, he could not just go to her and find out. He could have asked someone to carry him to her hut, of course, but he refused to leave his house other than on his own two feet.

A second knock, more forceful, made it clear the visitor was not going to be dissuaded so easily. Torsten wasn't sure he wanted to answer, only to be seen in such a pitiful state by someone who was not a close friend. Nevertheless, he called out.

"Enter."

Feeling more powerless than ever, he watched Sven walk inside the hut with his usual swagger. What wouldn't he give to shoot up to his feet and give him a slap on the shoulder, as they usually did.

"Brother. Good afternoon."

To his credit, Sven behaved as if nothing was amiss, as if it were normal that someone his age should lie on his pallet like a crippled old man in the middle of the day.

"What do you want?" Torsten asked none too graciously. Unlike his carefree brother, he was having difficulty pretending everything was as it should be.

"Mother came to see me this morning. She gave me some roasted trout for my dinner tonight. But I've been invited to eat with Elwyn and Bee. I didn't have the heart to tell her but I don't want the fish to spoil. So, here, you can have it."

With those words he deposited a wooden plate on the table. On it was the roasted trout, as well as a chunk of rye bread and some freshly churned butter. Mm. This seemed like a ploy to provide him with food, but Torsten didn't comment. His brother was only trying to help without making him feel bad. He was a good man, one of the most personable he knew, which was probably what had drawn countless women to him, including Aife.

Aife. The thought of her was a punch to the gut. Was she still in love with Sven?

After their heated encounter the other day he had done his best to ignore the question, but spending his day lying on his pallet with nothing else to do than think meant that he'd tortured himself wondering if her feelings for his little brother had changed. He'd also wondered if Sven was interested in her. And if he was, did he intent to act on his desire? It was not impossible. Torsten had changed his mind about a woman who'd been a childhood friend. Why wouldn't his brother, who had a notorious roaming eye, not consider bedding another beautiful, willing conquest? Aife had done all she could to attract his attention.

So, had she succeeded?

Taking a deep inhale, Torsten decided to ask the difficult question. He might not be able to will himself onto his feet, but he could at least set his mind at rest once and for all. And perhaps knowing he had nothing to worry about would help motivate him regain his strength. He refused to think of the other option—that he would have his worst fears confirmed and lose Aife.

"Tell me," he said while Sven started to brush the cold ashes from the fire pit into the small wooden shovel he'd taken from the hook on the wall. "What do you think of Aife?"

"Aife?" The arched eyebrow and the surprise in his tone were enough to indicate that Sven didn't think much of her, aside from the fact that she was a friend. "What do you mean? That I should resent her for what happened to you? Well, I don't. It was an accident."

"No, I don't mean that. I know she is not to blame, as you say, it was an accident. I mean, have you ever considered bedding her?" There. It could not be clearer.

"*Aife?*" There really was no mistaking the shock in Sven's

voice. He had not entertained the idea once, would likely never do. The knot in Torsten's chest started to loosen. Perhaps he could set his mind at rest. He wouldn't have to watch as his charming brother whisked her from under his nose. "Sigurd's daughter? No, of course, I have not! Why would you even think such a thing? Have you gone mad? Next, you will be suggesting I bed Eirik."

Torsten's mouth quivered at the idea of the two brawny men in bed together. "Well, no, I would not, for it is not quite the same, is it?"

"It is to me." Sven straightened back up, pan in hand. "We are friends, have been forever."

"I know, but things can change." They had already changed, in fact, as far as he was concerned. Aife was much more than a friend to him now, he definitely had no problem imagining bedding her and he didn't think himself mad for it. It was the most wonderful thing that had happened to him in a while, perhaps ever. She had given him his confidence back, and hope that he could lead the same life as any man.

If he recovered from his injury, of course.

"Yes, things can change but not with..." Sven shook his head, indicating that no matter how much he tried, he just could not see Aife in a different light. "No. I mean, you know, I like her well enough but I will never..."

Instead of finishing his sentence, Sven went outside to dispose of the ashes.

Torsten relaxed. There was no need to insist. His brother would never see her as a possible conquest, never mind wife. Not that he was looking to settle anyway. Poor Aife. She had been fighting a losing battle from the start. Nothing she did would ever make Sven see her differently. She would never stir his interest, whether she laughed at his stories or kissed other men. It had all been in vain. Except...

Except that it had not. It had made *him* see her differently. And he was most definitely ready to settle.

Ready to fight and give himself, and her, a chance at a life neither of them had hoped to have.

"Now," he said with decision, lifting himself onto his elbows once Sven had come back inside. "Please go get Steinar. You two big brutes will hold me up while I see what strength I have left in my legs, if any. It's been three days since the accident, plenty of time, I should think, to restore some semblance of vigor to my body and start moving about. Just...you know. Don't say anything to Mother or *Faðir* in case we find out that there is no hope of me ever being able to walk again."

There was no pity or doubt in his little brother's eyes. He merely nodded, as if he'd expected the request all along and had every faith in his ability.

"Well, you had better get yourself back into working order because I'm not carrying you around like a babe. Don't get me wrong, I'm strong enough to do it, but we would both look ridiculous. Besides, I still need to make you pay for the beating I received the other day."

The short nod Sven gave would have brought a lump to Torsten's throat if he'd allowed it. "Yes, you do."

"Very well, then. Let me go get Steinar."

15

"Look who we have here, Girard."

At the sound of the hated man's voice Aife could not help a shudder. Though they were in plain view of everyone and Wolf was not far, ready to defend her, she was instantly transported back to the meadow, when she had feared for her life and Torsten's.

While she steeled herself for the conversation she had hoped to provoke, the other man—Girard, she assumed— answered, rather unnecessarily. "The Norsewoman."

It wasn't hard to look afraid when she stood up from the fence she'd been leaning on and turned to face the two men closing in on her. It had been her plan to confront them and it was a good one, but it didn't mean it would be easy. The way they were glaring at her froze the blood in her veins. She had expected them to be delighted to have another chance at getting their hands on her but they looked angry. Why? Were they suspicious to have encountered her in town? This was bad, she could not afford to give them time to think, at the risk of having them conclude that yes, it was too much of a coincidence that they should meet her moments after they had been released.

And so she did what she would have done had she not been actually waiting for them.

She ran.

Looking afraid would be the best way to convince them this was a genuine encounter and move them into chasing her. Still, she made sure to choose her destination poorly, and allowed herself to be trapped in a narrow alley so as to give the Normans a false sense of security. Panting in genuine fear, she watched them closing in on her, blocking her only escape route. Having not really seen them that day in the meadow, since she'd pretended to be unconscious, she'd been unprepared for their size.

Hopefully, Wolf and the reeve men were following. If not, she was in deep trouble. They had seemed angry before; they now looked positively irate.

Enguerrand, who seemed to have taken the role of leader, spoke first. "You bitch! Did you really think you could escape us? You're going to pay for what you did. Because of you my cousin is dead."

"What c-cousin? What do you mean?" The stupider and more afraid she appeared, the more information she would coax out of them. Not that it was hard to appear either. She was petrified, and she had no idea who he was talking about.

"Hugues, the one who came back for you after we'd all left."

Oh, she certainly remembered *him*, his crushing weight, his foul smell, his frightening words. "He did come back to the clearing," she admitted, taking a step backward. She would have taken another but her back had just hit the wall. "But I didn't kill him!"

"You didn't plunge a blade into his heart, I'll allow that, but his death is your fault nonetheless."

So he was dead? "How can it be my fault?"

"Geoffroi didn't like to see that Hugues had ruined his

chance of finally convincing Ranulf we could be trusted and accepted into the clan. When the two of them found him tied up amidst the rocks instead of you and the Norseman, he ran him through with his blade without even giving him the chance to explain himself."

Not in the least sorry to hear about the man's demise, Aife fought her smile of satisfaction. The men were giving names, establishing their guilt beyond doubt. The more they talked, the more they corroborated Wolf's version of the story. This was good, just what they needed. But she still didn't see how Hugues's death could be attributed to her. He'd been tied up and unconscious when they had abandoned him to his fate, but alive. She should know, as she'd been the one stopping Torsten from killing him.

"Am I supposed to feel sorry your friend lost his head and killed your cousin?" she asked, feeling her courage returning at the idea that this confrontation would soon be over. "Well. I'm not. He intended to—"

"He lost his head, and all for a taste of your cunt," Enguerrand roared, cutting through her protests. "He was a good man, but lustier than most. You played on his weakness, you whore! If you hadn't lured him in while he tied you up, he wouldn't have come back to have a go at you. He would still be alive."

"I didn't 'lure him in,' as you say. I could not. I was unconscious while he tied me up to my friend and you know it!" Outrage had now replaced fear. How dare the man blame her for his cousin's decision to come back and rape her! How dare he call him a good man after all he'd done—and all he'd wanted to do! How dare he call the man's lack of honor a weakness and her a whore! "It's not my fault Geoffroi killed him. If Hugues wanted to live, he should have thought twice before raping an innocent woman."

"You mean he actually had you?" Enguerrand asked, his lips curling into a snarl.

Why did he want to know that? She ignored the question. "My friend and I were innocent, and you attacked us, with the intention of handing us over to—"

"We did not attack you. You fell from your horse if you recall, right in front of us."

This blatant demonstration of bad faith had Aife's blood boiling but she tried to control herself because it served her purpose. She was not here to convince the two men they had acted like despicable pigs, but to prove to the reeve and his man that Wolf had not lied. Let the Normans give as many details as possible.

"I did take a tumble when my horse was spooked by your sudden appearance. It couldn't be helped. That didn't mean you had to take me hostage. And what about my friend? *He* didn't fall from his horse, did he, yet you attacked him three to one, like the cowards you are! Well, not you," she spat, nodding at the second man, Girard, who still hadn't uttered a single useful word. He didn't appear to have the sharpest mind. "You twisted your ankle when your own horse bolted, didn't you?"

Would he admit to it? He didn't seem injured, which went against what Wolf would have told the reeve. She needed to get him talking, establish he was indeed the right man.

"'Twas nothing. I recovered quickly." He lifted his left leg to show he had recovered from the injury. Yes. That would do. "Why are you here in town anyway?"

"Why shouldn't I be?" she countered, relieved. Surely by now the two men's ability to speak the English tongue and their complicity in the crime they had been accused of had been well established. "I am free to go where I want. Or do you mean for us Norse people to remain in our village. Is that what your friend Ranulf wants to do? Park us like animals, use the men for sport and the women for his pleasure?"

"Well, you are barely civilized, so it's hard to blame him. What else would you have us do?"

"Leave us alone?" she suggested, stealing a glance to the entrance of the alley in the hope of seeing Wolf appear.

All she saw was a stray dog lapping at some vile substance on the ground. Where were the three men who were supposed to help her? By now, the reeve would have heard enough to justify arresting the men a second time. Why was he not intervening? Surely she had not lost him during the chase earlier? That would be a disaster.

"Enough of this," Enguerrand said, closing the space between him and her. "We just spent two days in a gaol doing our best to appear confused as to why we had been arrested. It paid off and the foolish reeve just freed us, so you will follow us. Before we hand you over to Ranulf, we'll make sure you know your place."

"*Oui*, under us," the second man leered.

"Shut up, Girard!"

"I'm not going with you!" Aife protested, starting to panic. Damnation, where *was* Wolf? She had not seen nor heard anything to indicate his presence during the conversation with the Normans.

"You are coming, unless you want to find yourself with a broken limb. I bet you want to give yourself at least a chance to fight us off, don't you?"

With those words, Enguerrand reached out to grab her by the arm. Before he could touch her, however, a blade had embedded itself in his hand. He screamed and fell to his knees cradling his wrist. Aife flattened herself against the wall while chaos descended into the alley. Wolf and the reeve's man pounced, their faces contorted with rage, and soon the two Normans were brought under control.

"Are you now convinced these are the men who attacked my son and my friend's daughter?" Wolf snarled. "I trust you heard enough to get Ranulf and Geoffroi the Norman punished for what they planned to do, what they no doubt did to others?"

"Indeed, I did hear plenty and so did John." The reeve turned to her, concern etched over his face. She'd had chance to see before that he was an honorable man and she was glad to be proven right. "Are you all right? This wasn't a pleasant confrontation."

"I'm f-fine," she stammered. This had been rather horrid, much more than she had expected. "Thank you. But I'd like to leave if I may. I don't want to have to look at these two men a moment longer."

"You won't have to. I will escort you home immediately," Wolf told her, before nodding to the Saxon who nodded in turn. "I'll come back to see you tomorrow, when you've extracted all the information you need from those two bastards. We'll talk then."

Aife didn't doubt the Icelander would make sure the men were suitably punished and the clan dismantled. She cared not, she just wanted to go, put this all behind her. An arm wrapped protectively around her shoulders, Wolf led her out of the alley and back into the busy street. Despite the acrid smell emanating from the various puddles, Aife took in a deep, steadying breath. Her plan had worked. It was over.

"So, you heard it all?" she asked, as they reached their horses.

"Yes. The alleyway was not so long. Placed where we were we heard it all." He gritted his teeth as he tightened Grendel's girth. "I'm sorry you had to go through this."

It had been hard indeed. She'd been accused of murder, of

having lured a man in, she'd been called a whore, compared to an animal only worth being good for rutting, she'd been told someone was dead because they had wanted a taste of her—

Aife shook her head, determined to forget the vile men and what they had told her. She would be avenged, that was all that mattered now. To steady herself further, she gave Grendel a hug. Against her cheek, the horse's coat was soft as silk. He nudged at her slightly, offering his reassurance. She wasn't surprised. Horses were notoriously sensitive animals, and though she had not known him as long as she had known Imp, he would have felt her unease.

"Please don't tell Torsten I met with the men," she told Wolf suddenly. "I'm not sure he would like to hear it."

"I'm sure he wouldn't," he grumbled, giving his own stallion a rub. "I didn't either, to tell you the truth. But you were right, it was the quickest and easiest way to expose the Normans. And it worked." With those words, he planted himself in front of her. "So can I now thank you for allowing me to avenge my son?"

Aife's lips stretched into a smile. "You may."

16

Should she go see Torsten this morning, Aife wondered? After so many days without him, she was dying to see him.

How would he be feeling today? Better, she hoped.

What if he was still unable to stand up? Then she would do her best not to cry.

Would he want to see her? She hoped so.

The questions came hard and fast in Aife's mind, swirling as fast as the leaves twirling outside her hut, whipped up by the fierce autumn winds. The weather had turned in the last few days, just like her life had recently changed. Summer was definitely over.

After much soul-searching, she decided to chance it and go see Torsten. There was no other choice. If she didn't, she would drive herself mad. She wrapped herself in her cloak and opened the door—only to find herself face-to-face with the very man she wanted to see.

Standing on his own two feet.

"Oh!" she hugged herself, sobbing, overcome by a wave of

relief so powerful it robbed her of all her strength. "Oh, Torsten."

Before she could fall to the floor, Torsten drew her against his chest with a powerful arm, holding her upright. She had the impression he would have preferred to sweep her into his arms but didn't trust himself not to collapse under the extra weight. With reason. Only a few days ago, he'd been told he might never walk again. That he was here was miraculous enough. Risking injuring himself would be foolish. She clung tight to him, running her hands all over his back, assuring herself he was whole, relishing in his warmth and strength, his wonderful scent.

"You can walk. You can walk," she repeated incessantly.

"Yes, I can walk," he soothed. "I've been practicing on my own for days, aided by my brothers and then by wooden staffs, following Helga's advice. And my first visit when I finally got out of the hut was for you."

Aife drew away, surprised. Surely he should have gone to reassure his parents, his siblings, first? He looked at her with such an expression that once again, her heart wobbled, something it only did in his presence. It seemed unable to function properly when he was in front of her.

"You came to me. But...why?"

Had Wolf told him about the encounter in town with the Normans? He had not exactly promised he would not, and it had been obvious he'd not approved of keeping it a secret from his son. So was this why Torsten was here? To remonstrate with her about putting herself in danger? He didn't look angry, but it was a possibility. She waited nervously for his answer.

"I came because I—" He stopped, as if thinking better of his first answer. Then he cleared his throat and started again. "I came because there is something I promised to give you days ago."

"What is that?"

Instead of answering, he led her back inside the hut, a hand on the small of her back. After closing the door behind him, he unfastened the brooch holding his cloak closed, folded the garment, and placed it on the back of the only chair. Aife watched his every move as if she had never seen him before, as if no one had disposed of his cloak in her presence before.

Then, to her surprise, he reached out to unfasten her own cloak. It was removed without a word and placed on top of his. This would not be a brief visit then... He clearly meant to stay a while. Her heart leaped at the thought. She had missed him so much. Would that he stayed forever, here in her hut.

Finally, unable to wait another moment, she asked. "Why are you here, Torsten?"

"To give you this."

He reached into the purse at his belt and extracted the most exquisitely crafted comb she had ever seen. The teeth were thin and regular, the antler shaft carved with swirls of leaves and berries that seemed ready to pop out. Of course, the comb. She had not forgotten his promise to give it to her, but she had not dared remind him of it when he'd lain in bed, waiting for his body to go back to normal.

"You remembered."

"Of course. Here, it's for you," he said, placing it into her hand. It felt smooth and warm, the size perfect for her to hold. Aife stared at it, then at Torsten in disbelief.

"Are you sure you don't want to keep it?" she asked, running a finger over the end of the teeth. It was so beautiful, he could have sold it for a good price or bartered it. Why was he giving it to her?

"I'm sure." He smiled the smile she had come to adore. "I already have a comb, and I only have one head so a second one would be quite unnecessary. Besides, I can always make another one if need be."

"Well, thank you. It was sorely needed. I've been using my mother's since Edita left." She ran a hand through her wild, tangled hair, feeling self-conscious. "As you can see, I haven't had the time to go see her yet this morning. The wind when I went out to let the chickens out didn't help."

His smile widened but he didn't comment. Perhaps she didn't look as frightful as she feared. At least he didn't seem to find her ridiculous. "Will you let me comb it for you now?"

Not waiting for her answer, he gestured that she should sit on the stool behind her. Unable to resist the temptation, Aife did as she was told. Her eyes fluttered closed as soon as Torsten lifted the heavy mass of her hair from her shoulders. This would be decadent, unlike anything else she had ever experienced, not so much an explosion of the senses, but rather a stroking of the soul. Carefully, he separated a long strand from the rest and began to comb, making sure to hold the hair near the scalp firmly until all the knots were loosened so as not to hurt her.

Aife was fighting the urge to groan and moan and sigh. Never had the simple act of combing her hair felt so good. The man really did have the most nimble fingers she could imagine.

"Here. All done."

Already? She could have sat there all day, being taken care of. She stood back up on slightly shaky legs and took the comb he was handing back to her. Unfortunately, she could not offer to return the favor. His luscious hair looked impeccable.

"Thank you," she said, closing her fingers around the comb possessively. She already knew it would be one of her most treasured possessions. "I love it. I will be sure to hide it the next time Edita comes."

Something hot and fierce flashed in Torsten's eyes. Anger? "Next time Edita comes, she will not dare steal anything from you, believe me. And she will not dare make you feel like a failure for being on your own. Because next time she comes, she will see you with a man."

Her breath caught in Aife's chest. Did she dare hope he meant what she thought he meant?

"With a...man?"

"Yes."

With me, Torsten wanted to add. Because, as true as it was that he had come to show her that he could walk and give her the comb he had promised her, he had, in reality, come for a much more important reason.

He was going to tell her what he felt and ask her to marry him. As he'd lain in bed alone in his hut, feeling his body get stronger by the day, he'd had time to think about his next course of action, and there had been only one he could agree on, only one that made sense.

He'd sworn to himself that if he ever recovered the use of his lower body, he would not shy away from what he felt. For the first time in his life, he'd found someone he wanted to be with, someone who allowed him to be the man he could be, someone who gave meaning to what he did and did not make him feel he was lacking in any way. He was not going to let this chance at happiness pass. Too much time had been wasted already, and after his brush with death, he knew that there were no guarantees he would get to live until a ripe old age. He could at least make sure he spent the time he had with someone who made his life complete.

But he could not ask Aife to be that person, not yet. There was one thing he needed to know first.

"Aife," he began, taking her free hand in his. She was still holding his comb as if it were the most precious thing she had ever held. "There's something I need to know. Do you still have feelings for Sven?"

There it was, the all-too important question. He knew his brother would never respond to her advances, but that didn't mean she had forgotten her intentions regarding him. Did the woman he'd come to love, love another man? Torsten's heart went in his throat while he waited for her answer. As much as he was desperate to be with her, and give what was between them a chance to blossom, he could not be with someone who was lusting after his brother. Any other man would have been bad enough but Sven... It was just impossible.

"No." The word tore through the silence with the precision of one of Magnus's double-edged swords.

"You don't?" It seemed too good to be true. Only a few weeks ago she'd been doing everything she could to make his brother see her differently, using him to attract his attention. "Because you were—"

"I don't," she cut in. There was such earnestness in her tone that he instantly knew she was not lying. "And in truth, I don't think I ever had feelings for him, not that kind of feelings anyway. I realized it the day we went to the beach together, because earlier that morning he'd asked me if he could come with me and I'd refused. I..." Her cheeks went a delicious red color when she made her confession. "I think I merely lusted after him, it was never...like it is with you. I lust after you as well, but I also laugh with you, I dream of you at night, I worry about you, I want to eat cockles with you, watch you sleep, confide in you, ask you questions, watch the sun set while nestled in your arms. It's everything with you. I—"

I love you.

She didn't say the words, but they still filled the resounding silence.

"Yes," he agreed, drawing her against him. It was exactly the same for him. "It's everything with you. Lust, hope, tenderness, gratitude, and just pure, unadulterated bliss. I think there is a simple way to describe this jumble of emotions."

"Love," she breathed, her face lighting up with a joy he had never seen on anyone's face before.

"Love. I suppose that after pretending we had become lovers, it was only a matter of time before we really did."

"I suppose so."

They stared at one another a long moment relishing in the realization that their friendship had transformed into something even more beautiful. He smiled to himself. Not so long ago he'd been hoping that fate would place what he needed in front of him and that he would be astute enough to recognize the opportunity and seize it. Against all odds, he had.

"You know, my mother told me the other day that I was in the hut with her and your mother the night you were born. I slept through the whole labor and when I woke up, I walked over to you. Apparently, the steps I took to reach the pallet were my first real ones. As soon as I saw you, I took your hand in mine. You grabbed my little finger and refused to let go."

The awe he saw in Aife's eyes mirrored the swelling he felt in his chest. "I did?"

"Yes." He closed his fingers around her wrist, encircling it. "It seems I was the first man to ever touch you and I want to make sure I'm the last one as well."

That was what his mother had tried to make him understand that day, Torsten now realized, that he would never want to let go of her.

She smiled. "I want you to be the last one, too. The only one."

"So what say you? We pretended to be a couple to make others believe we cared about one another. Will you marry me to show them that we do belong to each other? To make my life complete? To—"

"Yes. Yes and yes! I'll marry you, Torsten."

The kiss that followed was the best answer she could have given him, hot, passionate, full of pent-up need and love. Soon, however, it became obvious that she intended to give him much more than a kiss. Which forced him to address the issue he knew he could not avoid. He stilled.

"I... Aife, wait."

Sensing his anguish, she drew back. "What is it?"

This would be painful, but it had to be done. He placed his forehead against hers, putting his fate wholly into her hands.

"I've only just regained the use of my legs."

"Yes. Thank the gods you have."

He swallowed, for she didn't seem to want to see what he was getting at. But he could not help but fear his body would no longer be able to function like it had before. And even if it did... There were still no guarantees he would be able to bed her. He knew only too well that he'd had problems following through on the desire he felt for a woman. What if it happened with Aife, too, despite his very real desire, his love for her? What if, by marrying her, he was condemning her to a life of frustration? He would never forgive himself.

"What I'm trying to say is... Would you rather we tried to sleep together now, before we got married, to see what happens? In case I-I could not give you what a husband—"

"No," she instantly cut in. "I trust you. I want to be with you, no matter what you can or can't do. I want to be your wife. You love me, and you know I love you. We will not 'try' to sleep together when you're ready, we *will* sleep together. Everything will be fine between us, I know it. I already know of one way to bring you pleasure, I'm certain there are plenty others we can explore together." She took a step back, determination etched on her face, love shining in her eyes. "In fact, I refuse to sleep with you until we are wed."

"What?" he spluttered. This was not what he'd expected to hear moments after she'd given him the most scandalous kiss of his life. Not what he wanted to hear.

He'd just been telling her the opposite, that they should try to sleep together *now*, damn it all. He was ready for it.

"You heard me. If you really want me—and I think you do," she added, nodding at his groin meaningfully, "you will have to marry me first. You will have to be brave enough to accept that what you can give me is exactly what I need."

Torsten's chest squeezed at this proof of love and trust he'd desperately needed to hear, and in truth, he believed her claim that everything would be all right. He felt an all-consuming desire for her, and his body had responded as it should to their kiss. Right now he was hard as iron. Still, that was not the same as actual possession, he knew that all too well. Unfortunately, he could not be sure his body would cooperate once it was time to plunge inside her, but he would make damn well sure it tried his hardest.

"Let's get married tomorrow then," he said, drawing her back into his arms.

"So soon?" Aife giggled but she didn't refuse. "It's not even Friday."

"I'm sure Frigg won't mind."

Being the goddess of marriage, surely all Odin's wife was interested in seeing was that two people who were in love did get married? The *when* did not matter. He knew she would not begrudge them this breach with tradition. Tightening his hold on Aife, he gave her another kiss, just as hot and passionate as the one he'd interrupted earlier. She responded in kind, moaning into his mouth, sending shivers all the way up to his scalp and down to his toes. By the time they drew back, he didn't have any doubt whatsoever that when the time came to make her his, he would rise to the challenge.

"Tomorrow will be perfect," he rasped against her lips. "You haven't forgotten what day it is?"

"What d-day?"

Well, apparently she had. He smiled. His kiss had thoroughly undone her. Good. That was what he wanted.

"It's Michaelmas. I cannot think of a better day for us to get married considering it already is our special day."

"The day you first touched me." She grabbed his little finger, in the way she would have done all those years ago. "This time you will touch all of me."

Yes. Every delicious inch.

"Even if it was not our special day tomorrow, I would still marry you, because I don't think I'm going to be able to wait until much longer to have you," he said, rubbing his groin against her, making her feel how ready he was for her.

She ground back like the temptress she was. "Yes, I can feel that."

"Yes. So, the sooner the better. Unless you'd rather wait because you want to give your cousin Edita time to come to our wedding?" he added in a whisper.

"Mm, that's an idea," she answered in the same breathy tone.

"Well, too bad, I'm not waiting for her. She will just have to be told about it in a letter and think what she wants. Besides, Wulfric might not want to let his wife back into a village of 'simply too incredible to be believed' Norsemen, for which I don't blame him."

"No. Me neither." Aife let out the throaty laugh that shot straight to his cock. No, with this woman, he didn't think he would find it a problem performing in bed. "In any case, the only person I would like to attend my wedding, apart from the family who lives here, is my sister. But it would take months to wait for Hedda. So tomorrow is just perfect."

"Yes, perfect. And so now," Torsten said, straightening his spine. "All there is left to do is tell Moon."

"You don't look too shocked, I have to say."

Torsten arched one eyebrow in surprise. Moon was standing in front of him, a tranquil expression on his face, when he'd expected him to show at least some reaction.

"That may be because I'm not shocked," his friend answered. "I knew all along this would happen."

"Did you now?"

"Yes, because the alternative was unbearable." A heavy hand landed on his shoulder. "All the same, I will say this: 'Tis good to see you on your feet, my friend. Seeing you lying down on your pallet felt wrong."

Oh, he thought they had come to tell him about his recovery. Torsten gave a small smile. "It certainly did."

He had hated every moment of it. After the first few encouraging tries with Steinar and Sven, he'd practiced on his own, doing it at night so that no one could visit by surprise and see how weak he'd become. To his relief, however, it had not taken long for him to see that his body was indeed recovering well.

"Let me take this opportunity to thank you again for what you did for Aife. You protected her with your body, placing your own in danger, and you saved her life."

"Which is more or less what you did with Eyja when you both went to war," Torsten answered wryly. Moon had made sure that Eyja, who'd been foolish—some would argue, brave—enough to join the Saxon army, had made it back home unscathed. "It would seem we both cannot help but find ourselves embroiled with each other's sister."

"Yes. So it would seem."

Torsten cleared his throat in readiness. Moon had not expressed any surprise when he had seen him enter the hut on his own two feet, but he might be shocked by what was to come.

"Speaking of which, there is something you need to know."

He gestured to Aife, who'd been waiting for his signal outside the hut. She entered, bold and unashamed and immediately took his hand in hers. A burst of love surged through him at her unwavering support.

"What's this?" Moon asked, addressing her. Though it would be clear what was happening, he appeared reluctant to believe what his eyes were telling him. "I thought you two were only pretending to be together?"

"We're not anymore."

"I thought you were interested in Sven?"

Aife didn't hesitate, even if her cheeks flushed slightly. "I'm not 'interested,' as you say, in him anymore. I know I have been 'interested' in many unsuitable men over the years, but there is only one man I love."

"Love?" Moon repeated, taking a menacing step forward, his gaze fastened on their clasped hands. Torsten drew Aife closer to him in a protective gesture. If he had to fight with his best friend to prove the strength of his feelings for Aife, he would do it, just like Moon had taken a beating from him and Steinar to defend his feelings for Eyja, but he would not have her upset. "Wait, just what the fuck *is* this?"

"It is exactly what it looks like," Aife answered, squaring her shoulders.

"Aye, apparently. And you," Moon snarled, turning to face Torsten once more. "What is wrong with you? You let a woman speak in your stead? You hide behind her like a coward?"

"This is not 'a woman,' but the love of my life and I'm not hiding. But Aife is your sister and she insisted on coming in case you decided to, you know, pummel me to the ground, like you clearly want to do."

"Of course, I— You bastard!"

"He's not a bastard," Aife interposed before Torsten could even react. "But Wolf's true son, as we all know. Or are you saying it is impossible that a good man should fall in love with me? Are you saying that you don't trust his sincerity, even if I do, even if he's your best friend? Are you saying that Torsten should not have trusted your intentions when you fell in love with his little sister? That he should have accused you of only amusing yourself with Eyja before discarding her like an old sock? Should he have beaten you to a pulp simply for wanting to be with the woman you loved? Should he deny his love for me just because—"

"All right!" Moon exploded. "I think you've made your point! You're in love! It's all wonderful."

Torsten took Aife's hand back in his, sympathizing with his friend. Being a woman, and more sensible than men, she would not understand that it was not all that simple for a man to imagine his little sister as a woman in the arms of a man, especially if that man was a friend. But he knew his intentions were as pure as Moon's had been where Eyja was concerned, and he knew his friend would finally come to accept the change because he was a good man.

"I know how you feel because I felt the same when you started to see Eyja." He glanced at Aife and gave her a slanted smile. She would remember he had accused Moon of amusing himself with his sister at the time, and that he and Steinar had tried to beat him into a pulp, even if she'd chosen to behave as if it hadn't happened. "But we are in love and it *is* wonderful. I promise that I will strive to make Aife as happy as you make my sister."

Exasperation flashed across Moon's face but Torsten knew

he had won, because the muscles in his jaws had relaxed. It would be all right. In fact, his friend had shown more restraint that he'd had the right to expect.

"Well, if that's the case, I suppose there is nothing I—"

"What's this I hear?"

Eyja walked in through the door, her baby daughter in her arms. Her eyes were gleaming. At least Torsten didn't have to worry about her reaction. She was clearly delighted by this turn of events.

"You were there all along?" he asked, amused. Trust her not to intervene, even when she heard how irate her husband was getting.

"Yes, I was feeding Frida outside the window." With a smile, she handed the baby to Moon and then fell into his arms before reaching out to Aife for another hug. "I'm so happy for you both. Don't worry about Halfdan, he will soon come to see reason, if he hasn't already." She always called her husband by his real name when she disapproved of something he did, which, admittedly, was not very often. "There is no stopping two people in love."

Indeed there wasn't. "Thank you, sister."

"When is the wedding?"

Torsten smiled at this, for he had not mentioned any wedding yet but he knew Eyja would already be making plans. Moon inhaled sharply, but with the baby pressed against his chest, he did not dare let out the growl evidently building in his chest.

"As soon as possible," he answered, nodding at his friend. Would this proof that he was serious help appease him? Perhaps. "We'll go see your parents now, ask their blessing and tomorrow, we'll be married."

"Perfect." His sister beamed. "We'll all be there."

17

———

Aife woke up with her back nestled against Torsten's chest, bathing in his warmth. To know this was the way they would wake up every morning for the rest of their lives was enough to make her smile, even though she had yet to open her eyes.

"Good morning," he rumbled, tightening his hold over her. How had he known she was awake?

"Mm. It certainly is a good morning, for today we are going to get married," she answered, anticipation flooding through her.

"Yes." There was a wealth of joy, possessiveness, and impatience in this one word.

Opening her eyes at last, she turned to face him. He looked mighty fine this morning, with his gorgeous hair loose on her pillow. Unable to resist, before going to bed, she had unbraided it and used her new comb on him.

"Why are you smiling?" she asked, when his lips stretched into a lazy grin.

"When I lay on my pallet these last few days, I swore I would never again in my life linger in bed longer than necessary. And yet here I am, thinking that I would like nothing more than to remain here all day, snuggling in your warmth."

She laughed. Indeed she could well believe that after what he'd endured, the bed was the last place he wanted to be in, but circumstances had changed. "No doubt you made this promise because you were thinking you would be lying down alone," she purred, placing a hand on his naked chest. "But you will never be alone in bed again."

"No. I'll be with my wife."

Deep inside her.

The thought tore through Aife and a blaze of lust scorched her insides.

Though she couldn't wait to become his wife, it took all her inner strength to leave the bed and get dressed. She'd told Torsten she would marry him before she bedded him, and she would hold on to that promise however much it cost her. He needed to know she loved and accepted him as he was, and trusted him to be the husband she knew he would be. For that, she would have to resist until after they were married to make him hers. Mercifully, it wouldn't be long, less than a day.

Tonight they would discover how much pleasure men and women could give one another.

Outside, the wind had mercifully stopped blowing. Aife could hear that the preparations were already underway. Everything would be perfect, even at such short notice, since the villagers had spent the last few days getting ready for the end-of-harvest celebrations. Lost to her anguish while she waited for news of Torsten, she had failed to remember the day was approaching. But he was right, what better day to celebrate their union than the day they had both been born? Their parents had agreed it was a good omen, and not being the most organized person, Aife was grateful she didn't have to worry about anything. All she had to do was get dressed in her best dress and be at the big boulder when the sun reached its zenith.

This much she could certainly do.

"I'll go and get ready in my hut," Torsten told her, placing a swift kiss on her lips.

They had, of a common accord, decided to ignore tradition and spend the night in each other's arms even if, as promised, they had not done more than kiss and nestle in each other's warmth. She had also taken the opportunity to tell him about the meeting with the Normans in town the other day. At first she had been unsure whether it was the right thing to do, but Torsten deserved to know that their attackers had been punished and Hugues was dead. There would be no secret in their marriage.

"How could my father place you in danger thus?" Torsten growled, running his hands all over her body as if to ascertain that she wasn't hurt. "This could have ended up badly."

"Perhaps. But it didn't. Nothing happened to me." Seeing that he was already upset, she kept to herself Girard and Enguerrand's vile words. "Wolf agreed it was the best way, even if he didn't like it. I knew I could trust him to protect me. And thanks to our stratagem, the men have been punished, and Ranulf stopped. That is what matters."

Wolf had confirmed to her only the day before that the Saxon who thought he could harass the Norse people would not be able to hurt anyone ever again. When she'd asked what he meant, he'd explained what had transpired the day he and the reeve had gone to talk to Ranulf.

"As could have been predicted, he feigned ignorance when we asked him questions about his clan. Far from being cowed, he drew a dagger out and started to threaten the reeve. I had to intervene for he might well have killed the man otherwise. I tried to stop him without killing him, for we still had questions to ask, but it proved impossible. He would never have ceased until he'd killed me, and I had no intention of indulging him. And so he's dead," he'd concluded, his face grim. "With him gone, hopefully his clan of pathetic weaklings will see that there is nothing to be gained from persecuting us."

Aife had only nodded. The man who hated Norsemen and wanted them dead would not create havoc again. It was hard to feel anything other than relief at the news, and Torsten had not appeared distraught either.

"I'll see you later, by the boulder," she called out before he could walk out the door.

"You definitely will. There will be no escaping me, lovely."

Lovely. Her heart wobbled even more than usual. "No need to worry. I don't want to escape. Why would I? I'm right where I want to be."

After one last kiss, Torsten left.

In the silent hut, Aife smiled as she fastened the brooches holding her dress in place. How many times had she gone to weddings, seen radiant brides and proud grooms stare at one another with awe, and worried she would never know that joy? Dozens. Well, today was her turn. The moment seemed so significant that she'd asked to be allowed to get ready on her own. Usually friends and family helped the bride-to-be, but since Hedda was not here anyway, Aife had wanted this time to absorb the enormity of what was happening to her.

She was marrying the love of her life, a man who, up until recently, had only been a friend, a man who had showed her that she, too, could be desired and cherished. Now she wanted nothing more than to love and cherish him in turn.

Once she was dressed, Aife brushed her hair with her new comb, relishing the feel of the fine teeth gliding through the strands like spread fingers weaving through the rapid waters of a stream. Torsten's creation was a lot smoother than her old wooden comb had been, untangling the knots without once pulling at her scalp. Edita was welcome to the one she had stolen, this one carved of antler was a thousand times better and infinitely more precious. Finally, she placed on her head the crown of flowers she had fashioned the evening before with her friend Cwenthryth.

When she opened the door, Torsten was there, waiting for her. He had put on a tunic of dark blue wool she'd never seen before, and he looked utterly mouthwatering. This time, instead of wobbling, her heart sped its rhythm up to an impossible drumbeat. To think that this man would be married to her before the day was over...

"Aife. You look ravishing," he breathed, wrenching a smile out of her.

"I was about to tell you the same thing." Ravishing, and soon to be ravished.

"Come."

Taking her hand in his, he led her back into the hut, after checking they hadn't been seen by some old person set in their ways who would no doubt protest at this breach of tradition. It was better to avoid any problem.

"What are you doing?" she asked, once they were hidden from view. Did he mean to steal one last scandalous kiss? If so, she would be more than amenable.

"I know I shouldn't be here, but there is one thing I wanted to give you before our wedding, in private."

Delight and curiosity caused Aife to clasp her hands together. "What is it?"

"Close your eyes."

She did as she was told and Torsten took her hand in his. A moment later she felt him slide a ring on her middle finger.

When he asked her to open her eyes and she glanced at the hand he was still holding, she dissolved into tears. On the ring, encased in gold, was the amber-color stone he had found for her that day on the beach.

The day he had saved her life.

The day she had realized she was in love with him.

She'd dropped it because of the wretched seagull and thought it lost forever. It had pained her at the time, but in the aftermath of what had happened by the cliff she had quite forgotten about it. And now Torsten was restoring it to her in a nest of precious metal. It was too good to be true.

"But... What... How did you—"

He shrugged. "After you dropped the stone, I looked for it instead of looking for cockles. I thought you were doing a better job than me anyway, so there would be little loss." Yes, especially that in the end they had never even had the chance to eat the cockles. His time had been better spent trying to retrieve the little rock she had meant to keep as a souvenir. It was irreplaceable, whereas the sea was full of the shells. "I'd seen how upset you were when you lost it, so I thought it was worth trying to retrieve it. I had only just put it in my purse when you called me to come to the cliff. I asked Caedmon to put it on a ring as soon as we got back to the village."

The day they had come back here? This meant that, even incapacitated and fearing for his recovery, he had thought of the surprise he wanted to give her. She was more touched than she could say. Touched and more than a little surprised.

"But I don't understand... We didn't know we were going to marry then. We had even decided to stop, you know, kissing and everything." There would have been no reason for him to have a ring, or indeed anything else, made for her, especially considering that he had already decided to give her the comb.

"It doesn't matter. This wasn't about me, or even us. I just wanted you to have the stone as a souvenir, because I had seen how much you loved it."

Aife thought she might choke with emotion. This was true love, there was no mistaking it. If she'd had doubts that they were rushing into this union, they would have disappeared there and then.

"I don't know what to say."

Torsten lifted her hand to his lips and kissed the stone lightly. "Easy. Say you'll wear it always. On a different finger if it fits better. Or if you prefer, we could have it made into something else, a pendant or a brooch. I don't mind."

"No. It's perfect like this. I will wear it until I die," she vowed, closing her fingers into a fist as if to make the ring become part of her. "I love it. Thank you. This is the most thoughtful thing anyone has ever done for me." Overcome by emotion, she placed her hand over Torsten's cheek. "Do you know why I fell in love with this stone?"

"No. But this sounds like something I want to hear."

A heated kiss rewarded this heartfelt answer, a kiss that quickly became as hot and passionate as their usual kisses. When they finally drew away, Aife was breathless.

"Well?" Torsten purred. "I'm waiting. I still want to hear why you fell in love with the stone."

She blinked. He really expected her to have to ability to talk right now, after the kiss they had shared? She cleared her throat, doing her best to focus and give him the explanation he wanted.

"The color reminds me of your eyes." She suspected he had no idea how closely the rock mirrored the molten honey irises, having never seen his own eyes the way others could see them. "I've always found them fascinating, so unlike anyone else's in the village, even your mother's. And also, that day on the beach, I understood that I had fallen in love with you. I wanted a reminder of that moment."

"You have one now. Me." He placed a kiss on her forehead in a gesture that had now become familiar. "You'll always have me. I will make sure to remind you at least twice a day that you love me."

"Only twice a day? I hope that doesn't include the nights. I will definitely expect you to remind me then, again and again." Aife laughed, then stopped abruptly when Torsten burrowed his face into the crook of her neck and started to nibble at her like a starving wolf about to devour his prey.

"Mm, do you know why I love your laugh so much?" he asked, before taking her earlobe between his teeth, sending shards of delight all the way to her toes.

"No. But this sounds like something I want to hear as well." He had told her he loved her laugh before finding the stone, and it had sent her senses into a flurry.

"Because it makes me harder than steel. Feel it."

Bringing their two bodies in contact, he nudged at her. Aife gasped when she felt how aroused he was.

"Yes, steel indeed," she murmured. "But why would my laugh send you mad with lust?" It was the last thing she had expected to hear. She had never heard that laughter was what aroused men.

He groaned, his lips still at her throat. "Right now, we have to go and get married. I cannot tell you, because if I do, I will want to tumble you into bed. But one day soon I will tell you."

This sounded promising, and Aife almost begged him to do it there and then. The people waiting to go to the wedding could wait. She forced herself to reason. It wouldn't be fair on everyone who had worked ceaselessly from dawn. Besides, there was still something she needed to do. Now seemed as good a time as any.

"Before we go, I, too, have a surprise for you."

"Mm. Is it what I think it is?"

"I know not. What are you thinking?"

The look Torsten threw her was so evocative Aife went red to the roots of her hair. She knew he was imagining her on her knees, giving him pleasure in the most scandalous manner. "No. It's not that."

A mock sigh of resignation left Torsten's lips. "Very well. I guess I will have to wait until tonight."

Heat bloomed in her loins at the thought of welcoming him into her mouth again, so hot and heavy, so hard and smooth, so perfect for her. This wedding night would be memorable.

"I'll make sure you don't regret waiting. Now come," she said, taking him by the hand. "You will have to go outside to get your present."

Unable to resist, she ordered him to close his eyes as well. Then she led him to the back of the hut, and came to a halt in front of a newly installed wooden box. Smiling, she turned to him to see if he had recognized what it was. Of course, he had.

"You got me a hive?" He sounded both incredulous and delighted.

"Well, yes. I got it the other day, actually." Before they had decided to get married. "I meant to ask your father for help, as I have no idea how to get the bees inside it, but I didn't have time. But I thought that way you could have all the honey you want and be less at risk of being stung. It seemed the perfect solution for—"

She was prevented from finishing her sentence by Torsten sweeping her into his arms.

"Your back!" she immediately protested. Was he mad? What if he hurt himself again? "Put me down!"

"No. Not before you kiss me."

As if she would refuse such a request. Wrapping her arms about his neck, she gave him the fiercest kiss she could give him in that position.

As promised, he let her go as soon as their lips parted.

"Aife, my love, what would I do without you?" he asked, his forehead against her.

"You don't need to wonder, as you will never be without me."

"No. You're mine. So, come, let's go get married."

18

"My wife. Finally."

"My husband. At last."

Heat started to suffuse Aife's body at the idea of what was about to happen. It seemed as if her whole life had led up to that moment, and in a way, it had. She had known this man from birth, he'd been a constant companion, by her side in good and bad moments. Until he had become something even more precious than a friend and far more special than a lover.

A beloved husband.

After a moving ceremony during which Torsten had proudly carried his father's sword and a feast that had gone long into the night, they had retired to her hut, which was now to be their hut. In the flickering light of the fire, they stared at one another in wonder for a long moment, as if wary of breaking the spell, as if fearing that the last few weeks had been naught but a dream. It had not. The love in Torsten's eyes made that clear, and the heat between her legs gave her the nudge she needed to make the first move.

"Torsten—"

"Yes. Will you undress for me?" he started at the same time, speaking in a hoarse whisper.

"Only if you undress for me."

Having simple garments to dispose of, Torsten was naked in the blink of an eye. Naked and magnificent. Was there another man on this earth who could compete with him? Forget Knut's bulging biceps, Sven's muscular shoulders, Steinar's broad chest, or Haakon's chiselled stomach. *This* was what beauty was. And it was hers to admire and to stroke.

But Torsten made no move to go to her. Shadows cast by the flames danced on his skin as if to encourage her fingers to do the same. She would have done that and more if he'd come closer. But he remained two paces away from her, waiting. The fire crackled and popped, shaking her back into action. It seemed it was her turn to disrobe. Lost to her contemplation, she had completely forgotten she was supposed to get naked as well.

Feeling slightly self-conscious, but far too aroused to deny him, Aife unhooked the brooches holding her dress in place and let it pool at her feet. The shift of fine linen soon followed, then the woolen stockings and shoes. As naked as the day she was born, she stood there, watching him while he devoured her with his gaze.

"Perfection," he murmured, closing the space between them just like he had the night she'd been born. She could not resist grabbing his little finger and tears stung her eyes when he brought her hand to his mouth to kiss it reverently.

"I love you."

"I love you, too." His eyes had darkened with desire. "Lie down for me."

Aife understood how much it would cost him to ask this of her. She knew this was what he feared. But if he was nervous, he hid it well. True, in the Roman palace, he had touched her while she guided him, but he had not really seen her. It had been too dark and, more to the point, she had not lain back on the bed, legs spread wide, waiting for him to possess her, like the other women he'd tried to bed. There had been nothing to remind him of his past trauma. How would he cope tonight? There was only one way of knowing.

Slowly, she sat on the pallet, and then lay on her back.

"I should have stroked your breasts that night in the ruins," Torsten rasped, coming to kneel by her side. "I should have stroked and suckled them."

"Then what are you waiting for?" Why was he torturing her so? Surely he had just looked his fill? Being devoured sounded like something she would enjoy. "Eat me. Eat me as if I were covered in honey."

With a groan, he fell on her. The sensations were nothing like what she experienced in her life. Having a hot mouth engulfing her aching nipples and a wicked tongue licking them into peaks then rolling them around in slow, delicious flicks was exquisite. For a long moment, Torsten suckled her, moaning, seemingly taking as much pleasure in the act as she was. But of course, it was the first time for him also, and he was making the most of this new experience. Aife could not stop panting and writhing. Knowing she was the first woman he had stroked thus only added to her pleasure.

She closed her eyes and just allowed herself to be worshipped, holding on to his head and whispering words of encouragement.

Then a hand landed on her knee. "Can I?" Torsten asked, lifting his head from her breasts to meet her gaze. His lips were as wet and swollen as her nipples. The mere sight was enough to send her core into spasms. "I want to see you, see this part of you no one else has ever seen."

"Yes. And no other man than you will ever see it."

His other hand landed on her left knee. "Open for me. Please."

When she nodded, he started to ease her legs apart. Once she had bared herself to his gaze, Torsten positioned himself between her thighs and lay down on his stomach, his face inches away from her burning core. Slowly he parted her folds with his thumbs. Aife was holding her breath. How had she not predicted that she would feel exposed in that position? Exposed and aroused? Utterly powerful. Determined to watch as he explored her, she lifted herself up onto her elbows.

"So beautiful."

Well, she had no precise idea of what he could see. Was it beautiful? The expression on his face seemed to suggest he was not lying. She had been afraid he would be reminded of the women who had bared themselves for him, for surely they could not have looked very different. But he didn't seem to be thinking about them, or anyone else in that moment. His attention was wholly on her.

"Can I stroke you?"

"Yes."

At first, the caress was tentative. It became more assured when she sighed and rolled her head back. The wicked finger entered her, slowly parting her folds. When it came back out, it was glistening with the proof that she was more aroused than she had ever been in her life. Aife watched, fascinated, as Torsten's finger plunged inside her pink petals a second time, retreated and then entered her a third time, before another one joined in the sensual dance. He had such strong, masculine hands, she had never imagined they would ever feel so soft or handle her with such delicacy. The other day he had merely stroked the nub at the apex of her thighs, and skimmed at her entrance, as she had not dared tell or show him that she usually plunged her fingers deep inside her heat when she pleasured herself.

"So soft," he rasped, "so hot, so tight, so wet."

"Yes," she breathed back.

"For me."

"For you."

She did feel slick and ready. And with every thrust of his fingers, every word from his mouth, she could feel herself melt further, her body grow hotter. He teased her a long moment, then brought his fingers to his mouth and sucked them clean, wickedness flashing in his eyes.

"Mm, so good. Even better than honey." He gave a slanted, utterly naughty grin. "Can I get more? Lick you like you licked me the other day?"

Oh. She had been on the verge of begging for it, but wary of frightening him with her eagerness, had not dared. He had already stroked her once, but this was different, much more intimate.

"If you don't want me to, I won't," he hurried to say, as if worried by her silence. "Only I've heard about this and I find that I... With you, I want to try."

"Then yes, please, lick me. Do what you want with me. I'm yours."

He crept closer to her, placing his hands on her hipbones, lowering his head between her thighs. By the gods, but this was going to kill her.

"So perfect for me," he groaned, bringing his lips against her folds. "So sweet."

His tongue flicked out, once, twice. Then he flattened it and gave a series of long, luxurious, utterly scandalous licks along her seam, before engulfing the now throbbing nub between his lips and suckling in much the same way he had suckled her nipples.

Where had he learned to do that? It seemed he was a natural at pleasing women. At pleasing her.

Aife soon stopped thinking and wondering what she had done to deserve such a husband. All her strength deserted her and she fell back on the pallet. She couldn't watch anymore, she couldn't hold herself up, she could hardly breathe.

"Ah, wait, Torsten, stop! No, don't stop! I need more!" she cried. What was she saying? She would die if he stopped now. "More, I'm going to...*ah!*"

She did die then. But it was the best death anyone could hope for.

It took Aife a long moment to come back to herself. When she did, Torsten was kneeling between her spread legs, his shaft hard as rock and poised at her entrance, ready to push in. His long fingers had encircled her ankles, and he was holding her wide open. Her whole body spasmed in anticipation. How odd. Barely two heartbeats ago she would have sworn she was too spent to do anything, and yet here she was, undulating in invitation.

"Can I?"

Did he really have to ask? Couldn't he see how desperate she was? "Yes. Take me," she rasped.

Still, he hesitated. Something was obviously weighing on his mind. "You're a virgin." He made a grimace. "I am too, of course, but, unlike you, my first time will not hurt. It doesn't seem fair. I wish it were the other way around."

"I don't."

Not when he already had his own battle to fight. She might feel a stab of fleeting pain when he plunged inside her, but she was not the one confronting demons. Torsten would have to be far braver than she was. Besides, being taken could not hurt more than being denied was making her ache. She was ready.

"I'm sure it will be fine. I trust you. Please, I need you." She would never get enough of him, of this pleasure. They were husband and wife, and she already knew they would spend all their nights thus.

He pushed his way in, gently but confidently. The shaft entering her felt like tempered steel gloved in precious silk. No need to worry about him being able to perform, she doubted any man could be harder without hurting himself. A sigh escaped her lips.

"All right?" he asked, pausing once he was fully embedded inside her.

"Yes." It was more than all right. There was no pain, as such, only the odd but wonderful sensation of being stretched and filled, complete at last. Perhaps her nightly exploration had prepared her for a man's possession, perhaps she was simply too desperate to finally make love to Torsten to register any discomfort. Whatever the reason, she was glad for it. She could, in all honesty, reassure him that he was not hurting her. "It didn't hurt."

"I need to move." He sounded strained.

"Then do." She needed him to move also.

The more he thrust in, the easier it became. Soon he was gliding in and out with delicious ease.

Torsten threw his head back and let out a guttural moan. "Aife, this is...I'm not going to last. It feels too good. You feel too good. I can't stop."

"Don't stop. Take your pleasure," she whimpered. He deserved it, deserved to know what it was to erupt inside a woman. She'd already had her pleasure, and anyway, they had all night. And then the next. And the next.

Releasing one ankle, he bent forward and took her left breast in his hand. "Touch yourself," he ordered. "Do what you do when you're on your own. Help me. I will learn, in time, to please you, I swear, but for now I need—"

Aife saw how desperate he was to have her reach her pleasure with him inside, and she could feel she was not too far from blessed release. The fingers teasing her nipple, the shaft sliding in and out of her, the love burning in Torsten's eyes, it was all too much, and had brought her to the edge of ecstasy.

She put her hand over the place where the two of them were joined and started to rub with the finger adorned with her new ring. A few strokes were all it took. She'd been so well prepared by Torsten's hand and mouth that she erupted in no time, milking him when violent spasms overtook her body.

"Torsten!" she squeaked, shocked by the violence of this second, even more devastating release.

"Yes. Just like—*ah!*"

Liquid heat flooded her insides. Torsten roared, jerked, and a moment later collapsed by her side, looking utterly spent. For a long moment he just stared at the ceiling. Then he turned to face her and placed a possessive hand on her breast, smiling.

"My love. I fear you have married an insatiable man eager to make up for lost time, a husband who will give you little respite."

Aife smiled back. Was this supposed to scare her? It did not.

"Fine by me. As long as you don't mind having a wife desperate to explore every inch of you." A wicked idea formed in her mind. She had alluded to it earlier, and the notion wouldn't leave her. "I might even cover you in honey once the bees have done their work and lick you clean. Thanks to you, it has become my new favorite treat," she breathed in his ear.

"Fine by me. Every inch of me is yours, anyway."

THE KNOCK on the door broke through Aife's sleep with all the subtlety of a bucket of icy water thrown over her. In a distant part of her mind she heard Torsten open the door and whisper to their shameless visitor, hopefully to send them away. She hid under the fur covers with a groan, protecting her eyes from the admittedly still feeble light.

Really, who dared come visit at this hour? Didn't everyone here know last night had been her and Torsten's wedding night? Couldn't people guess they would be in no mood to be awoken at dawn?

"What was that? Who thought it all right to disturb us so early on such a day?" she grumbled once she'd heard Torsten close the door again.

"Early?" she heard him say from behind her, mirth in his voice. "'Tis almost evening, wife."

Aife threw back the covers and sat bolt upright on the pallet, looking at the window facing west. Indeed, the light was coming from there. She blinked in disbelief. Had she really slept all day? This had never happened to her before, not even once in her life.

"Evening?"

"Evening," Torsten confirmed with a smile so broad it unveiled all his teeth. Then he sat on the only chair to look at her, his long legs stretched out in front of him. He was dressed in the same blue tunic he had worn the day before and looked just as mouthwatering as he had then. "You did wake up at dawn, as usual, but so did I and...well, let's just say that once I was finished with you, you went straight to sleep."

Oh. Now she remembered. Indeed, he had not given her any respite, taking her over and over again until she couldn't remember how to say the word *yes*.

"Who was at the door?" she asked, doing her best not to let her embarrassment show, though she suspected her cheeks had gone flaming red.

"Moon."

Oh no. The heat burning her cheeks crept all the way to her ears. Now her brother would know she had been so well pleasured the night before that she had slept the day away. Well, at least Torsten still had all his limbs, which meant Moon had not taken exception to the idea.

"What did he want?"

"A visitor arrived in the village today. She's very anxious to see you so I said you would go see her as soon as you were ready."

His eyes were sparkling with delight. Or was it mischief? Aife frowned. A visitor wanted to see her. A *female* visitor. She had no idea who that might be.

"It's not... Please tell me it's not Edita?" Surely her cousin would not be back so soon? Unless she had decided she would rather have a Norse husband instead of the uninspiring Wulfric? Had she set her sights on Knut, who had made a strong impression on her? If that was the case, she would be disappointed, as he was now seeing Brenna, a woman he had hated all his life. But perhaps Edita would do all she could to break the two of them apart and—

"Calm yourself," Torsten cut in before she could get her thoughts into a tangle. "It's not Edita."

Yes, it *was* mischief playing in his eyes, she decided. Who on earth had come to visit? Unable to wait another moment to find out the identity of the mysterious woman, Aife jumped to her feet and gave a gasp of surprise.

The table was laden with delicious-looking food. A loaf of wheat bread was surrounded by bowls of various sizes containing smoked fish, slices of hard goat's cheese, cracked hazelnuts, wild berries, and thick cream. A handful of blue harebells in a wooden cup was lending a touch of color to the feast.

"You...you prepared all this while I slept?" Her throat was almost too tight for her to speak.

"I did. Sorry there are no cockles. I know how much you like them, but I am not the best at finding them, as we now know and they would not have been ready in time anyway. Besides, I didn't want to venture too far from the hut, so as to be there when you eventually woke up, all warm and soft for me to enjoy."

He took her hand to draw her to him, trapping her between his spread legs. It was only when his mouth closed around her nipple that Aife realized that she was still naked. Warm hands landed on her buttocks, bringing her closer to him. Mm, she could get used to this new life.

"Torsten," she moaned, taking his head into her hands to force her nipple deeper into his mouth.

Instead of obeying the silent instruction, he drew back, looking contrite. "Forgive me, I couldn't resist. But I know you are eager to go see who your visitor is."

The visitor. Of course. She was curious, admittedly, but for a moment she had completely forgotten about it. In fact, she had been about to reach out to the bowl of cream and ask him to feed the contents to her with his fingers. But he was right. Someone was waiting for her. She had better not let them wait.

As soon as she was dressed, they made their way to her brother's hut together. The setting sun had thrown a crimson banner across the pink skies, confirming that it was indeed evening. On the bench by Moon's vegetable patch, enjoying the last rays of warmth, were a man she had never met—and a woman she had not seen in years.

"Hedda!" Aife cried out, letting go of Torsten's hand to break into a run. A moment later she was hugging her sister in her arms. "But...but...what are you doing here?" she asked, laughing and crying at the same time.

"We've been wanting to visit for months. It was about time I introduced my husband to my family, don't you think?" Hedda gestured to the tall Dane waiting by their brother's side. "Here. This is Thorsten. Please note that he only speaks Norse," she added in that language.

"Thorsten?" Aife stared at the blond man in disbelief. As girls, she and her sister had always jested that they would end up marrying a man with the same name one day. It seemed that, against all odds, their fanciful prediction had come true. "Welcome into the family," she told the Dane, who gave her a warm smile.

"And what about you? Moon tells me that, had we arrived a day earlier, we would have been able to attend your wedding?" Hedda said, her eyes wide with excitement. "But the wretched man refused to tell me who you married. Is it someone I know?"

She craned her neck to look past Torsten, who she had naturally assumed was still only a childhood friend. Except that he was now so much more.

Aife smiled and took his hand back in hers.

"It is someone you know. Here. My very own Torsten."

EPILOGUE

"Oh, God, Sven! Harder. Yes! Just like that. Ah, yeeeessss..."

Aife went red to the roots of her hair. How many times had she said those exact same words just before she erupted in exquisite pleasure? Dozens of times. Well, with one notable exception, of course. She used her husband's name instead of Sven's. But there was no denying that she was a very vocal lover, something Torsten loved.

The click of the door behind her shook her out of her reverie, then a moment later two arms wrapped themselves around her, holding her tight against a warm body. Just then the moaning in the hut next door was joined by a series of masculine groans. Torsten gave a resigned sigh.

"Hearing those moans and grunts used to drive me mad with jealousy and frustration, you know," he whispered into her ear. "But now that I have my own beautiful, moaning woman in my bed, I don't mind."

"Mm." She had never before realized that if they could hear Sven and his conquests, he could hear them too. Not that she would be able to stop herself from expressing her pleasure the next time they made love.

There was one last mighty roar and then suddenly, everything went silent.

Torsten sat on the bench behind them, before dragging her onto his lap. "What's the matter, my love? Can't sleep?"

Aife nestled against him, inhaling his wonderful scent. "No."

"I expect the babe is disturbing you?"

"Yes. It's flipping around like an angry eel. Feel this." She took his hand and placed it just below her navel. Definitely a future warrior, eager to take part in his first sword fight, or a girl destined to become the finest archer the village had ever seen.

"Mm, yes, 'tis a veritable swarm of eels in there." Torsten chuckled. "Well, not too long to wait now until they are freed."

"Says you. But Cwenthryth and Helga, whom I trust more in these matters, say it will be another two months at least."

"Forgive me. I suppose I am so impatient to meet my child that I feel the nine months will be over tomorrow. But I understand it is harder on you."

He placed a kiss on her temple and Aife melted back into his embrace. He'd been so patient with her during these wonderful but difficult few months that she had no idea what she would have done without him.

"You don't need to stay here with me. There's no point in you losing sleep as well."

"There is every reason, since I was the one planting this babe inside you. We both shared in the pleasure of the conception, why should you be the only one suffering from the carrying of it?" he said roundly. It's bad enough that I won't be able to do anything when the time comes to bring it into the world. Let me do that at least."

"I love you, you know that?"

"I think I do."

Later, as the fat, silver moon started its descent toward the horizon, Aife and Torsten watched a woman creep out of Sven's hut. That she was a Saxon was obvious. Her disheveled hair was black as ink, and the dress she wore was in a style different to the one the women in the village favored. She looked slightly unsteady on her feet, like a woman whose strength had been drained, which was hardly surprising.

"I wonder who that is," Aife murmured to herself, cradling her stomach.

Torsten gave a soft snort. "No idea. And I doubt we'll ever get to meet her."

No. Probably not.

"Come. Let's go back to bed."

Coming next
Sven's Promise

ALSO BY VIRGINIE MARCONATO

Sons of the Wolf

Steinar's Gift

Torsten's Gamble

The Welsh Rebels

A Husband for Esyllt

A Savior for Branwen

A Second Chance for Carys

A Rogue for Siân

A Lover for Lady Jane

A Scot for Bethan

The Noble Norsemen

Taming the Wolf

Soothing the Beast

Wooing the Devil

Baiting the Bear

Tempting the Saxon

Seducing the Warrior

Loving the Blacksmith

ABOUT THE AUTHOR

As far back as I remember, I have been attracted to the Middle Ages, to knights in shining armour and their ladies in spectacular dresses. Now I get to write about them, I feel like the luckiest woman in the world. Being French and married to a Brit makes each book I write extra special, as our countries share a long and sometimes painful past. But in the end, in life as well as in fiction, love conquers all!

I have published several medieval romances under my own name, including series, and also have a pen name, Judith Falcon, for spicier projects, still in historical romance.

Join my newsletter and check out my other books on virginiemarconato.com.

www.ingramcontent.com/pod-product-compliance
Lightning Source LLC
Chambersburg PA
CBHW032245310726

48973CB00008B/2295